WRITTEN IN THE STARS

HELEN ROLFE

First published in Great Britain in 2024 by Boldwood Books Ltd.

Cover Design by Alexandra Allden

Cover Illustration: Shutterstock and iStock

A CIP catalogue record for this book is available from the British Library.

Paperback ISBN 978-1-83561-094-7

Large Print ISBN 978-1-83561-093-0

Hardback ISBN 978-1-83561-092-3

Ebook ISBN 978-1-83561-095-4

Kindle ISBN 978-1-83561-096-1

Audio CD ISBN 978-1-83561-087-9

MP3 CD ISBN 978-1-83561-088-6

Digital audio download ISBN 978-1-83561-091-6

Boldwood Books Ltd
23 Bowerdean Street
London SW6 3TN
www.boldwoodbooks.com

To Lauren Dyson, critical care practitioner with the Dorset and Somerset Air Ambulance, and to everyone who works with and alongside the UK's air ambulance charities to carry out lifesaving missions... thank you!

CAST OF CHARACTERS

The Whistlestop River Air Ambulance Crew (The Skylarks)

Red team
Maya – pilot
Noah – critical care paramedic
Bess – critical care paramedic

Blue team
Vik – pilot
Kate – critical care paramedic
Brad – critical care paramedic

Other
Frank – engineer
Hudson – patient and family liaison nurse
Paige – patient and family liaison nurse
Nadia – operational support officer

The Whistlestop River Freewheelers

Rita
Dorothy
Alan
Mick

1

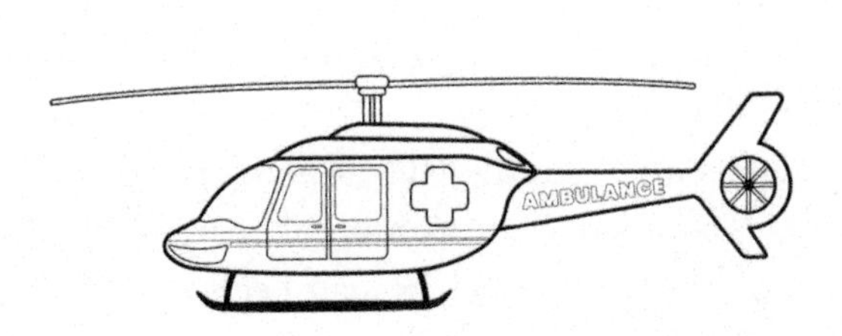

Bess's spirits dropped in much the same way as the post that came through the letterbox did when it fell to the mat. Given it was already late afternoon, she'd assumed that she was in the clear of any more unwelcome correspondence. Unfortunately not.

She picked up the two brown envelopes – nothing good ever came in a brown envelope. Each of them full-named her in brutal typeface. One of them even had the logo of the energy company at the bottom left-hand corner, as if that might entice her to open it sooner. But denial had become her modus operandi. In her job as a critical care paramedic with the Whistlestop River Air Ambulance, she was together, calm and practical in the most tricky of situations. Bess was known at work and around town as a chatterbox, bubbly, the life and soul of the party. But the truth was, she'd got herself into a mess and she wasn't sure how to find a way out.

Right now, she had no time for anything other than getting herself together and heading for her 4 p.m. shift with The Skylarks.

She threw both envelopes on top of the pile of similar correspondence on the table in the hallway. The top one was the credit card statement she'd received yesterday; underneath that was the notice to pay her television licence, and the rest... well, she didn't want to even think about what they were because she felt like she was drowning.

Could that happen? Could you drown under a sea of paper? Or could you suffocate?

Her thoughts were interrupted by a knock at the door.

Her insides churned again. Was she about to be handed a bill with so many pages, the envelope had been too thick to push through her letterbox?

'Parcels, love!' the post lady trilled when she came face to face with Bess. She pointed down to the side of the front door. 'They're not from me... I wasn't going to knock but I got to the end of the path and thought, well, I'd rather know if all my early Christmas packages were sitting outside my front door for anyone to nick.'

'Thank you!' Bess called after the post lady's already retreating back. It was no wonder the woman still wore shorts in the latter part of October given the pace she moved most days and the loads she carried.

Bess bent down to get the first parcel. She'd been in all day so had no idea how she'd missed these arriving. It would've been nice if whoever made the deliveries had thumped on the door to give her a heads up – she'd rather be woken or disturbed than have packages go walkabout.

She picked up a heavy parcel and a lighter one, guilt already rearing its ugly head. She set them down in the hallway – no time to rip any of them open now. Inside the first, given its identifying design on the package, would be the Christmas present for her mum: a luxury hamper. She could picture the wicker basket with leather straps holding the calming, nourishing treats she'd carefully selected. She wanted to spoil her mum in the way she deserved. Bess didn't feel quite so terrible about that package, the last of her Christmas shopping she'd made sure to do super early. It was the rest of her deliveries that prickled her conscience. Inside the lightest package would be a new dress that had been a quarter of its full price – the company logo was on the front of the postage bag – in the other would be the new toaster, a proper Dualit one this time that would look so much better in the kitchen than the cheap one she'd had since she moved in. Her reasoning had been that it would last for years; it was an investment.

She picked up the last parcel from outside just as her mum started walking up the front path. 'Mum! Wasn't expecting you.' She shunted the remaining deliveries into her hallway, reached for her keys, bag and coat and closed the door all in one swift move.

She almost collided with her mother on the front step.

Taken aback, Fiona Gardner gave her daughter a peculiar look. 'Aren't you going to invite me in?'

'Sorry, Mum. I've got to get to work.'

'You've plenty of time yet.' Fiona checked her watch. 'Don't you clock on at 4 p.m.? I thought I'd be early enough to say hello, have a bit of a chat.'

While Bess and her mum saw one another regularly, for her to show up unannounced was out of the ordinary. Mostly, she called first, especially if she wanted something – last time, it had been to ask to borrow Bess's lawnmower; the time before that was when she needed Bess to take her black cat, Liquorice, to the vet because she had a last-minute commitment with the WI at the town hall. Bess didn't mind dropping what she was doing to help out but occasionally, she showed up like this, without warning, and that usually meant she was worried about Bess or wanted to do a deep dive into Bess's emotions – those were the drop-ins that Bess couldn't handle. She'd rather do a thousand humdrum chores for her mother, cook a hundred cakes for a town hall bake sale, mow her lawn every week over summer than have one of *those* conversations.

'I need to get in a bit before start of shift today.' Bag between her knees, Bess had managed to shrug on her coat. She did up the buttons. The silver fob of her keyring shone as a beam of sunshine caught it when she turned the key in the lock to secure her house. The words *Live every day as if it were your last* were engraved on the fob along with the outline of a daisy – she'd found it at a craft fair on holiday last year and she'd grabbed it because those words encapsulated the way she lived her life. It was the way she wanted to keep living it too. Life was too short to do anything but, wasn't it? She saw so much devastation at work and she'd had enough of it in her personal life as well.

She hugged her mum tightly. 'I'm sorry, Mum.'

'I understand, you're busy. Another time, soon.'

'Definitely. I promise. Are you out on a walk?' On the cusp of turning seventy, her mum was pedantic about keeping active and that meant getting her ten thousand steps in each day and thrice-weekly yoga classes. For her job, Bess had to have a good level of physical fitness; she needed to be strong enough to walk rough terrains with heavy equipment and to lift patients on the stretcher. She only hoped she kept her fitness and had half the same energy at her mum's age.

'I am. Just heading home now.' Fiona indicated the wrapped gift poking out the top of Bess's bag. 'What have you got there?'

'It's a birthday gift for Nadia and the reason I'm going in early.'

'What did you get her?'

'It's a gift set with her favourite perfume, body lotion and shower gel,' Bess smiled. In its box, it wasn't easy to fit in her bag, but Nadia would love it and she deserved a treat. She worked hard and kept them all organised and in check. She wasn't part of either crew at the Whistlestop River Air Ambulance but she was integral to the team as their support officer. 'We're planning to surprise her with a celebration at start of shift when the red team coincides with the blue at changeover. That way, everyone gets to be a part of it.'

'Do wish her a happy birthday from me.'

'Of course.' Bess unlocked her car on the driveway, leaned in and popped her bag on the passenger seat. 'I really wish we could do coffee.' She felt bad that she had to race off. 'How about tomorrow? I could pop over to yours around lunchtime so we'll have a few hours before I'll be on shift. Let Liquorice know I'm coming.'

Fiona chuckled. 'I'll be sure to do that. And tomorrow sounds perfect. I'll make a cinnamon tea cake: your favourite.'

'Love you, Mum.'

She wasn't wrong about the cake – it was Bess's favourite, or at least one of them. And that had Bess even more inquisitive as to why her mum had dropped by on a whim. 'Is there something going on?' she asked. 'Something worrying you?' To be forewarned was to be forearmed, wasn't it?

'It'll keep,' Fiona told her and with a wave she left Bess to climb into the car and set off for work.

So there was something... *it'll keep* told her that much. And Bess didn't have a particularly good feeling about it as she cranked up the heat dial in the car to warm her from the October temperatures that in the last week had been a reminder that summer was well and truly behind them.

She drove the short distance to the airbase and pulled into a parking space just as her friend and colleague Maya, pilot with The Skylarks, was attempting to balance a crate on her knee and reaching into the boot of her car for something else.

Bess grabbed her bag and quickly got out with an offer of help. 'Where's Noah?'

'He's already here. I was running late. And besides, we're not joined at the hip.'

'No, but sometimes, I bet you wish you were. And you arrive together more times than not.'

Maya couldn't deny it so simply smiled.

Noah and Maya had been an item ever since the summer. They didn't flaunt it at work, both of them were too professional, but it was good to see Maya looking so happy after finally moving on from her waste of space ex-husband.

Bess leaned into the boot for the other crate. 'Whatever you've got in these smells heavenly.'

'Don't worry, I didn't make any of it myself.' Maya led the way to the main entrance. She made no secret that she didn't particularly love cooking and definitely didn't enjoy baking. Nadia was the keen cook of the team but they couldn't very well ask her to do the catering for her own birthday. 'We've got sandwiches, croissants, pains au chocolat, an assortment of cakes. There are quite a few of us; I didn't want anyone to go hungry.'

'How come they didn't deliver?' Bess hoisted the crate up again after opening the door to the building behind which was the helipad and open space as far as the eye could see.

'Their delivery van has broken down.'

'Well, you've saved the day.' They scooted through reception, hoping Nadia wasn't walking the corridors to catch them at it.

'She's in the office,' Vik, pilot with the blue team, said as he breezed past with a pile of paperwork.

'Thanks, Vik.' Bess led the way to the kitchen. Her tummy

was growling already, having only had a small bowl of cereal for breakfast to take the edge off her hunger, anticipating all of this, the sort of fare that, judging by the aroma, could turn even the fullest person hungry again.

As Vik kept guard at the door, Maya took on the task of decorating the kitchen. Bess found large platters from the cupboards and began to get the food transferred from the crates. Beyond the window was Hilda, the red and yellow air ambulance helicopter, ready and waiting on the helipad for The Skylarks' next job.

Noah didn't take long to arrive, followed by the rest of the blue team, whose shift was ending right about now as the red team prepared to take over for their stint, which would run until the early hours of the morning.

'Good job with the bunting.' Bess watched as Maya and Noah hung up the last of the rows of brightly coloured small flags as well as a big *Happy Birthday* sign.

'All right, time for someone to get the guest of honour,' Vik announced, volunteering for the role. The red team could be called out at any moment – they never could predict when a job would come in so they needed to make the most of the time they had.

Bess adjusted the band on her tightly ringleted hair, which sometimes had a habit of escaping its low ponytail. Not that much seemed to stop the ringlets at the sides hanging loose; they never did like to behave themselves. She, Maya and Noah huddled with the blue team in the kitchen until Nadia showed her face.

They yelled, 'Surprise!'

But there wasn't much time to enjoy the celebrations because they were interrupted by the shrill ringing of the multiple phones at the base, indicating another mission for The Skylarks.

'Worst timing ever,' Bess groaned as the whole crew leapt

into action. Noah went to take the call from the HEMS – the Helicopter Emergency Medical Services – desk, Maya headed out to the helipad to get Hilda ready and Bess squeezed her way past the birthday girl to go to the adjacent room and retrieve the cool box containing blood and plasma, and the drugs they'd take with them on board.

'You'll have to make do with the blue team,' Bess hollered into the kitchen once she had what she needed and walked past again. 'Don't let them eat all the food!'

'Thank you, everyone!' Nadia's voice trailed after Bess as she went to get her jacket on and her helmet. Noah was already geared up in his same kit, recounting the details of the job as they made their way out to the air ambulance.

As the technical crew member, Bess sat in the front of the aircraft next to Maya and helped with navigation and instrument reading. She programmed the GPS system in the cockpit and soon The Skylarks were soaring high up above the town on their way to the mission.

The Skylarks were afforded priority over other air traffic in line with aviation laws, allowing them to get to the patient as quickly and efficiently as possible, saving more lives in the process. Noah sat in the rear of the helicopter, already scouting for possible landing sites. Between the three of them, they concluded that a farmer's field would get them closest to the road traffic collision, which was on one of Dorset's windiest roads. It wasn't yet dark but it was getting there. They had night-vision goggles to allow them to fly at night but those came with different and complex challenges and it was always harder than attending a mission in daylight.

Moments later, Maya set Hilda down. She stayed with the helicopter and Bess and Noah, along with their kit bags, the drugs, monitors and the scoop, which would allow them to transport the patient back to the air ambulance should that be required, hurried to the edge of the field. They had to cut away at bushes and climb over a wire fence, but police had closed the road to traffic in both directions, making it easier for them and the fire brigade who pulled up on the other side of the two vehicles involved as Bess and Noah approached.

Bess smiled when she saw her good friend Gio Mayhan, firefighter from the Whistlestop River fire station, step down from the engine as they drew adjacent to it on foot.

'Hey, Gio,' she called out.

'How was the date?' He didn't bat an eyelid that they weren't alone.

'Mind on the job,' she scolded, half-joking. 'I'll tell you about it later,' she assured him. She'd kept him abreast of her dating situation plenty of times over the years. He knew all about boyfriends who hadn't lasted, all about the more serious relationship she'd had when she first graduated, only to find out the man was married. That one had stopped her dating for a while.

'I'll hold you to that,' he declared.

Gio and Bess had been friends since they lived in a house share in Lancashire where she was at university studying paramedic science and he'd moved out of his family home. They'd known one another more than fifteen years. Gio was a good guy, fun, nice to have around since he relocated here from up north, but he wasn't the sort of man you dated. At least not the sort of man *she* dated.

When they shared a house, there had been the odd time when Bess had thought Gio might become more than a friend. If she was honest with herself, she'd been a little infatuated with him at the start, not that she'd ever admit it to him. Four years older than her, he'd always seemed unreachable, wild, fun. He was good-looking, strong, the whole package in some ways. But his playful side came out whenever he was in a relationship and she'd seen enough girls broken-hearted by him not calling them back or by him not wanting to commit that she knew it was best to keep their relationship what it was: a friendship. She couldn't deny that sometimes, she felt a spark with Gio but when Bess fell in love, when she found the right person, she wanted what her parents had once had as soulmates, both committed to each other.

She thought of the picture of her mum and dad on their wedding day, the photograph that stood on her mother's mantelpiece cementing the beginning of their family. And if you looked really closely, you could see a small baby bump beneath Fiona's dress that the bouquet she was holding didn't quite disguise. Bess had always loved the fact that in a way, she'd been a part of their wedding too.

Gio was soon focused on the job and as Noah led the way towards the first vehicle, one of the two involved in the road traffic collision, Bess shared what she knew already. Gio would know some of it too but sometimes due to updates en route, one first responder knew more than another and those little bits of extra information could make all the difference.

'The female caller told the call handler that her car had skidded into the path of an oncoming vehicle. Maybe the mud caused the skid.' Bess held her footing in her clumpy boots as they passed over an enormous patch of mud at the edge of the tarmac, something that wasn't uncommon in this area given the surrounding fields. This part of the county saw regular passage of farm vehicles and the deposits they left behind created a hazard, especially given the default speed limit for the single-carriageway road. You only had to hit a build-up of mud too fast, or when you were applying the brakes, for it to cause trouble.

A road ambulance was already in situ the other side of the

second vehicle – usually it was the air ambulance who got to a job first. Given the nature of the remote location and the winding roads, they must have been in the area when they got the call to have arrived already. The road paramedics could deal with a lot on scene but often required the assistance of a critical care paramedic to administer stronger medications and sometimes to perform surgical procedures in the field. The air ambulance was also often the best option to transfer the patient to a medical setting, especially if they were time critical.

Gio and his crew assessed the scene while Noah and Bess attended to the patient in the closest vehicle.

Once Noah and Bess had evaluated the patient's condition, Bess fitted a c-collar to the woman's neck to prevent any potentially harmful movements should she have injuries they hadn't picked up on. She appeared to have escaped without many at all.

'I'll go see if I can help with the occupant of the second vehicle,' said Bess just as Gio ran back past them.

'Road paramedics need you,' he bellowed as he headed for the fire engine.

'You got this?' Bess asked Noah. The woman wasn't far off being helped out of the car now her vitals had been checked and they were sure she didn't have any injuries that would prevent her from being moved.

'Yep, you go.' Noah's voice continued to comfort the young woman, who was obviously still in shock. Bess had told her a few times how lucky she was but she hadn't wanted to listen. Her only concern was that she'd caused this; she wanted to know how the other driver was.

As soon as Bess started off for the second vehicle, a red saloon, she could see it had come off worse than the other. The driver's door looked as if it was caved in to a fraction of its size. It must have been hit at speed to do that kind of damage.

Gio caught up to her again, this time armed with a tool called the jaws of life, which enabled the extrication of a person from their vehicle. He carried the piece of machinery on his shoulder as though it was nothing heavier than a handbag rather than a powerful tool designed to cut and spread metal.

They were almost at the vehicle when Bess did a double take at the woman sitting at the side of the road wrapped in a blanket.

Usually calm in a crisis, Bess experienced a different feeling when she called across, 'Mum?'

Fiona's eyes filled with tears as she spotted her daughter. 'Please, help Malcolm.'

Malcolm? Who was Malcolm?

'Mum, are you all right?' Bess hovered there momentarily while Gio strode on ahead, his mind able to remain on the job, unlike hers, which had an unexpected distraction.

'Please, go, Bess. Help him. I can't lose him too.'

Bess's mind went back to the day they'd each held each other tightly, the day they'd lost her dad. But her brain squashed away her emotions. She had no time to address the blatant fact that her mother had just announced that she had another man in her life.

And knowing that felt to Bess like losing another part of her dad, another piece of their family past that she was never going to get back.

2

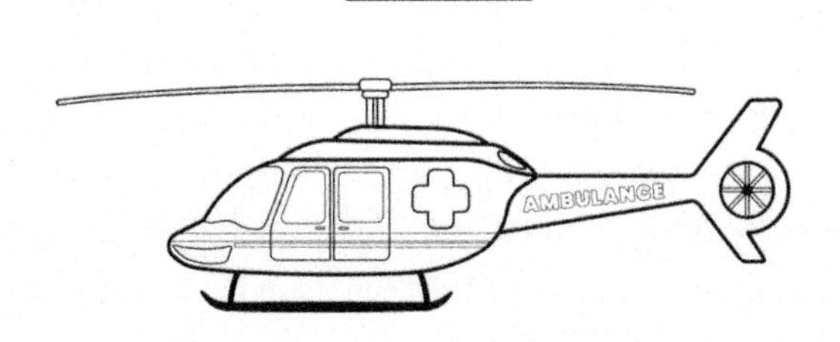

Bess reached the car and the road paramedic updated her on what they knew so far. The man, who Bess had to treat like any other patient, even though she now knew that he and her mum were involved in some way, was talking a bit. That was always a good sign. But he was trapped inside the vehicle and they couldn't fully attend to him until he was freed.

'Malcolm...' Climbing into the vehicle through the passenger side on her knees, Bess's voice rose above the noise on scene, the first responders, her mother still crying out to help this man. 'Malcolm, my name is Bess, I'm with the air ambulance. Do you remember what happened?'

'A car...' he croaked. 'Hit us. Knocked us sideways.'

His response proved he was lucid.

'I understand you have pain in your chest, Malcolm.'

Malcolm opened his eyes to Bess's voice.

As a critical care paramedic, Bess's job was to provide pre-hospital emergency care. It involved quick thinking, fast decision making, often in the most challenging environments with limited resources.

'I'm going to take a look at you,' she assured him. Pain in the chest could be due to a fracture, organ damage or bruising so she wanted to rule things out wherever she could. She needed to ensure he was stable, get him out of the vehicle, and transport him to the further help he needed.

Daylight was beginning to fade and even though Bess had a head torch on her helmet, she asked the road paramedic to hold a bigger torch and shine it into the car so she could better assess Malcolm. As she worked, she couldn't help picturing him with her mother, holding hands, talking, starting something new without her even knowing. Only three years had passed since they'd lost Bess's dad; it felt like no time at all in so many ways.

But right now, she had to block all of that out and do her job.

Once she was as sure as she could be that his injuries weren't life threatening, she administered a stronger pain relief than the road paramedics were able to give. 'The fire brigade are going to get you out of here, okay, Malcolm?'

'Okay.' He even managed a smile as Noah came to assist, a smile that seemed kind to Bess.

To Gio, she said, 'Slow and careful with this one; keep everything as still as you can.'

'Right you are.'

Sometimes, the instruction was the opposite – the patient was in such a critical condition that she told the firefighters to work fast, get the patient out by any means necessary.

As Gio got to work, one of the road paramedics came over and informed Bess that they would soon be taking Fiona to the hospital to be checked. 'She says she won't leave until Malcolm is extracted from the vehicle.'

'But she's okay?' Bess checked.

'It's a precaution,' the paramedic explained. 'I think she's fine, but it's always good to be safe.'

'Thank you.' Bess's words rushed out of her in relief as the jaws of life crunched and tore away the steel from around the patient while she and Noah stood by, ready for action again.

Once Gio had done his part, two other firefighters put protective boards inside the vehicle to stop injury to any party from jagged metal or broken glass as the patient was freed from the wreckage.

Malcolm was no longer very coherent which wasn't surprising given the stronger painkillers that had been administered. But, as Noah and Bess got Malcolm onto the scoop, one thing he kept saying stood out – Bess's mother's name.

'Fiona,' he said again.

'She's fine,' Bess explained, the weirdness of talking to this stranger about her mother not lost on her.

Noah radioed in that they would be transporting the patient by air to the nearest trauma centre and with their equipment gathered together, it was almost time to head back to the aircraft. Daylight had faded completely now, but with the lights of the emergency services vehicles plus the head torches she and Noah had, the visibility was manageable.

Fiona cried out Malcolm's name yet again, jolting Bess between her job and her personal life. She yelled over to Bess from the side of the road where she stood with a police officer. 'I want to go with you!'

'Mum, he's in good hands,' Bess called back.

'You okay?' Noah asked softly from beside her.

She hoisted the first bag onto her back. 'Yeah, let's go.' This was her job but it didn't stop her feeling torn, with part of her here with the patient, the other part desperate to go to her mother's side.

Gio, another firefighter and a second police officer offered to help with the scoop and the rest of the equipment so Bess and

Noah could get everything back to the helicopter in one trip. This happened a lot on scene and they were always grateful for any assistance, whether it was from another first responder or a member of the public.

Bess focused on putting one foot in front of the other. Her mum wanted to be sure that Malcolm was okay; Bess wanted to know her mum was all right and she needed to know who Malcolm was.

Was Malcolm the reason behind Fiona's visit to her house today? Was he what she'd wanted to talk to Bess about?

Her thoughts were drowned by the blare of sirens from the road ambulance that left the scene to take the first patient to the hospital for thorough checks and hopefully an all-clear.

Cold winds whipped Bess's ringlets across her face as Gio dropped back to walk alongside her. He had the other equipment bags; Noah and the two others had hold of the scoop heading towards the fence they'd have to get over to access the field and the air ambulance.

'You all right?' he asked.

'Why wouldn't I be?'

'Easy. Just asking.'

'Sorry, don't mean to snap.'

They'd reached the fence and Gio and Bess held one end of the scoop while the others took turns to climb over the fence before they could take hold of it again.

When Malcolm said, 'Fiona,' yet again, Bess called out to him before the scoop was on the move.

'Fiona is fine, don't worry.'

It was what she'd do if it was any other patient and they were worried about their loved one. It happened often that one victim was worse off than another and so they didn't travel to hospital together, especially when the air ambulance was involved as it had limited space and required everyone on board to comply with weight limits.

Bess told Gio to climb over the fence first. 'I'll hand you my bags once you've cleared it.' She ignored the hand he held out once he was over.

'Perfectly capable,' she said but with less of the snappiness of her previous remark.

'Did you hold hands with your date the other day?' he asked with a hint of the cheekiness she was very familiar with.

'I didn't.'

'That bad?'

Laden with equipment and gear, they trudged towards the helicopter.

'I don't think there will be a second date, put it that way. He was forty-five and lives with his parents.'

'Cost of living is steep.'

She added, 'And he has no intention of moving out; rent is cheap, meals are free.'

Gio's laughter lifted her stress for a moment, especially when she caught sight of his smile as they both negotiated the slippery mud. His rugged, dark good looks probably had most women turn to putty in his hands, but not Bess. She'd put him firmly in the friend zone a long time ago and it was probably for the best. He'd likely used his charms on plenty of Whistlestop River's female population since he moved to town and she didn't want to be just another number to him or anyone else. She wanted something long term; she wanted stability.

Gio caught her arm when she slid and stopped her falling on her behind. 'You needed me that time.'

As they followed the others, the bags not getting any lighter, he asked, 'So that's your mum's boyfriend?'

Maya had spotted them and headed over to help with the kit.

'It seems that way,' Bess replied.

'And I take it you didn't know about him.'

'No, I didn't.' The wind almost whipped her voice away.

The three of them caught the others up. Noah and Bess got the patient from scoop to litter, ready to transport, and with all the equipment on the helicopter, Bess thanked Gio, agreed to meet up with him again soon, and climbed into the cockpit.

Gio stood back to avoid the downdraft from the aircraft as they lifted up into the sky and Bess gave him a wave as she radioed through an update to the HEMS desk. Noah monitored the patient in the back and as they flew, Bess assisted Maya as needed, all the while the spinning rotors not quite loud enough to drown out the niggling thoughts in her head.

The patient – Malcolm – a man who was not her dad, was involved with her mum.

Ron had been Fiona's one true love. They'd been each other's perfect; that was how they'd described one another often. Bess's dad died suddenly three years ago and thinking of her mother with any man other than him...

Of all the things she'd expected her mother to want to talk to her about today, she'd never anticipated a new man in Fiona's life to be it. Her dad wasn't replaceable; he never would be.

Bess updated the hospital on their approach and when they arrived and hovered above the helipad on the roof, she pushed everything else aside other than this night, this job, everyone's safety. She climbed out of the aircraft once they touched down and were clear to do so and it was time to hand over the patient. She had to yell above the sound of the wind this high up, Noah gave them further details, and soon they were back on board ready to return to base.

Tonight, there had been no fatalities, and for that, Bess was grateful. But deep down, she was thinking about her dad, the man nobody would ever take the place of, the man she missed so much, it hurt like a head-on collision.

He'd be disappointed if he could see the way she'd been living her life lately, but as they cruised over the town's ribbon-like river, which looked completely different in the dark and yet was still magnificent, she couldn't regret her choices completely. Maybe she should, but there was always that little voice in her head that said, *Live every day as if it were your last*, the words on the silver fob of her keyring.

Life was precious; life could be taken away from you in a moment.

And she wanted to make the most of hers. She had to.

3

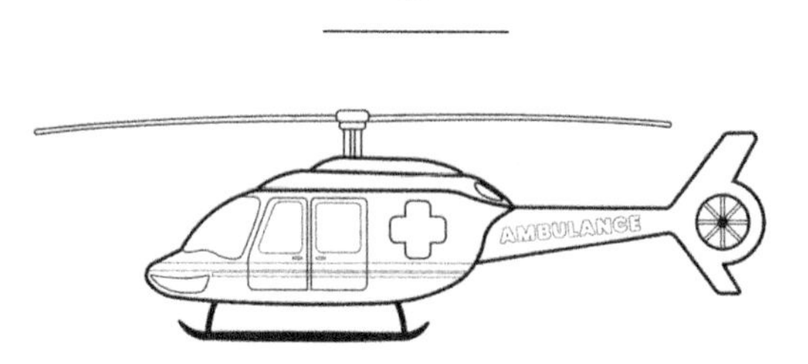

Gio switched off the shower but promptly turned it back on again to clean the dirt gathered in the corners of the white tray. Apart from what went on in his head, depending on whether lives had been saved or lost, dirt and grime was the other part of his job he couldn't help bringing home with him.

He wrapped a towel around his waist and wiped the back of his hand across the mirror. He'd missed some grease from the side of his face. No matter the temperature of the water or the steam, sometimes dirt remained stubborn. He rubbed at it with the hand towel for the friction and dumped the towel in the wash basket when he was done.

Gio loved his job; he buzzed on it: the adrenaline, the excitement, the demands and the need for fast reactions. Today's late shift had been quiet until a couple of hours ago. The crew had finished supper and embarked on a theoretical training session – not his favourite sort because it meant sitting in a bland room talking about what may or may not happen when he'd rather be in amongst it, doing the job or job simulations rather than talking about them.

Then a shout had come in, the piercing alarm at the station taking them all out of that dull meeting room, down the stairs, to their kit, which they pulled on before leaping aboard the fire engine and roaring out of the Whistlestop River fire station.

A house fire in a rural cottage five miles from town had had the potential to claim casualties but the family of four were all outside as Gio's crew pulled up. Bruce, the officer in charge, spoke briefly to the family and did a 360 of the property to get as much information as he could while the crew began to run out the hoses and waited for instructions to be given.

Gio had his full breathing apparatus on and with no one inside the cottage, the hoses were filled with water, checked and then taken into the residence. They would hit the fire directly at its source: the lounge at the front where candles had been left unattended.

The flames, fierce and unforgiving, could've taken the entire property. Nobody would know at this stage the extent of the damage, but the main thing was that everyone escaped with their lives. That was always a good day in Gio's book. Possessions and property could be replaced; people couldn't.

When Gio and the others emerged, the little girl from the family was freaking out. Her dad's arms were the only thing stopping her from running back into the house. Gio had lost count of how many fire talks they'd done where they reiterated personal belongings were not worth risking your life for.

But then he heard something about a dog and he realised she wasn't after something that could easily be replaced. He was right back inside to look for it, his teammate Jeremy following close behind as his back-up.

They went from room to room and eventually found Ziggy, the cockapoo, cowering under the stairs.

He brought Ziggy out in his arms and handed him to the

little girl. Her tears immediately stopped and the smile on her face as her whole world brightened was priceless.

'Do you all have a place to stay tonight?' he asked them as he pulled off his mask.

No sooner had he asked the question than the folks from the nearest property who had likely seen the flames, heard the sirens, came and assured the family that they all had beds for as long as they needed.

As Gio and his crew had left that job, he'd looked back at the property as they drove away and watched the family. They were devastated, it was quite likely that their house wouldn't be the same nor liveable for quite a while, but their faces said it all. They were safe. They had each other.

And Ziggy, of course.

He smiled as he readjusted the towel around his waist. He thought about the little dog, shaking in his arms, wagging its tail as soon as it saw its owners. Gio had never had a dog as a boy. He always wanted one, but it had never happened and when he got his own place, he'd told himself maybe one day, but with his job and the shifts, he knew it wouldn't be fair to leave it for long periods of time. He knew what it was like not to feel a part of a family and he wouldn't wish that on anyone, not even a canine.

Gio put the main light on in the bedroom. It was approaching midnight but he was still buzzing. You didn't just come down from a shout and the last one had been so close to end of shift that the adrenaline was still pumping through his veins.

He reached for the charger cable to juice up his phone but it came alive in his hand and his mum's name appeared on the display.

Midnight was late for most people but not for Marianne Mayhan. Whenever he saw her name on the display, he was tempted not to answer but knew that if he didn't, she'd keep on calling and calling until he picked up.

'Did I wake you?' She put the same question to him that she did every time – it didn't matter whether it was midnight or midday, she'd always ask.

'No, I got off shift an hour ago, just finished in the shower.'

'You work so hard; I worry about you.'

'I'm forty-four, Mum. No need.' And why start now? *Not mother material*, wasn't that the phrase people used when a person was unsuitable for the role? He'd tried to accept what she was like over time because he was a grown-up, but she didn't make it easy.

'You'll always be my little boys, both you and Marco.'

He didn't have time for a lengthy woe-is-me conversation, which he sensed she was about to embark upon. He knew exactly how it would go too – she'd say she would always be their mother, then she'd bemoan the fact that Gio and Marco didn't need her these days, then she'd tell him it was hard when you felt as though you had no purpose.

'What's up, Mum?'

'I just wanted to hear your voice.'

Pull the other one, he thought, but he'd go with it.

He gave her the gist of his day. It was something to talk about that distracted her from asking him for money or him asking her whether she'd quit drinking yet.

'You saved a dog; that's so sweet! You always did love dogs. I hope that family were grateful to you all for putting your lives at risk.'

'Kind of in the job description, Mum.'

'Well, anyway... I have a bit of news.'

He braced himself for what was next: new boyfriend? (Usually a loser and down-and-out scrounger who'd leave her when they got bored.) Or perhaps she was moving. (The last time it was in with a friend but, translated, that meant sleeping on someone's sofa because she was behind with her rent.) Of course, the most frequent 'news' she had was that *this time it will be different*. Which meant she'd stopped drinking – again – and it never lasted.

'I have a job,' she announced with a great deal of glee for this time of night.

'Mum, that's great.' And it was a relief.

But the doubts soon crept in. He could already anticipate the peak when she started work and loved it and the money coming in, then the trough when it went wrong. She'd never had much staying power, her track record was abysmal and the only saving grace she had in her corner was that she'd never pissed off an employer so much that she was left with only bad references. Usually, she walked away without much fuss, made an excuse for leaving so it wouldn't look to them like she just couldn't be bothered any more.

'Aren't you going to ask me what it is?' she prompted.

'Of course. What's the job?'

'Now don't freak out.' She paused. 'It's a cleaning job.'

'Why would I freak out about that?'

'It's in a pub.'

A pub. Great. Say no more.

'I'm not drinking, Gio.'

'Okay.' He'd heard that one before.

'I'm not, I promise you.'

He wondered how long she'd last before this job went the same way as every other job she'd had over the last decade.

'When do you start?' He didn't have the energy to voice his doubts. It never did any good.

'In the morning... well, late morning.'

When there was an awkward silence, he almost made his excuses to hang up. He was sitting in a towel on the edge of the bed and was starting to get cold.

'I bought some sparklers the other day,' she said, trying her best to carry the conversation on. It happened now and then – not every time – sometimes, she wanted to go almost the moment the call connected, even though she'd been the one to phone him, but tonight, it seemed she wanted to talk.

'Sparklers?'

'For bonfire night! Well, I've used them already even though it's only October, but they remind me so much of you boys. I'll bet Matilda and Billy love sparklers.'

Gio's brother Marco, also a firefighter, was married to Saffy and they had two kids: seven-year-old Matilda and six-year-old Billy. Gio's niece and nephew were real little characters and Marianne adored them when she got to see them. Marco, however, was reticent at having his kids spend too much time with their grandma given the times he'd taken them to visit and she'd either been on her way to getting drunk or she was hungover and a mess.

'I'm sure they do, Mum.'

'Do you think they go crazy for them like you boys did?'

Gio touched a hand to a sting on his upper lip that must've been hiding beneath all that grime on his skin. He went into the bathroom to check and it was a cut he hadn't realised he'd got, but man, it was sore now. He dabbed tissue against it to stem the small amount of blood that had come to the surface.

'I used the whole packet. Of sparklers,' Marianne rambled on.

Gio could imagine her twirling around in her bedsit, holding her arm out like she was a kid with her own sparkler, not thinking of the fire risk, especially if she'd had a few drinks.

'I tried to do what you boys used to and wrote my name in the sky.'

'So you were outside?'

'Of course I was outside. What sort of silly question is that?'

She'd bristled so he pulled it back quickly. 'It sounds fun, Mum.'

Her voice gave away that this was upsetting her now. 'You don't remember us doing it together.'

'I do remember. But it was a long time ago.' And unfortunately, as well as remembering her giving him and Marco sparklers, he also remembered her being so drunk one time, she'd picked up a discarded sparkler and burnt her fingers. It had been her two boys who'd raced her inside and held her hand beneath the cool tap to reduce the pain, swelling and risk of scarring.

'Do you remember that it was me who bought the sparklers, me who took you boys to firework displays?' she persisted.

'Of course I do.' But that was before their dad upped and left more than thirty years ago. She'd been relatively together up until her husband Antonio left her and their sons without so much as a backward glance. He'd found a new life with another woman. That was when alcohol had wormed its way into Marianne's life and, by default, her boys'. Gio's older brother Marco had ended up being more of a parent to him than either of his actual parents. Marco had been the one to take Gio to after-school sports, he'd done the weekly shop, he'd helped Gio with his homework. Both of them had waited for the drinking to stop, waited for the toughest times to pass, but they never had. At least not until they both left home.

'So will you get yourself some sparklers?' Excitement laced her voice once again.

'I'm not twelve.' But he managed a laugh; she was so enthusiastic. 'Maybe I will.'

'Do they have a big display in Whistlestop River?'

'They have one just outside town, but I'll be working.'

'You work too hard.' She began to chuckle. 'Remember all work and no play is bad for you.' She was teasing but it didn't work, not with their history. Because that laugh of hers made him want to crawl beneath the duvet and never come out again. He didn't associate it with kindness or happiness. It merely reminded him of his younger days when he'd stay in his bedroom, away from her and the chaos her drinking brought. And if she came into his room to say goodnight, drunk off her face, he'd pretend to be asleep.

He'd rather be dull than in the mess she'd got herself into. He'd rather be single and cruise through life than turn into either of his parents.

They'd tried as boys, tried to hold it together as a family. They'd thought their mum had hit rock bottom when their dad walked out on them but there was no upwards trajectory. Rock bottom had become a way of life for her. No matter how many times the boys bailed her out of situations – kept the house tidy, made her eat so she didn't get ill, fetched her medication when she did, made sure bills were paid on time, reached out to support groups on her behalf, only to be told by their mum that they were overreacting.

Marco had handled Marianne better in some ways – he was firmer than Gio, he'd started to say no to her more often, but as a consequence, Marco and Marianne barely spoke these days. Marco thought Gio was far too lenient with their mum. And maybe he was. But Gio had to believe there was a possibility that one day, she would wake up to herself. Unfortunately, it was akin to smashing his head against a brick wall, giving her chance after chance, listening to the same old gripes every time. Gio had given up lending her money when it became clear that the more he gave, the more she asked for. Some days, having her in his life in any way, even if it was just phone calls, felt as though he was trapped in a never-ending loop he couldn't escape from. But she was their mother. Neither Gio nor Marco, despite what he claimed, had it in them to turn their backs entirely.

'Working won't be dull. Although I would rather it was. Let's just hope people aren't too stupid this year.' He'd attended more than one shout at a residential property around Guy Fawkes night where the homeowner seemed to think it was a good idea to blast off endless fireworks rather than go to an official – and far safer – display. Those fireworks often ended up on other people's roofs or in their garden. He'd once attended a scene where the fireworks hadn't launched into the air but towards the back of the house. The house hadn't been the only thing to suffer; a little boy had been hit by one of them and experienced horrific burns. And then you got the idiots that set them off in the street, endangering their lives and those of others. If he could ban the sale of fireworks to the general public, he would.

'You're talking about me,' Marianne said snippily. 'One mistake and you won't let me forget it.' Paranoia was another thing she suffered from, thinking everyone was out to get her.

'I didn't mean you.' He should've kept his mouth shut, skated over her comment about work making him dull, but he'd gone into defensive mode, not something that usually ended well because it normally resulted in a verbal showdown.

'I told someone off last year, you know.'

'Yeah?'

'Well, I didn't tell them off, I gave them advice which they took and I saved a life. Two, actually. The man was about to light an enormous bonfire and I'd read something about hedgehogs, how a pile of logs is an ideal nesting place; they could hibernate there. I told him he needed to check, that he could be killing innocent creatures. Anyway, him and his wife inspected the fire while I watched on, and blow me down, they pulled out two hedgehogs. They did it carefully, released them somewhere safe, and you know what? They were ever so grateful. The man said he would never have known if I hadn't spoken up.'

He didn't have to see her to know she'd be chuffed with the compliment.

'Well done, Mum. Good on you.'

'I know I haven't been the best mother,' she said. And now he pictured her face, full of worry. He couldn't reassure her that she'd been a good parent either because she hadn't been and still wasn't. It felt as though he and Marco were destined to always be the ones looking out for her rather than the other way round.

'Tell me you remember some of the good times, Gio.'

She'd done this before too. She got emotional and needed to know she wasn't the worst person in the world and again, Gio's conscience got the better of him, as much as he wanted to hang up the ridiculously late phone call. 'Of course I remember some.' All of which were way before his dad walked out and she fell apart.

'Tell me.'

'You took us to see the Christmas lights every year. We'd drive to the best streets and we'd be out for hours.'

'You loved the Christmas lights. You'd wrap up all warm, mittens on, scarf across your mouth and nose – you needed it up north; it's colder there than where you are.'

Gio had joined the Whistlestop River fire brigade eighteen months ago, relocating from Lancashire to the county of Dorset. Last Christmas, he and the crew had been out on a shout and on the way back to the fire station, had driven down some of the best decorated streets he'd ever seen. Families crowded the pavements to take a look, fathers had kids lifted high up on their shoulders, mothers had their arms around excited toddlers, and everyone had a smile on their face. It had reminded him of the good times with his mum, when the three of them would take in the festive scene together in the local area no matter how cold it was, whether it was blowing a gale or pouring with rain. Their mum had always been excited for the Christmas lights every year – she'd never let the boys miss them either, not until the drinking started, anyway. Even the year he twisted his ankle, she'd insisted they still went out and she'd borrowed a wheelchair from the local hospice where she volunteered to read to patients once a week.

'What are the lights like in Whistlestop River?' she asked, leaving him discombobulated that they were having a proper conversation. 'I'll bet they're something to behold.'

Behold? His mother didn't use words like that and Gio's shoulders sagged with relief because he could always tell when she'd been on a bender and tonight definitely wasn't one of those nights. He wished he'd realised sooner so he could've enjoyed their conversation a little bit more but he'd been focused on keeping her calm, getting through the call from start to finish without a big blow-up.

'Last year, they were pretty spectacular.' He almost wanted to add *you should come and see them* but the words couldn't quite reach his lips. Should he feel bad that although he loved his mum, she came with so much stress that it was better to hold her at arms' length?

He shivered again. 'I have to go, I need to get to bed.'

'Silly me, I forgot the time. I was chatting away…'

'Mum, it's fine, honestly.'

'Gio, I…'

A pause. Which wasn't a good sign.

She was going to do it, wasn't she? She was going to ask for money; that's what the whole rekindling of memories about the Christmas lights had been about, the talk about sparklers and triggering nice thoughts before she went in for the kill.

So he got in there first. 'Goodnight, Mum.' And he hung up the call before switching his phone to silent to give himself a break.

He pulled on a pair of sweatpants and an old top, too wired to sleep. He headed down to the lounge, pulled the curtains, flicked on the television for some company and made a cup of tea.

As the kettle boiled, he took the rubbish outside to the wheelie bin before the inside bin overflowed. The cold bit at his arms and woke him up all the more but not so much as the noise of the air ambulance flying overhead.

He looked up into the night sky; he couldn't help it. He wondered, was Bess inside the helicopter?

Bess, a friend. A really good friend. At least from her perspective.

Gio had no shortage of women interested in dating him, he'd had more flings than he cared to remember – the uniform helped – but the one relationship that had stuck was the platonic one he had with Bess. They'd known each other since they were in their twenties and they'd lived under the same roof. Over the years since the house share, whenever they met up, he found himself thinking more and more about her: the way she smiled, her laugh, her constant chatter, her confidence and her calm and the intelligence she seemed to downplay. That was the thing about a woman like Bess: her appeal was in the things she didn't realise about herself. He'd delivered compliments enough times but she only ever seemed to accept them in a friend capacity. And for a while, he'd been thinking about more than a friendship. Ever since they'd both attended the wedding of a mutual friend where they'd danced and he'd held her in his arms, his feelings had shifted. Did she feel that way too?

Who was he kidding? She'd danced with someone else right after him that night and he'd gone to the bar for a beer, watching her from afar.

It had been Bess who'd suggested a move to Dorset, after a conversation they'd had at the wedding that alluded to how much stress he was under still living close to his mother. And while the deciding factor to head this way to Whistlestop River was when he received a job offer, he never would have even looked to move had it not been for the way he felt about Bess.

Sometimes, he asked himself whether with Bess, it was the thrill of the chase. Was he after her because she didn't fall at his feet, flirt with him or make it obvious she was interested? Was that why he couldn't get her out of his head?

Surely he wasn't that shallow, even though some people probably thought he was.

When they'd both attended the road traffic collision a few days ago, even those snippets of time with her had been something he valued. He'd always thought she was beautiful, not just the way she looked with her dark curls and captivating green eyes but her personality. And it was a special form of torture being with her but knowing it couldn't go any further.

He thought about Bess's reaction to her mum being at the scene. She was good at her job, she hadn't let her personal life get in the way, even though seeing her mum with someone new had been a shock. He could understand what it felt like too – he and Marco had seen their mother with new partners more times than he wanted to recall. None of the men she'd picked had ever been right for her. He wished she'd stop trying to have a relationship, wished she'd sort herself out first before she brought anyone else into the equation, but it seemed neither of those things were on her agenda.

Back inside and settled on the sofa, his eyes grew heavier as he finished his tea. An American cop show carried on in the background and although he should've taken himself off to bed, he made the mistake of lying down and pulling the nearby blanket over his body.

He was out for the count until morning when a knock at the door woke him.

When he opened it, he thought he was seeing things.

Life had just become a whole lot more complicated than it had been less than twelve hours ago.

4

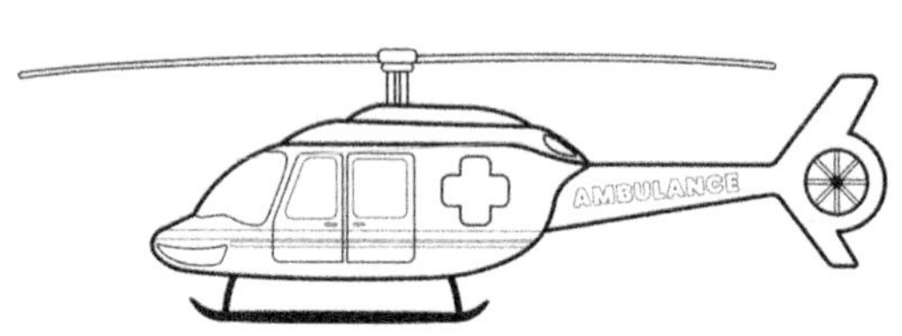

The cold wind against Bess's face as she stood on the helipad at the hospital was a good reminder that winter was on its way. She did the handover to the hospital staff of a male patient in his nineties who'd fallen down some steps at the local sports centre and hit his head. Lucky for them, the sports centre had an enormous rugby pitch and so landing Hilda had been easy for Maya, they'd got to the patient quickly and were here at the trauma centre eight minutes after taking off from the accident location.

'All clear and available,' Bess called through to the HEMS desk once she was back on board the aircraft and Hilda lifted into the air. At least it was a fine day without much cloud, and as they came in over the Whistlestop River, the sun reflected off its surface.

Bess loved her job, had a real passion for it. She'd been approaching the end of her school years and, after a work experience stint with the ambulance service, made her decision. She wanted to work in emergency care. She read up on different courses offered around the country and it was paramedic science that caught her eye. She'd done her degree, qualified as a paramedic, worked the job for a while and then, when she was hungry for more, she'd studied to become a critical care paramedic and never looked back.

'Always stunning,' Maya beamed as she flew over the river and took the crew back to base. 'We're going to try stand-up paddle boarding in the summer, aren't we, Noah?'

'Affirmative,' he called into his headset from the rear of the aircraft.

'I'll bet that's peaceful,' said Bess as they passed above the town. 'Well, unless you fall in, of course.'

Back at the base, as the whir of the blades came to a stop, Bess resisted the urge to look at her phone. She knew there'd be at least a few texts from her mum. Her mum was desperate to talk about Malcolm; Bess would rather put it off as long as possible.

The night of the accident, Bess had gone back to base with the crew but as soon as they got there, Kate from the blue team subbed for her so she could go to the hospital to be with her mother.

It was always weird going into a hospital not in a work capacity but as a relative, even when her relative had only been taken in as a precaution.

Bess found her mum sitting in one of the beds, eating a sandwich. Relief. She really was all right.

'How are you doing?' Bess hugged her and then sat on the nearby chair while she finished her food.

'I don't really want this but the nurses said I need to eat.'

'They're right, you do.'

Bess turned as one of the nurses came over.

The nurse took in her uniform. 'Ah, you're with the air ambulance; your mother has been telling us all about her wonderful daughter, the lifesaving work you do.'

Bess smiled. 'Right back at you – we're all one big team.'

'That we are,' the nurse said, then she was right down to business. 'I've been in contact with the trauma centre.' Because of his injuries, Malcolm would have been taken elsewhere for the specialist care. 'This is the number should you wish to call them yourself but Malcolm is doing fine – concussion, bruising, a few cuts from glass but other than that, he is one very lucky man.' She passed Fiona a piece of paper with a number on it.

Fiona put a hand against her chest. 'Oh, thank goodness. Can I go to see him?'

The nurse opened her mouth but Bess took it from there.

'Mum, not tonight. It's really late; I need to get you home.'

'She's right,' the nurse agreed and Bess appreciated the back-up because when her mum set her mind on something, it was difficult to get her to change course. Bess should know; she was the same way. 'I've got your discharge letter ready; you're good to go. You get yourself home, love, and you can go and see Malcolm in the morning.'

Or maybe a couple of days, thought Bess.

But when the nurse left, Fiona was already taking her phone from her bag.

'Mum, if he has concussion, he'll be sleeping.'

'He will?'

'He'll sleep a lot, it's the body's way of recovering, so leave it for now; let's get you sorted.'

It was only when they were in the car and driving away that Fiona burst into tears.

Bess pulled over. She hadn't even got out of the hospital car park. She put an arm around her mum's shoulders, held her for a moment and then found a tissue from the container in the glovebox.

Fiona took the tissue. 'I'm sorry, love.' She made that sound where you are trying your best not to cry but can't quite manage it.

'No need to apologise.'

'Bess, it was terrifying. One minute, Malcolm and I were laughing at something or other, I can't remember what now, and the next, a great big bang sent us hurtling to the side of the road. I thought we were going to hit the stone wall but we stopped just short of it.' Her voice wobbled. 'And that sound, the sound of metal being torn apart as they got Malcolm out. I don't think I'll ever forget it.'

'It's awful, I know,' said Bess. But it was the best way to get a person out quickly and without causing any more injury.

'You were all so calm at the scene.' She looked at her daughter. 'I mean, you told me what you do from day to day at work, but seeing it, like that, in reality...'

'You're safe now. And it sounds as though Malcolm is on the mend. You can try speaking to him tomorrow.' Whoever he was, she couldn't think about that now, or the way she might feel about her mother seeing another man. She was adept at doing this – pushing away stuff that could wait when a situation was urgent; she did it at work all the time. You couldn't bring too many personal worries with you or you'd never get the job done.

Fiona nodded but then calm gave way to fresh emotion. 'We could've been killed. Malcolm could've died.'

'You're both going to be fine.' Bess hated seeing her mum this way, reliving it all over again, not only the incident but the terror, the pain, that came with it.

'Did you see the size of the dent in his car? Oh, what a stupid question; you were right there, your fireman friend Gio helped to get him out.'

Her *fireman friend*? She kind of liked the terminology and she supposed that's what he was. Sometimes, when he looked at her, she wondered what it might be like if things ever moved beyond friendship but she couldn't let her mind, or anything else, go there.

They drove home in relative silence, both exhausted from the events of that evening. Bess stayed in her mother's spare room so she'd be there just in case. She wanted to feel the closeness of home too, the almost letting go of being a grown-up by stepping into her childhood bedroom, if only for a while.

In the morning, Fiona woke Bess to tell her she was getting a taxi to the trauma centre to see Malcolm. And she wouldn't have it that Bess could take her.

'We'll talk soon, Bess,' her mother said as she hovered at her bedroom door. She had on her favourite floral blouse and a waft of Anais Anais perfume came Bess's way. She was going to see her boyfriend and Bess wasn't really a part of that. And as soon as the taxi's horn alerted them to its presence outside, her mum was gone.

Now, back at the airbase, once Maya had refuelled the aircraft at the bowser, Bess climbed into the rear of the helicopter, which was separated by a sheet of heavy-duty plastic from the front. The inside of the air ambulance had the litter for patients, breathing apparatus, defibrillators, monitors, and blood transfusion equipment.

Bess retrieved the blood and plasma bags which they brought with them each time they went out on a job. They would need replenishing and the drugs they'd taken to the scene would need to be put away inside the airbase because legally, they couldn't leave those onboard. As she climbed out, she spotted Dorothy. Dorothy was one of the Whistlestop River Freewheelers, a team of fully trained volunteers who provided an around-the-clock, seven-days-a-week service transporting blood, donor breast milk, medications and other medical supplies to the air ambulance as well as hospitals, surgeries and patients themselves. The work they did was vital and words could not express how much this team of people were key to the operations here at the Whistlestop River Air Ambulance.

'You're right on time.' Bess smiled at Dorothy as they both headed inside the airbase. Bess slotted her helmet onto the shelf alongside the others, ready to grab when they were called out on another job.

'I have my uses.'

Bess put an arm around the woman's shoulders. 'You're always appreciated.'

'So is cake... Word has it Nadia has been making her scones again.'

'Don't worry, I'll sort you out once I've stored everything away.'

Dorothy gave Bess a fresh supply of blood and plasma in a special cool box fitted with a data logger that indicated if the temperature rose beyond safe limits. Sometimes, they kept blood on board the aircraft but not if it was too hot or too cold, and today, the outside temperature was questionable. Safer to keep it in here. And then any blood unused after twenty-four hours would be returned to the blood donation system to be used elsewhere. It was too valuable to waste.

Once everything was sorted, Bess and Dorothy headed for the kitchen and found Nadia as their welcoming committee.

'I thought I heard voices.' Nadia beamed. 'Dorothy, before you head off, you need a coffee and one of my freshly baked scones with jam and cream.' She didn't wait for an answer, simply loaded a scone onto a plate and handed it to Dorothy.

'Don't tell my doctor,' Dorothy whispered to Bess. 'I'm supposed to be on a diet.'

'A diet? Whatever for?'

'Oh, don't worry, I don't want to lose weight, but the doctor says I need to watch my sugar levels.'

'Watch them tomorrow,' said Bess.

Bess was good at convincing people to live a little, take a risk, whether it was with their waistlines, their love lives or money. She was good at doing the latter herself; the evidence of that was piling up back at home.

Nadia had Dorothy entertained and after Bess had enjoyed a scone herself, she went into the office.

Noah and Maya were in there dealing with paperwork.

'Eva loves the toy, Bess. Thank you again,' Noah said, looking up at her.

Noah had finally thrown Eva a very belated first birthday party, even though she was now getting on for seventeen months. His life and hers had been derailed somewhat as he settled into his role as a father and the process of adopting his late sister's daughter got underway.

'I'm glad she likes it,' Bess smiled. She'd bought Eva a toy school bus with little people inside.

'You shouldn't have brought a gift, though. I told you those weren't necessary.'

'And I told you I wanted to. Are you saying you want me to take it back?'

Pen in his hand, already scribbling on a form, he laughed. 'Are you kidding me? She'd kill me with her bare hands.'

Bess saw to her own admin – it was a good idea to get a jump on things before another job came in. Thankfully, today that didn't happen and she had it done it without interruption.

She'd just passed a file to Nadia when Maya came over, having finished checking weather and flight conditions. She perched on the edge of the desk. 'I haven't had a chance to ask whether you're excited? Surely it'll go better than the last one.'

'Huh?'

'The date tonight.'

Bess looked across at the calendar. 'Oh, God, it's Tuesday.'

'Don't tell me you forgot?'

'Kind of.' Even the brand-new dress hanging on the back of her bedroom door hadn't reminded her this morning. She'd bought it thinking it might be a good luck charm for yet another date she'd found on the app she was using. Surely at some point she had to meet someone half-decent. It was the law of averages, wasn't it?

She grabbed her phone.

'What are you doing?' Maya asked.

'Cancelling.' The guy from the other night was enough for now. She couldn't face any more disappointment, at least for a while.

In a few clicks, the deed was done. She swiped up to clear the screen when yet another text message came in from her mother.

'Why are you cancelling?' Maya asked.

'My head's not in the right space for a date.'

'Because of the last one?'

'Kind of.'

'You're still thinking about your mum,' Maya realised.

Maya knew the shock Bess had felt seeing her mum at the scene of the accident for a start but even more so, discovering the man she'd been in the car with. And ever since that night, Bess had done her best to push the facts deep down into the recesses of her mind.

'I need to get my head around my mother's "date" before I can go on another one of my own.' She put the word date in air quotes, having no idea whether it was a first date, a fifth, or whether the relationship had turned serious. She was sensing it was the latter, given her mum's reaction to Malcolm's injuries and the worry she had for him.

'Have you spoken to her about it yet?' Maya tied her chestnut hair up and out of the way as they headed out of the kitchen and into the hangar, which needed a tidy. 'Take it from me: the longer you put it off, the worse it seems. For the both of you.' She was speaking from experience.

Bess reached for the broom. 'She deserves to be happy. But it's a lot to get my head around. It's been three years since Dad, but it still feels so odd to me.'

Maya stopped what she was doing, a bin bag in her hands. 'After my mum passed away, I think it was years until my dad dated. And then, it was very on and off, and we weren't talking by then, so I could easily block it out.' She smiled kindly. 'I can't say I recommend that approach, though.'

Bess swept the main concrete floor, got rid of some of the debris from beneath cabinets against the walls. She couldn't begrudge her mother some happiness, some fun, but ever since her dad died, the man her mother had described as *one of a kind, the only man she would forever love deeply*, she'd thought her mum would be content with her daughter, her friends and acquaintances. And a man stepping into her mum's life meant he was stepping into Bess's too and she'd shocked even herself by how much it unsettled her.

She stopped sweeping and leant her chin on her hands against the top of the broom handle, crossing one ankle over the other. 'Seeing Mum crying about a man who isn't my dad, saying his name, her worry for him when I had absolutely no idea she was seeing anyone was hard. I reacted by not talking about it and... well, I've been avoiding her calls, sticking to text messages.' She'd used the excuse that she'd covered shifts for Kate, twice, and then that she had extra training sessions.

'I'm sure you and your mum will sort this out; give it time.'

'You're so wise.'

Nadia breezed into the hangar, bringing with her a waft of the floral perfume Bess had given her for her birthday. 'I think it's the scones.'

'Probably,' Bess laughed. 'What's with all the baking anyway, Nadia?'

'I've always enjoyed it but I took a few classes at the start of autumn, thought I'd do something different just for fun, and then I got addicted. Now I've started baking even more, I can't seem to stop myself.' Blonde and curvy, she was every bit as gorgeous as the cakes she kept bringing to the airbase.

'No arguments from me,' Noah hollered as he passed by from the direction of the office. The airbase building had a welcoming reception at the front, the hangar at the rear, an office, kitchen, locker room and briefing room as well as a small room with a few beds should any of them need to get their head down for a while on shift.

'Talk to your mum soon, Bess,' Maya urged when it was just the two of them again.

And she knew she had to. For both their sakes. She texted her mum there and then to say she'd be over after shift.

But no sooner had the whoosh sound signalled the text leaving her device, the phone at the base rang out, its shrill signal alerting them to another job coming in.

It was time for The Skylarks to drop everything and take to the skies again.

* * *

The job turned out to be a major one where the outcome was very unsure indeed. A schoolgirl had climbed a tree in her back garden to rescue her cat and she'd fallen, landing on her head. Her injuries were life threatening and Bess and Noah did as much as they could for her on the ground before transporting her by air to the trauma centre where neurologists and other doctors were on standby. If the young girl came through this, it would be a long road to recovery.

By the time Hilda landed back at base, it was well after the end of shift for the red team and Bess was shattered. The more difficult and traumatic calls where the outcomes might not be favourable were hard.

She called her mother so she could explain why she was running late. If she sent a text, her mum would assume she was putting the talk off again, but after she gave the gist of what had happened, her mum suggested they reschedule for lunch tomorrow instead.

'What can I bring?' Bess asked, keen not to dwell on the sadness and shock of her shift. 'I'll have to do a supermarket dash in the morning, I'm almost out of a few essentials.'

'I don't like to be a pain but could you grab me a few packets of cat food for Liquorice?'

'Of course I can. I'll see you tomorrow, around midday.'

No mention of Malcolm. Maybe her mum was as apprehensive about talking about him as her daughter was.

Bess headed home, the last job of the day still very much on her mind, all good thoughts going to the young girl and her family that their story would have a happy ending.

Nothing was ever guaranteed, though, and as she pushed her key into the lock of her front door and clocked the words on her key fob yet again, she was very much reminded of that.

5

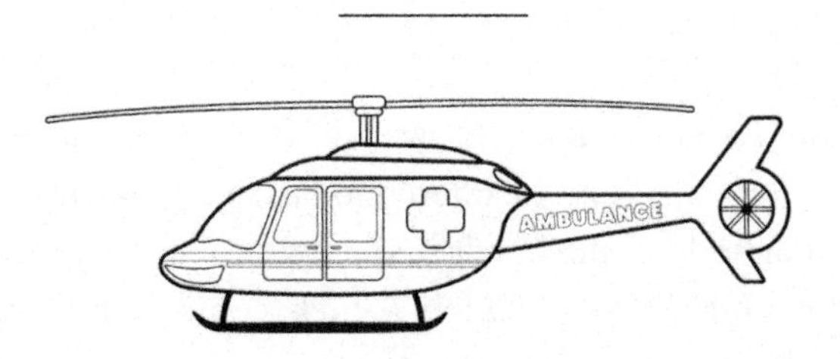

It had only been a few days, but Gio thought he might well tear his hair out soon with this woman here. All day, every day.

There was only so much patience Gio had.

And already, it was wearing thin.

The night he'd spoken with his mother on the phone had brought with it the usual stress but when he'd fallen asleep on the sofa, he'd had no idea of what was about to come his way.

His mother. In real life. At his door.

'Well, don't I get a hug?' his mother had said, opening her arms.

He rubbed a hand across his face as though he might be seeing things. 'Mum, what are you doing here?'

She dropped her arms but he quickly stepped forwards to indulge her with a hug, defusing the situation before it blew up in his face. 'You'd better come in.'

The sun wasn't even up yet and he wished he wasn't either. He felt all over the place – late shifts and night shifts often buggered up his sense of timing. And so did unexpected visits.

'Mum, what are you doing here?' He repeated his question

the second he closed the door after she'd hauled her bag inside. His heart sank at the size of it; it looked big enough for most of her worldly possessions from what he remembered.

She unwound her green, knitted scarf, the one she'd knitted herself in one of her better periods when she had steered clear of the bottle – at least for as long as it had taken her to knit the thing anyway.

'I know it's a shock.' She toyed with the ends of the scarf between her fingers until he offered to take it along with her coat. He put them both on the hooks in the hallway.

So much for the cleaning job. Which, come to think of it, she had either lied about or jacked in before she'd even started.

But then she must have planned this – thinking back to their conversation last night, she'd said something about how it was *colder there than where you are*. He hadn't registered at the time that she hadn't said it was colder *here*.

'Mum, how did you get here?'

Her grin spread. 'I got a lift in a lorry.'

She'd bloody well hitchhiked! What sixty-six-year-old did that unless she was trying to recapture some sort of youth? She'd missed out on a lot of years getting pregnant so young, barely out of school herself; perhaps that was a part of what had made her the way she was.

'It was all above board,' she insisted. 'The driver is a husband of a friend and we arranged it last week.' Well, that was a relief. 'He was very kind to bring me.'

'What about your job?'

She waved her hands as though that was unimportant. 'I'm parched, we didn't stop off anywhere; could I have a cup of tea after I use your loo?'

'Sure.' Why not? Why not act as though she was popping in like a regular mum, come to say a surprise hello rather than showing up on the doorstep of the son who she barely saw and who, a couple of visits ago, had gone to her place and had had to clean up vomit from her carpet and help her change her clothes.

The tea gave him something to do. But he needed coffee. A strong one. He dropped a pod into the little machine and positioned a mug beneath the spout.

When the drinks were made, he pushed the mug of tea in her direction. 'Why didn't you tell me you were coming?'

'You might have pretended to be out.' She followed him into the lounge.

'I wouldn't have done that.' He hid his own doubts about this claim behind a sip of coffee that burnt the edge of his lips. He wanted to know how long she was staying – the bag she'd brought could mean one night, or it could mean one month.

It took her a while to look at him and when she did, there was a reticence in her smile, a nervousness in her eyes. 'I'm back in AA.' Her fingers stroked the china of her cup. 'I know, I've been before, a few times. And it never worked. I never stuck with it. But it's different this time.'

It always was.

'I don't expect you to believe me,' she said.

'What about the job?' He set down his own mug, clasped his hands together, the knuckles squeezing down onto one another. 'Last night, you had a job; today, you're here. You must understand why I'm confused.'

'I still have the job. It isn't far from here – I found it online,' she said, proud of the fact, 'and it's only five minutes by bus.'

Oh, God, she was moving in!

'Five minutes... from here,' he said.

'Gio...'

He stood, paced, raked a hand through his hair. 'How can you do this to me? You turn up because you have nowhere to live. I can see right through you.'

'Don't shout at me.'

'Why did you lie?'

'I didn't. I just never told you everything. They put the rent up on my bedsit. I could barely afford it as it was. And then I found a job but the landlord wouldn't give me extra time to pay what I owed. They wanted me out. So I found another job here. All I need is a bit of time to gather some money, then I'll be out of your hair; I'll go back up north if that's what you want.'

'Do not turn this around to be me wanting you to go.' She was good at the guilt trip, he had to hand it to her. Or perhaps Marco was right when he said that Gio had a habit of shouldering the guilt for her regardless of whether he was at fault or not, just because she was their mother.

'I'm sorry, I know it's a lot to ask. But I mean it, Gio, when I say I'm not drinking. I won't be any trouble. And I'll pull my weight when I'm here. I promise. It won't be for too long. And it'll be good to spend some time with you, if you're not too busy.'

'Where exactly is the job?' Delivering the question, he did his best to calm down.

It worked. He was relieved when she told him it wasn't at the Whistlestop River Inn but an establishment in the next town. At least if she was to go back to her old ways, it would be one step removed from his local area.

'And they know you're not from around here?' he asked her.

'I told them I had lodgings.' She didn't meet his eye.

'Of course you did.'

'Gio—'

'You can't be surprised that I'm pissed off, Mum!'

She said nothing because she knew he was right. Both he and Marco had been there more for her than the other way round.

They did it because they loved her, but there were limits, which she continued to push.

Gio swore under his breath and left the room. He was likely to say far too much if he stayed too close to her right now. He stood in the kitchen, arms strained against the sink, angry, upset, worried, everything else their mother's presence brought with it.

When he went back into the lounge, she hadn't moved.

'I knew you wouldn't be thrilled.' Her voice, quiet, made him feel terrible, guilty. 'But I was looking online for work and couldn't find much locally and then, I don't know, suddenly, I was looking near here.' She shrugged. 'I miss you, both my boys; I miss my sons.' And Gio knew that he was the best one to target because Marco might not even let her in the front door of his home in Hampshire.

He almost went to her and hugged her but he couldn't.

'I'm sorry, Gio.'

'Do you know how many times I've heard that from you over the years?'

'The words probably don't sound genuine given how many times I've let you and your brother down. This won't be a second chance for me with you; it'll be a twentieth, thirtieth, I don't know... all I know is that I'd really like this one.'

She was trying, wasn't she? Perhaps this time, it really would be different?

'Gio, all I want is to get myself going with this job, and like I said, I'll pull my weight. I won't outstay my welcome... or have I done that already?'

'You haven't.' As hard as he knew this would be, he didn't have it in him to turn her away. He'd never forgive himself. 'You can stay. A few weeks.'

She smiled and her words rushed at him. 'Gio, thank you, thank you, you don't know what this means, I'll pay you board—'

'No, you won't. You'll save the money to find somewhere else. And after a few weeks, it'll be time to move on.' Not easy unless she had a steady job but perhaps this cleaning gig would turn out to be that. 'Will you be able to afford it?'

'I'll manage. Don't you worry about that.'

But he would, he always did.

'I suppose I'd better think of something for dinner tonight,' he said. 'Are you still vegan?' She'd turned vegan a few years ago, announced it to him the day he'd turned up at her flat with chicken sandwiches. He'd had to eat all of them himself.

'I'm not,' she smiled, recognising the olive branch, no matter how temporary, when it was handed to her. 'And I can cook if you like.'

'We'll see,' he said.

She looked at her watch, the watch he'd given her a few birthdays ago. She'd sold a lot of her jewellery in tougher times; he supposed he should be grateful that the watch had survived the cull.

'What time do you start?' he asked her.

'In a couple of hours.'

He went out to the kitchen, found his spare key and handed it to her. 'Don't lose it.'

'I'm not a kid, Gio. I have used keys before.' But her snappish remark softened to, 'Sorry, that was rude of me.'

'Look, maybe we should both try and relax a bit while you're here.'

'I'd like that.'

'How about I show you the spare room. I'll have to make the bed up.'

'Thank you, Gio.' She followed after him as he took her bag upstairs.

'You can unpack things into the drawers, the wardrobe.' He disappeared to get the bedding.

He came back with the duvet cover, pillowcases and sheets and as he made up the bed, she unpacked what little she had. He didn't miss the fraying at the bottom of the pyjamas she folded and put on top of the chest of drawers ready to put under her pillow – she'd always done that; he'd forgotten until now.

When he noticed how threadbare the towel she had was, he went and fetched a couple of fresh towels and left them on the ottoman at the side of the room.

She must've noticed him looking at his own watch this time.

'When does your shift start?'

'I'm due in in an hour and a half. I don't usually do shifts so close together but we've got a couple of guys off.' And as much as he needed space from her, it couldn't have happened at a worse time. 'I'd better get organised. I'll leave you to unpack.'

There was something he really had to do before he so much as contemplated leaving the house or more importantly, the house with his mother in it.

* * *

When it was time for Gio to go to work, he picked up his holdall and heaved the heavier-than-usual bag over his shoulder. 'You know where the bus stop is?'

'I do. It's left at the end of the road, then left again.'

He couldn't help but smile. 'Good.'

'And Gio?' she said before he reached the front door to head to work. 'Thank you for trying to be discreet by taking away the bottles.'

When he'd left her upstairs earlier, Gio had gone downstairs to the cupboard where he kept his booze. He'd stashed all of it inside the holdall on his shoulder now – as well as a change of clothes and his washbag, there was a bottle of whisky, two bottles of red wine and a six-pack of beers. He'd crammed them in but the noise when he picked up the bag had likely given him away.

'You can trust me here, I promise,' she said when she got no response.

To be fair, she'd never ever told him she could be trusted before. She'd lied plenty of times and gone back on her word, said sorry, but she'd never made that claim.

'What time will you be home?' she asked as he stepped out of the front door into the cold October day, unsure whether it really was a good idea to be leaving her here.

'After you.' A few weeks and that was it. He only hoped they could be civil for all that time, that he wouldn't regret this. 'Call me if you need anything.'

She rushed to him and hugged him, squeezing tight like a kid clung to their mother's legs when they didn't want them to leave their side. 'Thank you.' Her words were almost too quiet to hear. 'Stay safe, my Gio.'

He hugged her back just a moment longer. 'I'll do my best.'

And then he climbed into the car and drove away.

But he stopped around the corner once he was out of sight. He had to text Marco, who would think he was off his head letting her crash at his place, Marco who wouldn't believe her claims that she was sober and doing her best, Marco who like him, would be wondering how long before this woman who was in AA, who had a job and an income, would fall on her face again.

Usually, it was only a matter of time.

And now, a few days into her stay, Gio was on edge most of the time waiting for things to escalate, for them to have a big bust-up, because that was usually only a matter of time too.

6

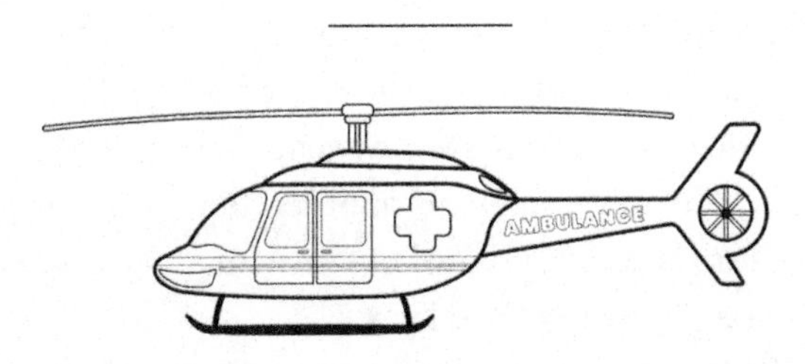

Bess had the cat food in her shopping basket and was perusing the flower arrangements at the supermarket when she saw him. Gio. Over by the books, with a woman who had to be a relative, given they both had the same smile. As Gio put a book in the basket, the woman took it out again and he put it right back in there.

And now he'd spotted her. She pulled out a lovely arrangement of bright winter flowers from the bucket they'd been displayed in as Gio headed her way.

'Good to see you, Bess.'

'And you.' She frowned. He sounded formal rather than his usual relaxed self.

'Those are beautiful,' said the woman.

'Thank you, they're for my mum.'

'How is she doing?' Gio enquired, again with more formality than they usually used around each other.

'Good, very good.'

'I'm glad.' He followed it up with an introduction. 'This is my mum, Marianne. Mum, this is Bess, she's a paramedic with the air ambulance.'

'All these people with important jobs,' his mum gushed, presumably mostly with pride for her son.

And now it made sense. Gio's mum was in town, and that likely came with a whole host of problems. Over the years, he hadn't shared the specifics but she'd got the measure on what Gio's home life was like and it wasn't good. When they'd shared a house, Bess had never met his mother but he'd disappeared sometimes for days on end and always came back quieter and more subdued than when he'd left.

Bess lifted up the flowers. 'I'd better get on, got a few other bits to grab.' She sensed Gio's discomfort and she didn't want to put him through any more of it than was necessary. 'Good to meet you, Marianne.' And to Gio, she said, 'We'll catch up soon.'

'Hope so.' He smiled. He didn't have to say so but Bess could tell how much his mother's visit was impacting on him already.

She got the rest of the things she needed and was at the self-serve checkout when he came up behind her.

'You're following me,' she joked. 'I should report you.' She looked around. His mum was over the other side of the check-outs, putting through their small basket of shopping. 'How's it going?'

His eyes lost their usual sparkle. 'I don't really know. Good... weird.'

'She's staying with you?'

'Yeah.'

'Did she tell you she was coming?'

'What do you think?'

'Gio...' his mother called over. She smiled at Bess but quickly looked away as if embarrassed.

'I'm needed,' said Gio, his voice soft and low. 'See you soon.'

Bess watched him go. If they hadn't been in the supermarket and his mother wasn't watching, she might have hugged him tight, told him to hang in there, that it would all work out in the end.

Half an hour later, Bess let herself into her mother's home; Fiona insisted upon it, although Bess had to wonder what would happen if Malcolm became a permanent fixture in her mother's life. Surely there'd need to be some ground rules then; she didn't want to walk into a situation she'd rather not see.

She shook away the feeling, called out her arrival and closed the front door behind her. 'Something smells good,' she added as she took her coat off.

'Cinnamon tea cake, your favourite,' Fiona hollered back as Bess made her way towards the kitchen.

As soon as Fiona saw the bouquet, she hugged her daughter and leaned in to smell the blooms. 'For me?'

'Of course for you,' said Bess. 'And for you,' she added to Liquorice, who had already jumped down from the kitchen chair to come over and wind around her ankles, 'you have a treat too.' She scooped him up and made a fuss of him as Fiona unloaded the pouches of cat food from the bag Bess had brought in.

Fiona emptied the rest of the bag. 'Thank you for bringing lunch; I could've easily whipped something up, you know.'

'I thought you could use the rest.' Bess had found Cajun chicken, a lovely side dish of herbed potatoes, vegetables already prepared. All that needed to be done was to heat it all up in the oven.

'You've spent too much on me today, Bess, what with flowers and food. I don't expect it.'

'You didn't ask, but I wanted to spoil you. You deserve it.'

The cat leapt from her arms and she put the oven on ready to warm everything through. They needed to talk but she couldn't do it on an empty stomach.

They got the lunch ready, dished up and it was only when they were part way through the meal that Bess's mum finally mentioned Malcolm.

'I know it was a shock for you, Bess, seeing me with another man.'

'How is Malcolm doing?' Perhaps it would be easier to approach this from a different angle rather than addressing her emotions about the new man in her mother's life. Medical details she could deal with.

'Thanks to the wonderful work of all the first responders, including my own brilliant daughter, as well as the hospital staff who took such good care of him afterwards, he's home already and recovering well.'

Bess swallowed a piece of chicken not quite chewed enough to go down smoothly.

'Bess, I know this isn't easy for you. It isn't for me either.'

She kept chewing.

'I've wanted to tell you but never found the right time.'

Bess rested her cutlery against her plate. 'How long have you been together?'

'About a month.'

'Is he moving in?'

Her mother seemed shocked at the question. 'No, of course not.'

'Are you going to go and live with him? Get married?' Her mouth was running away with her and in this moment, she felt like she was seven years old, sitting on the kitchen bench while her mother prepared a meal, asking question after question the way she had done back then, inquisitive about the world she was a part of.

'Slow down, Bess. I'm happy to talk about Malcolm but can we make it less of a firing squad of questions? I feel like I'm on trial.'

Bess shoved another forkful of food into her mouth to stop herself saying more. The last thing she wanted to do was upset her mum.

When she'd finished, she delivered another question, but a gentler one. 'Where did you meet?'

'At the town hall – I was with the WI and as I left, Malcolm walked past me. My dress caught on the bag he was carrying. We were attached to each other and one of the ladies had to bend down to set me free without tearing the fabric.' She began to smile. 'He asked me if I'd like to go for a coffee and...'

It was a nice story, sweet, serendipitous even.

'Bess... why don't I tell you a bit more about him, what he's like? It might help put your mind at ease.'

And so Bess listened, took in the facts and tried to dampen down her emotions about it all.

Malcolm was the same age as Fiona. He was widowed, he had three grown-up children, and he'd worked for three decades as a financial advisor.

'He's retired now,' Fiona finished.

In many ways, he sounded lovely.

'Bess, tell me how you're feeling.'

'I'm thinking about Dad.'

'You think it's too soon.' Fiona looked out of the back doors into the conservatory and the damp garden that was beginning to lose its colour, ready for winter to set in.

'I'm being ridiculous. It's been a while. Three years is a long time, but... somehow it feels like it was only yesterday.'

'I miss your dad every single day. It's not as painful as it was before, but that doesn't mean I don't wish things could have been different. I didn't expect to meet Malcolm and he won't ever replace your dad, but he makes me happy.'

And now Bess felt terrible. What right did she have to destroy any of her mother's happiness?

'He makes me laugh and for a while, I wondered whether I'd ever do that again,' Fiona admitted. 'Meeting Malcolm made me realise that a part of me was holding back. Now it's coming alive again. We share some of the same interests, I feel blessed to have him in my life and the night of the accident, well, it made me realise that I may be falling in love for the second time in my life.'

Love? Friendship and companionship were one thing, but love was a whole different game. This was serious. And Bess knew her mum deserved her support.

Her gaze drifted over to the photograph of her parents that stood proudly on the windowsill. 'I want you to be happy.'

'I think I am, Bess. Give him a chance, get to know him.'

'I will.'

Bess piled up the plates to take over to the sink.

'Do you have room for cinnamon tea cake?' Fiona asked.

Bess laughed. 'Silly question.'

Bess set off for home once they'd had a couple of slices of cake each and a cup of tea and she let the conversation with her mother settle. One step at a time. Maybe meeting Malcolm properly, and soon, might be a step in the right direction.

When she arrived at her house, she parked on the drive and stayed there for a moment looking up at her cottage-style home with its unassuming frontage.

Bess's place wasn't big but she'd made each room inside individual – all had walls in various colours, two rooms had a feature wall with wallpaper, the furniture fitted perfectly, she had pictures up from the holidays she'd taken over the years, trinkets she'd collected like the colourful sand timer she'd found in Spain which sat on the shelf in the kitchen next to the olive dish she'd brought back from Italy. She had a set of coasters she'd bought in France, the hard-knotted teal rug she'd found in Scotland last winter which she couldn't resist after seeing it in a shop window.

Bess's dad Ron had helped her choose this house. When she'd begun looking for her own place all those years ago, he'd gone with her whenever she asked. He quite enjoyed it and confided in her that he loved looking at property but he'd never persuaded her mother to move so he had to live vicariously through his daughter. Ron had vetoed four properties before this one for various reasons, including subsidence, proximity to an alleyway, a ridiculously high asking price, and a non-committed vendor. Then they'd come to see this house. It also came with a fairly high asking price but it was a sound investment if they could get the price down even a little bit. Ron had told her to think with her head as well as her heart – that was her dad all over. He always said emotions had to take a back seat when you were spending a lot of money. He'd been sensible up until his very last day – always paid into a pension, never put money on a credit card unless he knew he could pay it off, he had insurances for this, that and the other. He had money put aside too so that eventually, he and Bess's mum would be able to enjoy his retirement and do the things they'd talked about like the cruise around Norway, learning to play tennis together, heading to Europe.

And then he died.

Bess remembered the day her second and final offer on the property was accepted. She hadn't expected to be successful, she never thought she'd be so lucky, and even better, nobody dragged their feet and she moved in three months later.

Bess loved her home. She'd installed a wood burner, redone the kitchen with Cotswold grey cabinetry and solid oak benchtops, she'd stripped off the torn and very old wallpaper in the main bedroom and replaced it with something to her taste. She'd slowly put her stamp on the house and the labour of love was all recorded in a photograph album, the before and after pictures she and her dad had looked at many a time, hardly able to believe how different it looked now compared to when she bought it.

Bess went inside. She stepped onto the mat, picked up the post collected there as if she'd been away for a week, not out for less than twenty-four hours while she went to the supermarket and had lunch with her mum. Her feet sank into the pecan-coloured carpet as she made her way from the hallway and into the lounge but she didn't open any of the correspondence yet. She needed a glass of wine first, something to take the edge off. Because she knew what was waiting for her.

She snuggled on the sofa in what was usually the ideal reading spot, armed with a glass of wine for Dutch courage, and tore open the first envelope. Then the second, the third, each and every one of them. Some weren't too daunting; one wasn't even asking for money – that had to be a win, didn't it? But plenty of them were and she added them to the pile with the others. She retrieved her iPad from the shelf below the coffee table and logged on to her banking app. But where to start? When you had this many bills, it was hard to know, when you had so much debt you couldn't doggy paddle, let alone swim.

Her mortgage payment had been taken successfully – that was a plus; she didn't want to miss it. Losing her home was terrifying; surely she couldn't let things get on top of her so much that that happened? She remembered one of her blind dates last summer, a guy who was a roofer and, although nice enough, she'd had a feeling from the start that he wasn't her type. She'd stayed for the date – it would've been rude to leave just because she didn't feel any attraction towards him. She'd wondered whether things might improve; maybe if she gave him a chance, he'd surprise her. He definitely did that when, a few drinks in, his whole woeful story about a gambling habit and a recent drug addiction came out and it was a story without a happy ending because he lost his home as a result of those things. Was that about to happen to her? Was she about to get herself into so much mess that she'd have to turn up on her mother's doorstep with all her things in tow as if this, being a homeowner, had all been a game of make believe like she was a little girl again who'd been playing house all this time?

With the mortgage payment already made, it didn't leave an awful lot in her account by the time she'd also paid her water bill followed by the electricity charges that she'd had reminders for and ignored until today's demand arrived.

With a shiver, she got the wood burner going. Her dad had loved sitting in front of it when it was first installed. He'd said it went perfectly with this house and she'd had a sneaky suspicion that he might have tried to persuade Bess's mum to get one put in too.

It hadn't happened, or maybe he'd never got the chance to push the idea.

Ron Gardner would hate what his daughter had been doing since he died. He'd hate that she'd lost control – *Be careful with your money*, he'd always said, *Make sure you have a fund set aside for the unplanned things that might happen*. It was what he'd done. She still did the same job he'd always been proud of, but unfortunately, when she lost him she'd sought comfort from anywhere she could get it. And as much as it sounded laughable, she'd found comfort in buying herself things, treats here and there that over time had become more common. Spending money had become her way of life and her habits had run away with her.

She reached for the last piece of post she hadn't yet opened and ripped away the envelope before she could chicken out.

She read the letter.

This was the third time she'd been late with repayments on a loan she'd taken out last year to cover the cost of a new boiler when hers needed replacing.

She sat forwards, taking in the additional information at the foot of the letter, about debt collection agencies, legal action.

She threw the letter down and clipped the side of the wine glass, sending red liquid all over the coffee table. She grabbed a bunch of tissues from the box on the shelf beneath and mopped it up straight away, the tissues soon staining pink, never to be white again.

And then she put her face in her hands and cried, something she rarely did, something she hadn't done since the day they buried her dad.

This was very real. And if she didn't do something about it soon, she might end up losing just about everything.

7

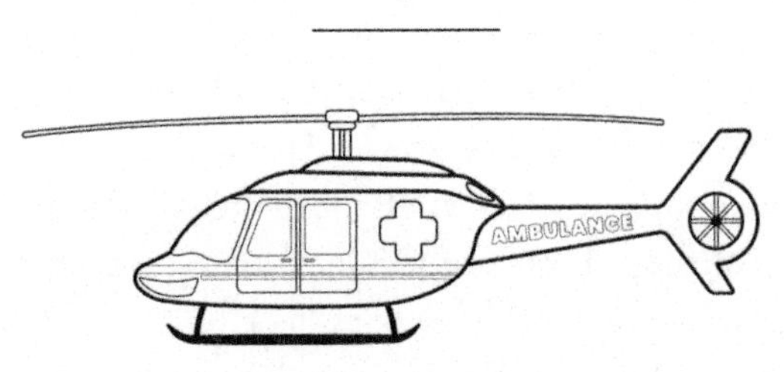

Gio wasn't all that comfortable with his mum being on her own at his place but he was slowly getting used to it. He was on a day shift that would finish when she was still at work herself, which at least meant they had some head space from one another. And it gave them something to talk about when they were both home other than focusing on the past – he told her about his day, she talked about hers, although she did tell him that there wasn't all that much to say about cleaning and steered him to talk more about himself. Fair point, he supposed, and he indulged her, told her about life at the fire station, what it was like to go out on a shout, the work they did and the lives they saved. But he'd also glowed inwardly at the thought of her going out every day, to a job. It sounded so trivial, but it wasn't for her, and it was a welcome change. She was holding down employment and after almost a week, things were looking good. He only prayed it stayed this positive.

Gio arrived on shift, changed into his uniform and stood with his crew on parade while the officer in charge detailed their duties. Then it was on to checking all their equipment including breathing apparatus, the fire engine itself and the equipment on board.

Halfway through the morning, they set off to the primary school for a community visit.

'What?' Mickey asked Gio, who gave him a look when he pulled up in the playground and set the sirens going and blared the horn to announce their arrival. 'Kids love it.' Sure enough, little kids' faces lined the low-down windows.

'Are you telling me that was all for them?' Gio laughed.

Mickey shrugged. He didn't deny that part of it was for him too.

The crew had the pupils trying out kit and using the hoses; it was a riot. Gio didn't spend much time with children aside from his brother's two but kids were usually a captive audience when the fire engine rolled into view and once the demonstrations started.

They were almost back at the fire station just in time for lunch when they were radioed to attend a job less than two miles away.

'Roger that.' Mickey, a skilled driver, had the engine turned the right way in seconds before they bumped along a side street and emerged onto the road to take them directly to the bed and breakfast down by the river.

The shout was one of their most straightforward – a kitchen fire which hadn't got too bad thanks to the owner's quick thinking to call the professionals. Too many times, the crew saw fires that had gone out of control and heard owners' stories of how they'd tried to put out the flames themselves first before calling 999. Unfortunately, some fires were a beast and wouldn't go down without a bigger fight than a simple fire extinguisher could handle.

Back at the station after lunch, the crew was onto a training drill, the physical kind rather than being in the meeting room, which was always Gio's preference. The crew challenged their physical ability, their use of apparatus, ensured their competence by pulling ladders from the top of the engine and putting them up against the training tower to simulate a rescue from the top floor. And before they left for the day, there was a lecture, a debrief, and more cleaning of equipment.

Gio didn't go straight home after shift; he went to the next town and the supermarket there because he knew they sold sparklers. He didn't approve of home firework displays but sparklers he could get on board with and thinking about his mum's face when he showed them to her later was enough to send him into the store.

He came out with four packets of giant sparklers. She'd love them. They'd wait until dark, though, when they'd look their best.

Gio drove home. He rounded the corner near the river to drive along the road parallel to the water, and stopped to allow a woman pushing a pram to get safely from one side to the other.

He pressed the accelerator to go on his way but at the same time saw a figure sitting on the bench overlooking the river.

He was about to pull into the parking space, head over and ask his mum what she was doing here when she should be at work, but he found his hands firmly gripping the wheel and staying on course for home.

Marianne was supposed to have another couple of hours at her job. Had she finished early? Had she been fired?

He'd usually sprawl out on the sofa when he got home and take a break but Gio couldn't rest, not until his mum came home and he knew what was going on.

He went out for a run. It was surprising the energy you could pluck out of thin air when you had something on your mind. It wasn't the first time he'd pounded the pavements to solve a problem, probably wouldn't be the last.

Following his run, he had a shower, burnt his tongue gulping down a mug of coffee, all the while watching the clock. She'd be back any minute.

And when he heard her keys in the lock, he was in the kitchen and braced himself.

He kept his back to her as he pulled out the two pieces of almost-burnt toast from the toaster and dropped them onto a plate. 'How was work?'

'It was fine.'

He scraped his knife across the top of the butter, the jagged, yellow pieces breaking rather than coming off in nice, smooth curls. 'Tired?' He heard her pull out a chair.

'I am. You must be too. How was work for you?'

'Busy.'

And when he ripped a hole in the surface of the second piece of toast, the butter way too firm to be doing this, he lost it. The knife clanked against the china. 'You're lying to me.'

'What?'

He turned to face her. He watched her. Had she been drinking? He couldn't tell, not from here, and he daren't take a step closer. 'I said, you're lying to me. I saw you by the river when you should've been at work.'

'You've been spying on me?'

'No, I haven't! But I think perhaps I should've been!'

'Don't yell at me.'

'Have you been drinking?'

Her chair scraped back and she picked up her handbag which, he wouldn't mind betting, had a bottle of something inside and she knew it because rather than walking away as he assumed was her intention, she yanked the sides of the bag and thrust it under his nose so he could see its contents. 'Take a look for yourself.'

He did.

'Satisfied?'

'Satisfied that you've lied to me? No way. You're living in my house; I deserve the truth.'

But rather than argue back, she looked about to burst and stormed out. He heard the front door slam.

He ate his overdone toast, made another coffee. He wasn't going to go looking for her. He thought about calling Marco but Marco would say *I told you so*. And he'd be right.

Gio was surprised when he heard the front door open less than ten minutes later and rather than sneak off upstairs to avoid him, Marianne came into the kitchen and sat down opposite him at the table.

'I promised myself that if we argued, I wouldn't walk away.' She looked up at him through eyes that were dry now but the red rims suggested she may have been crying before. 'Can I explain?'

He shrugged, tired of the same old routine.

'It turns out I couldn't stomach the smell of stale booze in that pub. I got there on the first day, opened the door and I almost threw up. I left, I called them when I got a couple of streets away, I told them that my accommodation had fallen through, that I had nowhere to stay. I apologised; they said it was regrettable. That was it.'

Was it believable? Yes. Was it true? He had no idea.

'Gio, I swear that's the truth.'

'Then why didn't you tell me?'

'Because... I had a job and then I jacked it in. I knew how disappointed you'd be.'

'And I am... but not when I know the reason.'

'I guess it was silly to have even taken the position in the first place but it was near you, I wanted a chance to see at least one of my boys and start trying to make amends.'

He wondered, was that the wording they used at AA? Did that mean she really did go to those meetings?

'What have you been doing every day, Mum?'

'I've been wandering around town, keeping a low profile in case, you know...'

'In case I found out.' He ran a hand across his jaw. 'Didn't you realise that sooner or later, you'd have had to tell me? Without any money coming in—'

'I know, you'd have found out. But I'm looking for alternative work, I promise. And if in a couple of weeks, I don't find any, then I'll move on.'

He let the words settle. She was shivering and he realised she had a coat but it wasn't thick enough to stand up to late autumn temperatures, never mind the winter chill once it arrived.

Without asking, he got the carton of soup from the fridge, tipped it into a saucepan and warmed it up for her. She sat there in silence, letting him digest her revelations.

As he served the soup with a bread roll on the side, he watched her. It was as though she'd removed a mask and now he could see vulnerability, the fear she'd likely kept hidden once upon a time behind laughs and smiles conjured up by the evils of alcohol. And instead of making her talk any more, he let her be, let her eat, let her feel as though she was safe.

He watched as she used the last of the bread roll to mop up the remnants of soup in her bowl. As she'd eaten, he'd thought about telling her to leave, to go back up north and find work there. It would get him off the hook, let him go back to the way things were; it would be easier. But watching her, he was sure she was telling the truth, that she was doing her best to get herself together. In all the times she'd claimed it before, he'd never seen her quite so determined. Or was it his wishful thinking making him view her that way?

Whatever one it was, he knew he wouldn't forgive himself if he didn't see this through. If she messed it up and eventually left then that would be it. He wasn't sure even he had it in him after this to give her yet another chance. There was being kind and then there was self-preservation and sometimes looking after yourself became the only way to survive.

She put her bowl onto her plate and took it over to the sink without looking at him. He heard the plate clatter against the draining board as she misjudged the distance.

'Gio, I promise I am trying.'

He said nothing.

'I'm looking for more work; I'm doing my best.' She turned around when she heard him push his chair back from the table. 'Where are you going?'

'I need to get us some dinner. I'll grab takeaway, save either of us cooking.' He paused in the doorway. 'Will you be here when I get back?'

'Do you want me to be?'

He walked out of the room briefly to retrieve the sparklers and back in the kitchen, he set them down on the table. 'I do, and we can use these.'

Gio expected her to smile, which she did. But what he didn't expect was for her whole face to light up, for her to put her hands across her mouth to hold in the emotion and for him to be transported back to his childhood in a way that almost knocked him off his feet.

* * *

That evening, after they'd eaten their takeaway, they went out into his back garden and lit the sparklers one after the other.

'Hold them at arm's length, remember,' he instructed.

'So bossy.' But she did as she was told.

With the lit sparkler, she did her best to write *Marianne* in the air. 'There are too many letters, easy for you with only three.'

'Why don't you just write *Mum*.'

His suggestion was met with a wide smile.

'M... u... m.' The letters sparkled against the night sky one by one and Gio sensed the poignancy of the moment wasn't lost on either of them.

When each sparkler was spent, they dropped it into the bucket of water he had nearby. 'Sparklers hold their heat for a long time,' he reminded her.

'Ever the firefighter,' she replied. 'You and Marco both love your jobs; I'm proud of my boys.'

Marco had gone into the profession first and Gio a few years after. Joining the fire service had appealed to Marco after a careers fair when he had no idea what else to do but knew he didn't want to be in an office. Gio was built the same way and so when it came to the time he had to make some decisions about his future, it seemed like a decent career. And he'd never looked back. Neither of them had.

Marianne balled up the empty wrappers from the sparklers and Gio opened the top of the wheelie bin for her to drop them inside. 'You both grew up to be fine men. And you did that in spite of me.'

She prompted him to close the bin when he stood there, the lid still up and in his hand.

He didn't address the last part of the claim – he wasn't sure what to say – so he went with, 'There's nothing else I'd rather do,' before they headed inside and into the warm.

* * *

'Are you sure you don't mind me going to the AA meeting tonight?' Marianne asked as Gio set the dishwasher to go a few nights later. 'It's at your local town hall; I thought maybe it's too close. It saves me the bus fare, see, and the extra time it'll take.' She pulled on her coat, ready to leave.

Gio and Marianne had spent three consecutive evenings together, just the two of them, and rather than Gio feeling suffocated, like he needed to get the hell out of his own house, they settled into a routine. Not working, Marianne had cleaned his house from top to bottom, she'd cooked meals that weren't too complicated, and better than that, she'd looked for jobs. He'd seen evidence of it in her email account, all the applications, the effort she was putting in.

'I've said it's fine, Mum. You go.' He had a sudden thought. 'I could maybe walk you there, meet you after.'

He'd expected her to say no, claim that he didn't trust her or tell him that this wasn't something she wanted to share with him. But she didn't. She zipped up the coat they'd found for her in the charity shop – a warm, faux-fur-lined one that would see her through winter – and told him to hurry up as she didn't want to be late.

The winds of the last few days had gone, the temperature was falling but there was something about being out in the crisp evening air that was pretty special.

While Marianne went to her meeting, Gio walked down to the river and sat on the bench he'd seen his mum on that day. If he hadn't seen her, how long would it have taken her to admit the truth: that she hadn't done a single shift on the job that had brought her this way in the first place?

He stared out at the river but he didn't sit on the bench for long – it was too cold – and so he walked alongside the water and back until it was time to meet his mum.

When he arrived at the town hall, she came running down the steps waving a piece of paper.

'What's that?'

'It's a cleaning company; they had those little tear strips on the bottom of an ad on the noticeboard.'

He looked at the logo. He'd heard of them. 'They're a big company.' Maybe too big – she'd likely need experience and references. But he wasn't going to put a dampener on it.

He'd made the right choice not to put any doubt in her mind because as soon as Marianne got home, she applied for the job online and the very next morning, she had an interview.

The interview was at the company's premises. Gio took her there and rather than waiting around to make sure she did what she claimed, he was instead waiting around and keeping everything crossed for good news.

She came out happy enough but it wasn't until the early evening that she got the call she'd been wishing for.

She came running at him when he came downstairs with his holdall, ready for work.

'I got it, Gio! I got the job!' She didn't know what to do with herself, doubling back into the lounge, hands on her hips, her breathing ragged. 'I have a job, Gio. A proper one. A real one, one that might last!'

He wrapped her in a hug and held her until she'd calmed down a bit. This was the kind of buzzy mood that reminded him of days when she'd been happy about something – anything – and usually, it had ended up with a celebration, with booze in amounts that would make most people's hair curl.

'Well done. When do you start?' he asked.

'Tomorrow lunchtime. Oh, Gio, it's for a reputable agency. I'll have a steady income, I'll have clients – that's what they call them, *clients*. And they'll train me up, the hours are flexible. I never thought they'd be interested in me, but they are, they really are.'

'Mum, it's really great.'

She'd already picked up her phone. 'I have to tell Marco and the kids.'

Gio left for work, hoping Marco answered the call, hoping he'd see what was happening with their mother, that she really was turning her life around.

Everything was changing and in a good way.

And by the time he arrived at the fire station, his brother had messaged him to say he was pleased about Marianne's new job.

Was it too much to hope that, finally, things were looking up in the Mayhan family?

8

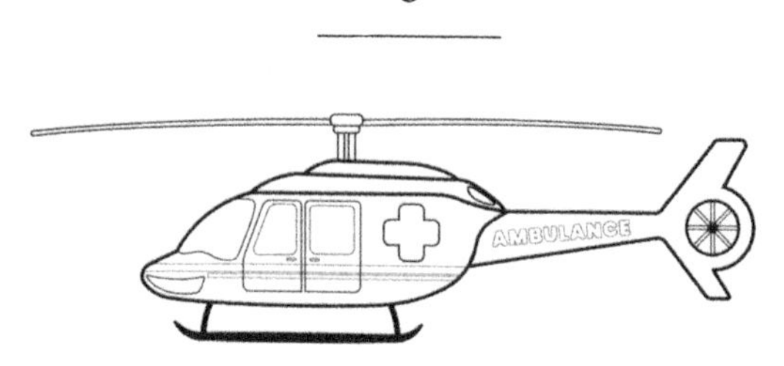

Hovering above the Dorset countryside in the darkness in Hilda, Bess felt her chest tighten like it had a physical weight on it every time she thought about what she'd done.

In the locker room before The Skylarks had got their first call of the shift, Bess had checked her bank balance. The payday loan she'd applied for online a couple of nights ago had been approved quickly, in her account swiftly, and without delay, she'd paid the amount owed on the loan she'd taken out for the new boiler, hopefully putting a stop to the loan company taking further action. At least for the time being. She still hadn't paid it off in full but it was enough to stop them hounding her for a while. Relief, however, was temporary, because now she had another loan of £1,000. And this one came with a ridiculously high interest rate that would increase her debt by a couple of hundred pounds even if she paid it off within the month.

But Bess couldn't let those thoughts invade her head too much right now, because The Skylarks were en route to a job.

The nights were drawing in all the more now they were well into November and the crew were wearing night-vision goggles as they made their way to the scene of a structure fire where there were possible multiple casualties. Bess took the radio update from the HEMS desk – the initial fire was almost out, half a dozen people had been inside the building and all had made it to safety as the firefighters continued to put out the blaze in the building next door to the original structure affected. Proximity of the industrial estate to an ambulance base meant that the road paramedics were already in attendance along with the fire brigade, joined by the police, and the air ambulance had been deployed in case they were needed for transportation or help at the scene. The Skylarks hadn't been out as quickly on this job as they would have been in daylight hours because in order to fly at night, they had to follow extra protocols. Before lifting into the air, they had to establish two or three possible landing sites, all of which were required to be larger than they would be in daylight in case online maps failed to identify something which may now be occupying the area such as a new building or campers or temporary structures. Once they were in the air, they had continued to recce landing sites from overhead as usual.

Bess hoped the crews managed to put out the fire quickly, unlike the personal fires she kept creating for herself – it was as though her debts were one big blaze and embers kept flying off and starting little fires everywhere.

'Two minutes to go,' Maya announced into her headset.

They'd already decided back at base that they could land in one of three car parks, the biggest being at the north end of the industrial estate. The crew kept everything crossed that that car park would still be empty as they'd been advised.

Maya hovered the helicopter above the centre of the car park. The downdraft blew a dilapidated fence to the right, sent a few cones on the other side flying, but with the guidance of a police officer down below using hand signals to assist with the helicopter's landing, they set down safely.

As soon as the doors were declared clear, Noah and Bess leapt out and hauled their bags onto their backs as well as the rest of the kit and the scoop. It was a short distance away from the fire engines and police had blocked off both ends of the road so there was no passing traffic.

The police officer who met them in the car park updated them further as they made their way towards the site. The surrounding premises had been evacuated. Six casualties were already being treated by road paramedics but the fire was still blazing and as they got closer, thick, grey smoke billowed into the air. Bess could see jets of water behind the structure as they approached. There were a lot of buildings and businesses along this road, plenty of livelihoods at risk as well as the threat to life.

Bess wouldn't have known the firefighter out front was Gio until she heard the crew member he was standing with yell to him, 'Do not go in, that's an order, Mayhan!'

It must be the officer in charge and there was obviously a clash about something. Gio had always been a strong character, never a pushover; those were among the many traits of his that she admired. She wondered then how it was going with his mother. They hadn't had a chance to catch up since bumping into each other in the supermarket that day. Both of them had such busy lives with demanding jobs. If she ever found a life partner, they'd have to understand that too.

Bess and Noah took a wide circle around the scene to keep themselves as safe as possible as they tried to reach the patients and the road paramedics further along.

One of the road paramedics advised Noah and Bess that all victims were good to go by road ambulance. There were only minor injuries, some smoke inhalation, and no co-morbidities to worry about.

But Bess didn't have time to feel relieved about that or respond because they all turned at the roar of a voice.

'Mayhan!'

And Bess saw a brief glimpse of what could only be Gio's form running towards the building they had evacuated.

What the hell was he doing? Obeying orders didn't mean you were a pushover. Those orders were usually given for a reason. He should be listening.

Mind back on her own job, she and Noah continued to talk with the road paramedic and agreed they would wait to see if they were needed for anyone else on scene.

But what happened next had everyone's attention.

Bess felt the enormous explosion from the building Gio had run into shock and pulse through her entire body.

Bess and Noah didn't hesitate. They got closer to the danger zone to see what they could do. Bess hoped Gio hadn't been caught up in the explosion; he had to be okay.

But her hopes were dashed as she and Noah saw two firefighters drag one of their crew away from the danger zone, away from where the explosion had happened.

One of their men was down.

And Bess knew before she even reached the casualty's side that it was Gio.

'Explosion knocked him off his feet,' another firefighter yelled amongst the mayhem. 'Silly bugger went in there against orders.'

A young woman who didn't look much older than twenty was crying nearby, watching the scene unfold; a road paramedic was trying to check her over and would call Bess or Noah if they were needed.

Flames still billowed from the rear of the building, the fire crews were still tackling what needed to be done, the officer in charge cursing at Mayhan's disobedience.

And all of Bess's attention right now went to Gio. Her good friend, Gio – kind, strong and stupidly stubborn.

Every second counted.

'What are the chances of another explosion?' Noah asked the officer in charge loudly over the commotion.

'Highly unlikely but never impossible,' he shouted back. 'Do what you can for him. Please.' And he shoved his emotions back down and went on with his own job, directing his own crew.

Bess went through the motions. It was as if muscle memory told her what to do, had her doing her checks, reaching for equipment, conversing with Noah.

Gio was mumbling on and off and his pain level was clearly severe. From examination, it appeared injuries were confined to the lower limbs, mainly his left leg. His face was covered in soot, mud, or a mixture of both and for once, Bess didn't want to see his smile because that would make this even harder. She was doing her best to not think about the sound of the explosion, the thought of Gio being knocked flying by a force he hadn't seen coming.

In a bid to get him to talk more, to assess his pain levels more accurately and maybe ascertain what happened from him which could bring to light new information, she put a hand on his. 'Gio, it's Bess.' Her heart thumped more than it had at the thought of her stupidity, her mounting debt. Self-induced problems rather than a hero taking a battering he absolutely did not deserve. 'Can you hear me, Gio?'

He groaned.

'We're going to take good care of you,' Noah put in because Bess said nothing else; she'd frozen.

But not for long. She snapped into action again, and so did Noah.

They wouldn't rush; rushing could compromise their patient and so it was vital they took one step at a time. An apparent injury could mask another so it was important to be thorough. They did their observations – ECG, oxygen saturations, blood pressure, temperature – and administered paracetamol and morphine.

But it did little for his pain.

'We'd like to give you something a bit stronger,' Bess explained to Gio.

But Gio's response this time was clear. 'No.'

Bess leaned over him. 'What do you mean, no? It'll help. We need to stabilise your leg, Gio, and believe me, it will be better if you have some stronger pain relief.'

He gave another grunt.

He may not have even understood about his leg; it wasn't obvious he knew there was anything wrong other than that he was lying on the ground in pain.

Noah and Bess got Gio onto the scoop once he had blocks at either side of his head as well as the c-collar to support the spinal cord and head. The sound of him in distress didn't make the job any easier as Bess used the scissors from her kit bag and cut off the clothing covering the lower half of Gio's body.

'He's in so much pain,' she reiterated to Noah. It didn't help that he was trying to move his body rather than letting them take control. She wondered whether Gio was trying to be macho in front of her and that's why he was refusing the extra pain relief.

The fire officer in charge, who introduced himself as Bruce, came over and recapped on what he'd seen happen. While he talked, Bess administered antibiotics for Gio, necessary because of all the dirt and debris around the compound fracture to his kneecap which was likely the result of hitting it against the concrete as he landed on the ground.

According to Bruce, Gio had gone back into the building, against orders, because one of the onlookers insisted a young woman was still inside. There was some disagreement as to whether she was or wasn't but Gio hadn't cared about that; he'd not wanted to risk leaving anyone behind. And he'd come out with her in his arms, put her down outside the building and as they walked away, he'd been the one at the rear. The explosion had knocked him off his feet. The young woman hadn't been caught in the blast at all.

When Gio tried to move again, Noah adopted a stern tone. 'You need to keep still for us; we can't work unless you do. And you could make things a whole lot worse for yourself.'

Bess moved above Gio so she could look him in the eye. 'He's right, you know. Bossy, but right.'

Eyes glistening with tears, Gio looked up at the moon hanging above them all in innocence. He blinked, closed his eyes, settled, but not for long; he was clearly in agony.

Bess squeezed his hand again. 'We're going as fast as we can, Gio, but at the same time, we have to be careful and thorough. We'll have you out of here soon. I promise.'

Jeremy, another of the firefighters, came over and knelt down next to Gio as Bess got the splint for stabilising Gio's leg ready.

'You're a bloody hero.' The firefighter looked up at both Bess and Noah. 'That girl would be dead if it wasn't for him.'

'You hear that?' Bess asked. 'You're a hero, Gio.'

Noah frowned and asked Gio again about his pain. 'Give me a level, mate. On a scale of one to ten.'

Noah's question got a swear word before a begrudgingly uttered nine.

'Nine... are you sure?' Bess asked.

Gio gritted his teeth, the pain almost overpowering him. 'I lied...' he croaked, 'pain is a thirteen... didn't want to admit...'

She knew it. And to actually make the admission, it had to be bad.

Noah reiterated the suggestion of stronger painkillers and this time, Gio agreed, to Bess's relief. Getting his left leg into a splint was going to hurt like anything.

As Noah prepared to give Gio ketamine, a more powerful drug they as critical care paramedics were allowed to administer, and one that in larger amounts could be used for sedation or anaesthetic, Bess looked Gio in the eye again, hoping that the eye contact might help him stay calm. 'You're about to get some of the good stuff. Are you ready?'

'Bring it on.' He managed to get the words out along with a tight smile before it was taken away on another wave of pain.

While everyone reacted to drugs differently, ketamine had been known to cause hallucinations so it was important to keep Gio thinking positive thoughts and so Bess told him again that the girl he'd rescued was safe, uninjured, he was her hero.

Noah put the pulse oximeter – the probe with infrared light to measure how effectively his blood was carrying oxygen – to his foot and leg. Happy there was no circulatory compromise, he administered the ketamine before they could do more. Once it took effect, it would give Bess and Noah enough of a chance to stabilise the leg and spare Gio from the horrendous pain that came with it.

'Bess...' The way Gio said her name this time told Bess that the ketamine was already happily buzzing its way around his system.

'Still here,' she assured him.

'I'm a hero,' Gio rambled, making both Noah and Bess grin. It was hard watching patients suffer and to be able to give them some relief was rewarding and, she had to admit, sometimes amusing when the drugs took effect.

'Told you I was a good man,' Gio went on. He probably wouldn't remember much of this conversation, if any, later on. 'I could be good enough for you.' Even in his predicament, his smile had the ability to melt Bess at a thousand paces if she let it.

Noah laughed. 'I really hope he means you, Bess, because you're not really my type, Gio.'

And he wasn't Bess's either. Was he?

When she met someone, she wanted it to be for keeps. Gio was a good friend, they'd never pushed it any further, and she wouldn't dare because if they dated and it didn't work out – because Gio's relationships never did – it would ruin their friendship.

With the help of three other firefighters, they took the scoop, the equipment and their bags back to the helicopter, transferred Gio onto the litter, and climbed on board, ready to head for the hospital.

Maya didn't say much when she heard it was firefighter Gio Mayhan – there was no sign of the teasing that often came Bess's way when Gio's name came up or he showed up at a job at the same time as The Skylarks – Maya was too professional for that and so was Bess.

As they took to the skies, they could both hear Noah's commentary from the rear of the ambulance; the patient was talking on and off, which was a good sign. It wasn't so great that Gio vomited on the way but it was a common occurrence with patients either from injuries, from drugs or because of the helicopter ride, but apart from that, he was comfortable and stable. He'd likely need orthopaedic surgery given his injuries and he was being flown to a hospital team who were the best in the business in that regard.

Within five minutes, they'd touched down on the helipad on top of the hospital and handed over the patient.

Except he wasn't just any patient. It was Gio.

'You all right?' Maya asked Bess once they lifted into the air again and headed back to base.

'He's a good friend.' And part of her had wanted to stay right there by his side.

'He has the best team looking after him.'

And although Maya wouldn't see, Bess nodded her head before flipping back to professional mode as the technical crew member on board. 'What's the fuel situation?' she asked. As pilot, Maya was obsessed with fuel but it was Bess's responsibility to prompt also.

'Fuel is all good. Refill back at the airbase. Hilda could use another clean too.'

'Affirmative,' said Noah from the rear. 'I didn't like to say, but she could, especially back here.'

Upon arrival at the airbase, Bess took the bloods and the drugs to store in the fridge.

As she came out of the room, she bumped into Paige, one of the patient and family liaison nurses, who gave Bess an update on the kid who'd fallen out of the tree the other day. They didn't always get to know outcomes or progress but it was good when they did.

'I've got the family some suitable accommodation nearby,' Paige explained, 'so they can be by their daughter's side as much as possible.'

'Well done, and thank you for letting me know,' said Bess. The young girl wasn't in a good way but she was expected to recover.

Bess went to the locker room, used the toilet and went to the sinks to wash her face. They still had the helicopter to clean and when she'd pulled herself together, she bypassed Maya in the office doing her paperwork, and the laughter between Nadia and Paige about something or other. She wanted to mop the inside of Hilda, so offered to take the task from Noah and he willingly handed it over.

Anything to stop the thoughts whirring in her head.

Gio. The man she was good friends with. But seeing him like that, lying on the ground, writhing in pain, her feelings had hit her unexpectedly.

She couldn't help it. She knew now that she wanted more than friendship. And if she was being totally honest with herself, she'd wanted more for a while.

As he'd lain there on the ground, he'd said something too and the words came back to her now. *Told you I was a good man... I could be good enough for you.* She hadn't heard him say anything like that before. He'd looked at her on the odd occasion as though he might want something more than what they had but she'd always dismissed the notion as flirting or wanting someone he couldn't have.

Could she really be with a man like Gio, who never went in for long-term commitment?

She was pretty sure the answer was no, but fighting her feelings was another matter.

As she mopped Hilda's interior, her imagination conjured up Gio again, at the scene. She heard the explosion in her head, pictured him sent flying through the air and crashing to the ground.

She dipped the mop into the water, cloudy already despite having only just started the clean-up job.

Thoughts of her own problems filled her head. The payday loan was the latest example of her stupidity. She'd used it to deal with some of the debt she'd managed to accrue but in doing so, she knew things really weren't any better.

The payday loan might have put out a fire in one area of her life but what about what followed from now?

She was in a mess. And it was all her fault.

What had happened to Gio not only had Bess's feelings all over the place; it made her own problems seem foolish. Gio's downfall had been trying to save a life; hers was living one where she didn't want to let herself feel hurt and pain and so she spent money like her final day was coming.

And for that, she was ashamed of herself.

9

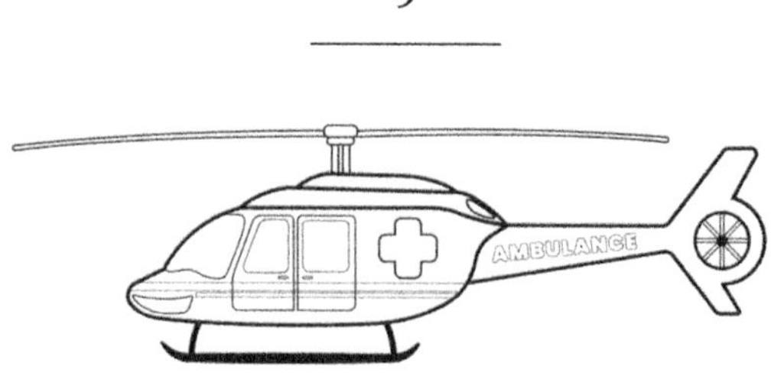

Gio felt tranquil and frequently sleepy with the decent painkillers he was on. He'd had his shepherd's pie, which wasn't bad for hospital food, at least visually, although the same couldn't be said for its texture, which reminded him of pureed kiddie food. He'd finished all of his apple strudel and ice cream, and his leg didn't hurt too much after his knee repair surgery.

What pained him now was his mum and the nurse's conversation about Christmas shopping, Christmas trees, all things festive. Not that he had a problem with the festive season; it was just that he worried his mum wasn't at work and all the talking and attention was beginning to feel suffocating.

His boss had come to see him yesterday. Apparently, the source of the fire they'd attended the night of Gio's accident was an electric bike left on charge inside the building. The explosion had been due to a faulty gas appliance. The details had mostly washed over Gio, who was half awake at the time, and it hadn't helped the situation he was in, but it was a kind of debrief, the sort the rest of the crew would have got back at the station as they went through what had happened, used it to learn from. His boss had reiterated what Gio knew, too: that he'd be on full pay for six months while he recovered. His boss talked about what happened after that, should Gio need longer to recuperate. By that time, his pay would reduce and his boss skated over some of the details for him. Gio only hoped it wouldn't come to that because if it did, dealing with less money every month would be the least of his worries. Mentally, he'd lose it if this job was taken away from him.

When the nurse went on her way to attend to another patient, he had to ask Marianne, 'Why aren't you at your cleaning job? You've been here a lot since my accident.'

'Of course I'm here. And work have been very understanding.'

Really? She had only just joined them – surely their understanding would only go so far.

'I was in this morning, 7 a.m. I'll be in again tomorrow, same time. I've been juggling both.'

'You never said.'

'I did, but those drugs have made you forget.'

Usually, he'd suspect her of lying but he had woken earlier thinking he was in a bed at the fire station, and last night, he'd had a dream he was a tortoise doing his best to win a race. He supposed his mother had a point.

He hauled himself up against his pillows, which Marianne adjusted for him. 'I don't want you to lose this job.'

'I don't want to either.' She checked her phone when it pinged. 'That's your brother; he's home safely. I insisted he text me when he arrived.'

'Where did he go?'

'He was here last night to see you.'

'I don't remember.'

'I only knew because one of the nurses told me. She said he came right at the end of visiting hours; they almost didn't let him in. I called him once I'd spoken to the nurse and he said he hadn't been able to hang around for long because Saffy is away at her parents' and he'd left the kids with a sitter.' She tutted. 'I said he should've brought them here and I could've looked after them.'

'You have a job.' And there was no way Marco would've trusted Marianne with his kids.

'I suppose.' She pulled his phone from her bag. 'Here, all charged up – you and he can message each other or FaceTime.'

'Cheers, Mum. Did you and he talk?'

She shook her head. 'I think that's why he came so late: so he could avoid me.'

When the doctor came around, the focus turned to him rather than his mum or Marco. They talked about the operation to repair the patella, the triangular bone at the front of the knee. The doctor answered his questions and also the surprising amount his mum asked. They discussed what his recovery would involve and by the time the doc left, Gio was exhausted. His mum went to get a coffee and he must have fallen asleep because when he woke again, she was settled in a chair at his bedside reading a magazine.

'You've been asleep a while,' she told him.

'Feels like five minutes.'

'That's because your body needs to heal. I don't mind; go back to sleep, I'll be right here when you wake up.'

There was something about her words and the way she said it that almost had him choking back tears. It was the sort of thing he would've liked to have heard as a boy when he fell over and cut himself, if he was struggling at school, when he was missing his dad after he walked out on them.

'Sleep is a waste of time,' he claimed before he closed his eyes yet again and didn't wake until it was dark beyond the windows of the ward. Bleeping from machines – his and others' – the low hum of nurses conversing beside the bed opposite his, the louder voices passing by outside the ward, all of it a new landscape right now and for at least another couple of days. Then he'd need physiotherapy and occupational therapy to get him moving around and eventually back to work.

'So, work tomorrow morning,' said Gio after his mum passed him the cup of water from his tray table and he took a sip. 'You should get going, get some sleep yourself.'

'I'd better.' And she leaned over, kissed him on the forehead.

'Goodnight, Mum.'

He FaceTimed his brother next, still unable to believe he'd missed his visit. But it was good to see him now. He brushed aside Marco's lecture that he shouldn't rush his recovery, that he had to take it easy whether he liked it or not. It reminded him of how his brother had always looked out for him over the years.

And then he slept yet again, surprising even himself.

The following day, with his mother hopefully at her job – she hadn't shown up at the hospital, which was a good sign – the surgeon came by to examine Gio's knee.

'How are you feeling?' he asked.

'Not bad at all.'

'Good.' He nodded, taking off the disposable gloves now he'd finished his exam. 'And now the truth.'

'All right, there's a bit of pain and swelling but it's honestly not so bad.'

'The physiotherapist will come and have a chat with you later, discuss what happens from here.' The surgeon had done his bit; time to move him on to the next person on the rehabilitation conveyor belt.

By the time the doctor finished with him, Gio had been about ready to fall back to sleep but his next visitor had him more alert than he'd been since he was airlifted here what felt like aeons ago.

'I knew you wouldn't resist me for long,' he grinned at the curly-haired beauty approaching his bed. Dressed not in her Skylarks uniform but in jeans and a roll-neck jumper that hugged her body in ways that had him feeling things he'd rather not be feeling in a ward filled with five other patients, Bess came over bearing a gift box.

'You've still got your sense of humour, I see.' But she was amused, he could tell.

'That for me?'

'Courtesy of Nadia, who has been baking again – I nabbed these brownies before the other team came on shift and she was all for me smuggling them out of there for you.'

When he opened the box, the smell confirmed that Nadia was no novice in the kitchen. 'Want one?'

Bess hooked her bag on the back of the chair. 'Not for me, thanks; there's the dreaded weigh-in next shift.'

'They weigh you? Brutal.' Nothing wrong with her weight from where he was standing, or more accurately, lying.

'Helicopter fuel is calculated taking into account weight on board, which includes us as well as equipment. The whole team dreads a weigh-in, especially post-Christmas. We do our best to blame it on winter jackets and layers rather than indulging – it's usually quite amusing.'

'Have a brownie... Go on, you know you want to.' There was something about Bess that made him feel instantly better, like he could jump out of bed at any moment. Although on a recently damaged knee, that probably wouldn't be the best idea he'd ever had.

She reached for one, her smile addictive. 'Go on then. I'll wear lighter layers at the next weigh in,' she joked.

He liked that she savoured it and wasn't hung up on her weight or what she ate; too many women were. He'd once dated a woman who had only ever ordered a salad when they went out but then ate half his chips when the food came.

'The rest are for your pleasure,' Bess told him after she'd licked her lips following the final mouthful.

But then she looked away as though her choice of words had all kinds of thoughts soaring through her mind, exactly like they were doing in his. Over the years, he'd thought about asking her out more than once but he had to admit, he wasn't sure he was good enough for Bess. He certainly hadn't been back in his twenties or thirties when he'd have laughed if anyone had suggested a long-term relationship. He'd thought he wasn't built for them, he'd thought he'd never go the distance, but something about Bess had made him want to try. And yet he'd held back from making a move. Their friendship was too important to him.

'How are you feeling?' she asked before taking the box of brownies back and setting them on the shelf near his bed.

'Not too bad. Thanks to The Skylarks coming to my rescue.' He held her gaze for a moment. 'My knee was pretty smashed up but it's all fixed now.'

'Might be a while until you're on your feet. Literally.'

'The doc says I'll be leaving here in a couple of days, got the physio making all sorts of plans for me.'

'That's good.' She flapped the front of her jumper. 'It's hot in here.'

'Yeah, glad I'm not the one who has to pay the energy bill for this place.'

She didn't seem to find that particularly funny. Perhaps he was losing his touch; usually, he could make her smile easily.

When she wriggled her jumper up and over her head, he didn't mind the glimpse of the flesh on her tummy and her belly button. But she caught him staring.

'What are you smiling at?' She sat down, swept her curls from her face.

'You have a tattoo. How did I not know that? We're friends.'

'I didn't have it when we were sharing a house.'

'But still...'

'We're not that close,' she teased. She didn't elaborate on the dolphin to the right of her belly button and, instead, changed the subject. 'You were really lucky, Gio.'

'So they keep telling me.'

'You disobeyed an order. I heard it; everyone heard it.'

'Not great to do that,' he admitted. 'But I'd do what I did again to save a life.'

'Why didn't the young woman come out with everyone else?'

'I think she got disorientated. She said she'd been in the bathroom when the alarm sounded and she panicked. She tried to run to the back door but couldn't find her way – she was an intern; it was her first day. Someone said she'd left already; someone else was adamant that she hadn't. I would never have forgiven myself if I hadn't checked the building was definitely empty.'

'And I never would have forgiven you if you'd died.' She pushed his arm gently, the warmth of skin on skin sending sparks of euphoria zapping through him in a way not even a strong medication had managed to do yet. He and Bess had hugged as friends plenty of times, been in close proximity to each other, they'd danced at their mutual friend's wedding. And yet, now, every look and every touch felt more intimate.

'I'm not sure what shook that young woman up more, you know – the fire or me in all my breathing apparatus finding her and scooping her up to take her to safety.'

'She's alive and kicking thanks to you.'

'Yeah, and apparently I'm a hero.'

'So you told me after we gave you the good drugs.'

He put a hand across his face. He didn't remember. God, what else had he said? Nothing too incriminating, he hoped.

'What else did I say?' he asked her.

She grinned. 'That's for me to know…'

'Come on, you can't leave me to think the worst.'

Just then, a nurse popped in to check his blood pressure and ask whether he needed more painkillers, but right now, he didn't. Seeing Bess seemed to be bringing on enough feel-good endorphins.

'Did you talk to your mum yet?' he asked when the nurse left them to it. They hadn't talked much since they'd met on scene that day and Bess had found out in a difficult way that her mum was dating. 'Have you met the boyfriend? Malcolm, wasn't it?'

'Yes, it was. And no, I've not met him yet. I should, though.'

'You still don't like the idea of her having a boyfriend?'

'I'm not too happy that I didn't know about him,' she said, 'but I'm getting used to the idea.' She flipped the questioning around. 'Talking of mothers, how long is yours in town?'

He was momentarily confused with the unexpected question, and it took him a moment to cast his mind back to the meeting in the supermarket. He gestured for her to pass the spare pillow sitting on the windowsill he couldn't reach from his bed.

'Where do you want it?' she asked.

'Behind me will do.' He wished he'd made more of a fuss and that she wasn't so efficient because the pillow was in place quickly and he wouldn't have minded feeling her hands against his shoulder for a bit longer as she wriggled the pillow behind him.

Now he was more propped up, the fluorescent light wasn't firing directly into his line of vision and he answered her question. 'I'm not sure how long Mum is staying.'

She would remember from their days in the shared house that it was a constant worry for him that his mother would show up unannounced. To be fair, she never had; he'd always been the one to go to her. Back then, he'd felt an attraction towards Bess but with his family hassles and his family history, he didn't have the headspace to go in for anything serious. He'd met the odd boyfriend of Bess's during that time – one total knob who gave her the run around, another more serious type she'd ended it with because he wanted to move back to Ireland and she didn't want to go with him.

'I know you two have had your problems over the years,' she said.

'That's putting it mildly.' An exasperated sigh left his lips. 'Our family has been through a lot; you know some of what happened. She claims to have reached a turning point this time, though.'

'That's a good thing, isn't it?'

She was good at this: liaison with her peers. He'd seen it with people at the scene on a job, how she was a comfort to a patient, the fact she always seemed to know the right thing to say. Not everyone did.

Bess picked up her jumper when she saw three of his colleagues coming into the ward. 'That's my cue to move on.'

'Please stay a bit longer.'

She paused briefly, maybe considering it.

'Don't make me beg.'

'I won't, but remember it's two visitors to a bed and I'll let this trio get in trouble rather than me.'

With a smile and a wave, she left.

And despite the handshakes and camaraderie from his colleagues, he'd much rather see a lot more of Bess right now than anyone else.

It felt like it really could be the start of something between them.

10

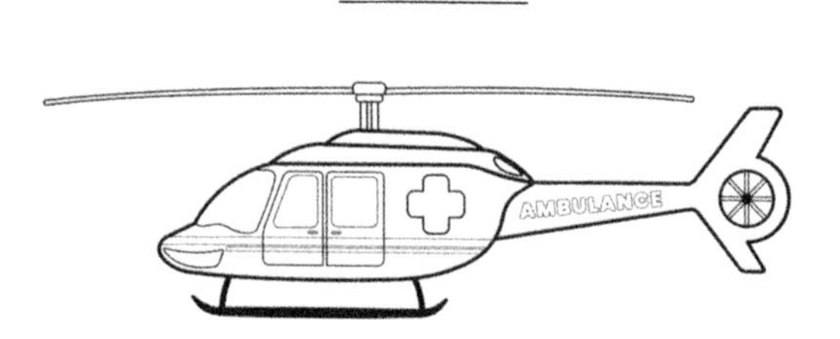

The day Bess heard her father had died, she'd been in the same place she was right now: sitting in her car outside her parents' home, about to head in for dinner. That day, her phone had rung and she'd snatched it up with a chirpy, 'I'm here! I'm outside, give me a minute to get out the car and in the door,' which was met not with the laughter she'd expected from whichever parent had called but with her mother sobbing down the line. Bess had run inside and been handed the devastating news, breaking down alongside her mother as she listened to the police officer explain it all over again. Her dad had had a heart attack driving home from work one day and, just like that, he was taken from them.

Bess's hand was against her tattoo beneath her winter layers – her coat and jumper got in the way but putting her hand there still connected her to her memories.

When Gio had spotted it at the hospital last week, it should have been simple to say she'd got the tattoo of a dolphin following her holiday to Florida. He knew she'd been there. She could've explained it away by reminding him she'd swum with dolphins, remembering the crystal, blue waters, the friendly, social animals who'd captured her interest. But that was only part of the truth and she wasn't sure she could've got all those words out without emotion bubbling over.

Bess had taken as many holidays as she could since her dad died; it was part of what had contributed to her ever-increasing debt. The need to escape had been almost overwhelming at times. If she had a few days between shifts, she'd plan to get out of town. If time was limited, she didn't leave the UK; if she'd accrued enough days, she went further afield. Florida had been one such destination and seeing dolphins was always going to be a part of it because it made her feel closer to her dad. Her dad had always been fascinated by dolphins; he'd bought her first soft toy dolphin when she was too young to register what it was, he'd read her books about them – both fiction and non-fiction – he'd talked about his summers as a boy at Cardigan Bay and told her he'd got so close to dolphins, he'd talked to them. She wasn't sure how much he embellished but she'd sat with him and made him tell her over and over again about the graceful creatures she'd grown to love as much as he had. You would never have thought it to look at him – a serious man in a business suit through the week, but a much more relaxed character come weekends and holidays. And when she was ten, he'd taken her to Cardigan Bay and she'd fallen in love with the dolphins in their natural habitat, their acrobatic displays, the splash of water on her face as they came up close to the boat. And whenever she saw a documentary clip or read an article about dolphins, she'd always told her dad about it.

After he died, it became all the more poignant. She'd reached for the phone more than once to call him and tell him about what she'd seen or read. And following a trip to Florida, she'd been out with friends having a few drinks on a balmy summer's evening when a girl had walked past and there on her shoulder was a tattoo of a dolphin. Less than a week later, Bess had her very own dolphin tattoo etched onto her skin forever in memory of a father who'd been taken away too soon.

Bess looked at the well-kept home she'd grown up in with its spring blooms all gone out front and only greenery remaining apart from the few winter flowers in the pot beside the front door. She hoped her dad wasn't looking down on her today to witness her having to go inside and admit to her mother that at age forty, she was in financial strife. In the four decades of her life, she'd never had to do this – not unless you counted the times as a teenager she'd borrowed money in advance of getting her monthly allowance so she didn't miss out on things with friends. She didn't want to do it now, but what choice did she have? She was drowning in debt and the personal loan repayment, the payday loan, the credit card debts and charges, the bills still waiting to be paid, were all reminders of just how much trouble she was in. Around about eleven thousand pounds' worth of trouble to be precise and that figure was rising by the day.

She climbed out of the car, her thoughts going back to Gio. Thinking about him gave her some temporary relief rather than constantly stressing about her finances.

When Gio had asked her about her tattoo, it had given her another hint that he might be interested in more than friendship. It wasn't so much the question as the way he'd looked at her, the softness of his voice, an edge of flirtation despite lying in a hospital bed. And when he spoke about his mum, it reminded her of their days in the shared house, the times he'd been distraught at his mum's latest drama, the vulnerability he'd tried to keep hidden from as many people as possible. She'd had boyfriends on and off but she and Gio had always stayed friends; she'd always been ready to listen. Perhaps Bess had always known that there were more layers to him than what she saw on the surface. But maybe at the same time, she'd decided to play it safe, keep him as a friend, nothing more.

A mewling at her feet signalled Liquorice's presence.

She bent down and scooped up the black cat with huge, round eyes. 'You crept up on me. How did you manage that?' He didn't seem to mind the puffy coat, and she knew he'd start purring in a minute and put his claws into the fabric, which wouldn't be so good. She wouldn't feel it but the material would take a battering.

She set him down inside the front door after she let herself in with a call of, 'Hey, Mum, it's me.'

'In here, darling,' Fiona trilled from the direction of the kitchen.

Bess found her mother with her apron on and flour dusting the front pocket as she wiped her hands. 'I wasn't expecting you today.' But her beaming smile as she came to hug her daughter was enough to know her drop-in was a good thing. It didn't make Bess feel any better about the reason she was here, though.

Bess peered over in the direction of the kitchen worktop. 'What's cooking? Quiche?' She noted the pastry her mum had fashioned into the pie base, imagined the way her fingers had pushed the mixture into the little grooves that would cook that way and create a pretty pattern.

'It's tonight's dinner if you'd like to stay? You're more than welcome.'

'Can't, I'm on shift at four, but thanks, your quiches are always delicious.' She watched as her mum lined the pie base with parchment and poured in ceramic baking beans, ready to blind bake the crust.

Many a time as a little girl, Bess had sat in this kitchen and helped her mother cook. She knew that blind baking the crust first before the filling was added avoided the crust getting soggy while the quiche baked. Some of the filling should also be pre-cooked, hence the little bowls on the side of cooked mushrooms, bell peppers and broccoli which would be added along with the milk and egg mixture once the crust had had a head start.

'Remember the day you made your first quiche as a surprise for your dad?'

Bess burst out laughing. 'Do I ever?' She'd tried to add in his favourite things – spinach, tomatoes, mushrooms, and basically overloaded what wasn't a great pastry base and the whole thing was a sloppy combination of waterlogged vegetables. 'He did well to eat as much as he did. I couldn't manage it and I was terrified it would be one of those dinner times where you both made me sit and finish every last mouthful.'

Fiona's laughter mingled with her daughter's as she closed the oven and set the timer for the crust before pulling out a block of Gruyere from the fridge and batting away Bess's attempts to help her.

Oh, how Bess wished her dad were here now, sitting at the table reading his newspaper, or in the study beavering away on his computer. The house had run well with her parents both at the helm but her mum seemed to be managing just fine even though it was only her now. Both of them would be ashamed at the shambles Bess had made of her own life.

Her mum slapped away her hand when she reached for some of the grated Gruyere and she handed Bess the edges she'd cut away from the block. 'Nibble on those; you could always get more off.'

Bess wasn't going to argue. She wished she could stay doing this and not have to confess a single thing. Let her mum believe she was the strong, capable daughter they'd raised, the one who had a good job, her own home, rather than a daughter who could be about to lose a very big chunk of all of that.

Bess made tea for them both as they chatted, mostly about the weather and the frost that had graced the roofs of Whistlestop River that chilly November morning.

'I think we'll get snow before Christmas.' Fiona poured the egg and milk mixture into the baked crust to cover the vegetables and slotted it back in the oven. 'There, one hour to go. I'm early.' She finished her mug of tea. She'd always been good at multi-tasking in the kitchen and chatting at the same time. 'I should get on with peeling some potatoes.' She pulled a bag of potatoes out and took quite a few to place in the colander next to the sink.

'I can't stay, remember.'

And that was when she realised her mum wasn't planning on dining alone tonight.

Her mum turned at the sink and faced her daughter. 'Malcolm is coming over.' She looked up at the clock on the wall. 'Soon.'

'Right.' She tried to sound a lot brighter than she felt.

'Oh, darling, I'm sorry. I was so pleased to see you, I didn't want anything to upset you. And I'd like to introduce you two properly.'

Bess supposed she needed to get used to her mum forging a new life. She wasn't a kid any more. 'Listen, before he gets here—'

Her mum put down the potato peeler. 'What's wrong?'

'Nothing is wrong.' Well, it was, but even though she'd been rehearsing a spiel in her head on the way over here, her mind had suddenly gone blank.

Then the doorbell went and her mum gathered herself like a sixteen-year-old waiting for a prom date, all upright posture, shoulders tensed in excitement, a giddy smile on her face. 'He's here.'

While her mum went to answer the door, Bess realised the signs were here when she turned up at the house that Fiona was expecting company. Her mum was wearing her favourite red shirt beneath the cooking apron, the silky one she only wore if she was going out for coffee with a friend or having someone over. Bess had assumed it was the former; she should've realised it could easily be the latter given how out of sync the pair of them were with each other's lives at the moment.

Bess turned round to meet Malcolm and when she saw how nervous he looked, it made her feel a bit better. It shouldn't, but it did. Meeting someone new at any age was daunting, at their age probably even more so, and meeting the family had to be hard. She wondered if it was as bad as when you were a teenager and went to your boyfriend's house for the first time to meet their parents.

Malcolm handed over a seasonal bunch of flowers with reds, inky blues and plenty of foliage. His hands were shaking and so was his voice as he reeled off the names of some of the flowers. And he only made eye contact with Bess once Fiona had made a formal introduction.

She made the snap decision to make this as easy as possible for him. 'Malcolm, it's nice to meet you.' She used the voice she had in team meetings, especially when potential sponsors came to meet The Skylarks and find out about the lifesaving work they did, and she shook his hand too, all very sensible and formal.

'Well, we have met once already, remember.' He seemed to be fighting the urge to put his hands back in his pockets. He probably wished he still had hold of the flower arrangement.

'Roadside doesn't count,' Bess smiled. 'How are you doing?'

His shoulders relaxed a little. 'The bruising has almost gone, the headaches have stopped, and I think I've processed the shock.'

'The shock is often the worst thing.'

'I was very lucky. We both were.'

When her mum and Malcolm smiled at each other, Bess felt like an intruder until Liquorice weaved between her ankles to remind her that this was the family home. She picked up the cat and tickled him beneath his chin.

'It's been a pain trying to find a new car,' Malcolm carried on now he'd found his voice. 'I don't live on a bus route. I've borrowed a friend's today, but I need to sort one out soon before I talk myself out of driving altogether.'

Bess sat at the table first, Liquorice curling up on her lap, and Malcolm followed suit. 'Don't let the accident destroy your confidence,' she told him.

'That poor lass in the other car.'

Bess liked that he sympathised with the other driver; it showed integrity.

Their talking evolved to road safety, which led to a bit about her job and then onto driving lessons each of the three of them had had and their experiences – both terrifying and funny – and Bess found herself warming to the man despite the slightly porn-star-style moustache and the chin dimple. His grey hair was combed back and Bess spotted a tiny hearing aid in one ear, one of the discreet ones you could get that meant most people didn't even realise you were wearing one.

'What are you looking for, Mum?'

For the last couple of minutes, as she and Malcolm talked about what it was like driving on the wrong side of the road when you went to Europe, Bess had watched her mother rummaging through every single shelf in the food cupboard.

'I can't find the custard powder. I was serving apple crumble and custard for dessert. Not much good without custard.'

'We could have ice cream,' said Malcolm.

'I don't have that either.'

Malcolm got up. 'I'm all about practising my driving to get my confidence back. I'll drive and get some now. What's it to be: custard or ice cream?'

Bess looked away when her mum came to his side. She felt sure Fiona had been about to kiss him but realised at the last minute that her daughter was sitting right there.

'I tell you what,' said Malcolm, picking up his keys from the Welsh dresser, 'I'll get both.'

The second he left, her mum looked worried.

'Mum, he's really lovely.'

And now she looked relieved. She sat down next to Bess. 'Once you get to know him, you'll like him all the more.'

'I'm sure I will.' She glanced up at the kitchen clock. She was going to be late if she didn't get going soon. So far, her mum hadn't told Malcolm that she wasn't staying for dinner and he hadn't asked because he'd probably been so nervous.

'I know you have to go soon.' Fiona must've seen her looking at the time. 'What was it you wanted to talk to me about, love?'

'It'll keep.'

'I know my daughter and I know there's something, so if you don't tell me, I'll be thinking about it all evening.'

Her mother had read her well.

'There is something but it's awkward and I don't think I can get it all out quickly with someone else here. Or someone due back any second.'

'Spit it out, Bess.'

She looked down at her hands, her curls fell either side of her face to hide away her shame. 'I need some money.'

'Money?'

'A loan, Mum.'

'Oh, is that all?' She sat back against the kitchen chair. 'I thought you were going to tell me you were sick.' She put a hand against her chest to settle her breathing.

Two years ago, Bess's world had been rocked more than they thought possible on the anniversary of her dad's death when she found a lump in her breast. She'd ignored it for almost a week, thinking perhaps it might disappear, that it might be hormonal and go away all on its own, but after Maya's persuasion she had made an appointment with her GP. She'd assumed he would say the same, that he was sure it was nothing, to come back if it hadn't gone in a few weeks. But instead, she'd been referred for breast screening with a mammogram and ultrasound, they'd taken a biopsy to be sure they knew what the lump was, and the doctor had wanted to remove the mass to stop it from growing and to prevent it from developing into cancer.

Every stage had involved a wait and with every wait had come the agony of time ticking by, not knowing what she was going to be faced with. Her mum had almost crumpled when Bess had told her about it after Fiona spotted her coming out of the doctor's surgery. But after that, she'd been a tower of strength, gone with Bess to every appointment, held her hand through it all.

And now, Bess apologised. 'I'm sorry, Mum. I should've started out by saying it's nothing to do with my health.' Not her physical health, anyway – her mental health was another thing entirely.

When Bess first found the lump, she'd been in denial, but after screening and being told a biopsy was necessary, plus removal, she'd started to feel an ever-increasing sense of fear creeping up on her. She knew that for some women, thoughts would have immediately gone to their spouse and their kids, but she didn't have either of those things. All Bess had been able to think as she'd walked out of the doctor's office was *I'm not done, I'm not finished, not yet!* And so began a cascade of choices that had led to her getting in a total mess.

'I can help you out, Bess.' Fiona went to the Welsh dresser and took out her iPad. 'How much do you need?' She sat back down.

'Mum, it's not that simple... It's a lot of money.'

'Well, how much are we talking about?'

Bess shook her head. 'Too much.' She was ashamed to say the amount out loud and by the time she looked up, her mother was tapping at the iPad intently.

'Done,' said Fiona, setting the device down. 'I've transferred £500 into your account—'

'Mum, I—'

'It's done. No arguments. You're my daughter, of course I want to help. It's all I have for now, but I can get more.'

'Mum, have you left yourself enough?'

'I will manage just fine.'

Bess had come here wanting help, wanting to talk about the level of her debt and get advice, possibly borrow some money to get on top of things. But the last thing she wanted was for her mum to struggle financially as a result. Her face had said it all, that she'd made the transfer and would *manage*. She didn't want her mum to *manage*. She'd been through enough.

'I'll pay you back every penny,' said Bess. 'As soon as I can.'

'You just get yourself straight. Will £500 help?'

The hope in her mother's eyes almost destroyed Bess. 'Of course it will, thank you.' She flung her arms around her mother, hugged her tightly.

The fact that her mother thought £500 would be enough to

get herself sorted made Bess feel ten times worse because it would barely scratch the surface and telling her mum that would only transfer some of the worry onto her shoulders. She didn't need that either.

When the front door went, the conversation stopped there. She put a smile back on her face in time for Malcolm to arrive in the room.

They joked about Malcolm's search for normal vanilla custard powder when the shelves were filled with all these fancy things, the effort to find vanilla ice cream when the flavour combinations had almost left vanilla behind.

'It was so much easier to shop when there wasn't so much variety,' he concluded. He looked a bit bewildered that Fiona wasn't really joining in the conversation. She was at the sink filling a pan of water for the potatoes, which didn't need to go on yet unless they wanted a really early dinner.

Bess picked up her bag, looked around to say goodbye to Liquorice, but he'd got bored of them all and was probably curled up on her mum's bed upstairs, his favourite place since Bess had left home. 'I need to go; work beckons.'

'You're not staying?' Malcolm didn't look relieved, he looked disappointed, which gave Bess a good feeling.

'I'm afraid I can't – another time.' She gave her mum a hug, whispered the question of whether she was all right into her ear and her mum nodded against her cheek. 'I'll nip upstairs and use your bathroom first.'

'You know where it is,' her mum said with false joviality.

Bess trotted up the stairs. She used the toilet and washed her hands, pausing at the sight of her mum's single toothbrush in the little cup, the women's shower gel and shampoo in the frameless shower her dad had had put in. There were no signs of him left save the few photographs around the house, the little things like his shaving foam and aftershave had gone, his slippers were no longer at his side of the bed, there was no shoe horn propped up beside the front door for the smart, leather shoes he'd worn to work. There was even another man here now in his place at the table this evening.

But he seemed a good man. She had to remember that.

She stopped by her mum's bedroom and, sure enough, Liquorice was curled up at the end on the old cardigan Fiona had left there for the cat. She kissed his forehead and he barely opened his eyes, so content in one of his favourite spots.

Bess went downstairs and was almost at the bottom when she thought she heard her mother crying. She stopped; she wasn't sure. But after another minute, she knew she was right and it broke her heart.

She froze. She couldn't intrude. It sounded like Malcolm was comforting her. And she sensed it was probably out of fright that Bess had been about to share another health worry.

Bess put on her coat, sat on the bottom stair. Should she sneak out and get to work? Or would that be worse? Should she not poke her head around the door but rather just call out her farewell?

She was still thinking when she heard them talking and she realised her mum had only gone and told him Bess had money troubles.

Bess didn't know whether to fly in there all guns blazing or head straight out of the front door. He wasn't her dad! He wasn't in this family! If she'd wanted a stranger to know her business, she would've told him herself.

She crept back up the stairs and then made a show of coming down heavy footed, rounded the corner and called her goodbyes from there before grabbing her coat from the hook in the hallway.

'Stay safe, love,' her mum's voice followed her.

'Good to meet you,' came Malcolm's as she got to the front door and opened it before either of them could catch her up. And she didn't look back; she got in the car and left.

Bess drove to the airbase. Part of her was fuming; another part wanted to fall in a heap and cry. Her dad had instilled the same messages over and over: that she should think about the future, not just the present, to be careful with money and save in case something unexpected happened. She'd tried to do that, the same way he had for years, before he'd died suddenly. He'd worked his arse off and for what? To leave a load of savings in bank accounts that he'd never get to use? He took holidays but could've had so many more and to further afield, he hadn't updated his car even though it was getting old, he'd never bought that fancy barbecue he'd always talked about having *one day*. He hadn't spent much on the family home either apart from to keep it comfortable – a new bathroom suite when it began to show a lot of wear and tear, an upgrade to the kitchen when things began to start falling apart.

Her father's death had started the ball rolling with Bess's spending but it was the breast lump and the scare that she could be terminally ill, because that's where your mind went when you were waiting to find out, that had really done it. She'd been faced head on with her own mortality and had begun to wonder, what really was the point of it all? You worked hard to put a roof over your head and food on the table and you saved, you saved hard, but for what? In the end, what was the point?

And just because the lump hadn't turned out to be cancer, Bess's head had been embroiled in the fear that another lump might appear, or that something else might happen to her. And so her mantra became, *live each day as if it's your last*. It wasn't like there was a day when she decided that was going to be the way she lived her life; it became a feeling that engulfed her – it became her purpose.

A few weeks after she had been given the all-clear, Bess had found herself driving to a shopping centre away from Whistlestop River where she could be incognito, grab a coffee, sit and watch the world go by. Since the scare, she'd found herself needing to do that more and more.

The café she tried to go to was packed, as if everyone was in need of the same comfort that day. And so she'd ended up in a posh restaurant nearby, ordering herself a slap-up meal of lobster and after that, she'd thought she'd better walk off the heavy meal, and she ended up going in and out of shops, browsing turning to buying, and buying making her feel better. She'd got home and felt a buzz when she got a text confirmation with the delivery time for her new plasma television she'd bought when she saw it on special offer. She'd smiled as she put away the designer-label jeans she'd splashed out on, excited to wear them soon, the cashmere jumper, the beautiful silk pyjamas, too. And she'd admired the totally unnecessary purchase of a new handbag, a bag that she never would've justified under normal circumstances with its buttery-soft leather, its smell, its feel of extravagance.

Bess pulled into the parking space at the air ambulance base. It was time to push away her worries, get ready for her shift.

She waved across to Frank, the engineer as he emerged from the building.

And just like she did every other day, she put on a smile which she knew she'd have to keep in place unless she wanted to fall apart.

A smile she was getting tired of wearing when her life was well and truly up shit creek.

11

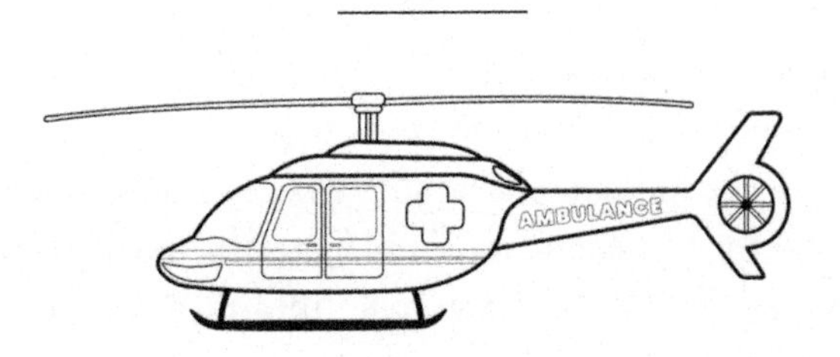

Gio had been discharged from hospital almost a fortnight ago and December had crept up on them all with one day much the same as any other now he wasn't at work.

To say he was frustrated was an understatement. He'd had surgery to fix his knee and allow for the return of function but whenever he asked the healthcare team, nobody would tell him when or how long before he got back to the job.

Gio's healing could now be done from home with visits from the physiotherapist. He was diligently icing the knee to stop pain and swelling – which would've been a hell of a lot more pleasant in summer than winter – the bruising was beginning to subside, but he had a brace on his leg when he moved around to stop it twisting or being subject to unnecessary impact. He was told he had to have the brace for at least two but possibly as many as six weeks, but it was better than wearing a cast. At least he could remove the brace when he was sitting or lying down – it meant he didn't have to imagine his limb shrivelling up beneath plaster either; his muscles were still there, he could see them rather than think about them.

Gio was doing his utmost to stay positive, to think about getting back on the job, but the whole situation was making him far rattier with his mother than he needed to be and she was watching him like a hawk, something he was neither used to nor needed.

'I thought you were working until six,' he said when she came through the door at four.

'Not today; I started at 7 a.m., remember.'

'I forgot.' He was still on the sofa, this morning's session with a physiotherapist basic to onlookers but even moving his foot up and down at the moment was painful and a unique kind of torture.

He watched his mother closely as she unlaced her trainers, her face hidden as her ponytail of dark-grey hair that was once the same colour as his fell over her shoulder. 'How was work?'

'Tiring,' she said, not making eye contact as she lifted her shoes in her fingers and took them back to the hallway and the rack.

He had a sinking feeling in his stomach that had nothing to do with his recent surgery or the fact he was facing a long time before he could return to the job he loved. He looked at her when she came back into the room, but rather than the eyes he expected to be dancing with an alcohol-fuelled enthusiasm she was desperately trying to hide, she really did look exhausted.

She caught him looking as she set down her handbag. 'You want to ask whether I've had a drink.'

'No.'

'Gio...'

Having her here was a pain, a worry, but in the moment, he found himself smiling. 'I don't want to ask you but I was suspecting.'

She sat down on the armchair opposite the sofa. 'I suppose I ask for that with my history. It's what you boys probably came to expect.'

'It's what we saw, Mum.'

'It's hard for you to shake off your doubts. And it's hard to get rid of my own too. I'm always waiting to fuck up again. Sorry, excuse the language.'

Having listened to him swearing his head off since he came home, he couldn't very well complain. He'd moaned about everything – the pain, the swelling, not being at work, not being able to stand and make himself a meal, sleeping on the camp bed in the small dining room next to the lounge, the inconvenience of not being able to use the shower upstairs because he couldn't get up there. He was having to make do with the one downstairs that he'd never got around to replacing. He was pretty sure that the owner before had used it to shower their dog after long, muddy walks and the thought, despite the fact he'd lived here for a while and the shower had seen many cleans, made him feel even worse every time he got under the weak-as-piss jets of the shower head.

He pushed himself upright, looked at the crutches resting against the wall. Already, he couldn't wait to see the back of them.

She must have seen him do it. 'What do you need?' Her hands were on her knees as if poised and ready to leap into action.

'I need to do things for myself, that's what I need.'

'Stop being so hard on yourself. What do you want?'

Reluctantly, he admitted, 'I could murder a can of Coke from the fridge.'

Marianne went to get the drink and brought it back along with a couple of painkillers.

'Don't need those.'

'Yes, you do. I saw you wincing when I came in the door.'

The physio had reprimanded him earlier for saying he no longer needed painkillers. She'd explained that it would hinder him in the long run if he didn't take them; it would leave him in pain and unable to do the exercises. That meant he'd suffer more stiffness and a slower recovery. He'd also been told not to do too much too soon, so he couldn't really win, could he?

His mother disappeared and for a blissful moment, he enjoyed the cold, fizzy drink. The heating was on and it didn't matter that it was almost winter beyond the doors and windows of his home; for now, he could close his eyes and imagine himself anywhere. Tropical preferably, with fully functioning legs.

He opened his eyes when he heard his mum come back. She'd brought down a pillow. 'Sit up a bit more, put your leg on the sofa on top of this. You should elevate it when you're sitting.'

He should but sometimes he forgot, or he didn't bother.

'Thanks.'

She pulled the blanket from the other sofa – the purple blanket from the end of the bed that she'd tried to cover him with yesterday and the day before and the day before that – and she tried to wrap it around his shoulders.

'All right, that's enough, Mum,' he snapped, almost adding that it was too late to start fussing around him now when she hadn't bothered when he was a boy, but even he wasn't that much of a tosser, despite the fuss doing his head in.

'Sorry, just trying to help.'

'The heating is on, I'm plenty warm enough.'

She huffed and puffed and busied herself taking out a lunch box, which he heard her washing up, being none too delicate with anything in the kitchen, taking out his resistance to her helping on anything she could find. And then she went for a shower while he settled back and watched television, the ridiculous number of programmes doing nothing to make him happier about his current position. If anything, they made him feel worse, particularly when he found a show set in a fire station; it was as though broadcasters had put that on on purpose.

'Mum, could you do me a favour?' he called over to her when she came back downstairs. He hoped the request would settle things between them. He didn't want to be the one to piss her off, the one who drove her to distraction, risked making her want a drink.

'What is it, love?'

'Can you get the key for the back door – it's in the junk drawer – and open it up for me? I'm going to use my crutches and go outside for some air.'

'Are you sure that's…' She broke off at his expression. 'Okay. I'll open it up. But at least put a coat on. I'll get that for you.'

'Appreciate it.' He'd rather do it all himself, but if it placated her, so be it.

Within five minutes, he was bundled up warm, and he managed to use his crutches to cover the fifteen or so metres from the lounge to the back door and went outside to sit on the bench that sat on the highest part of the patio in front of the steps leading down to a lawn.

It felt good to be out in the cold, early-evening air. He looked into the darkness and he hadn't been sitting there long when he heard the familiar sound of a helicopter. Sure enough, when he looked up, he spotted the yellow and red Whistlestop River air ambulance passing overhead. He almost wanted to wave, as ridiculous as that was – who would spot him all the way down here? He wondered whether Bess was on board. He wondered whether she'd been thinking about the day she'd come to see him in the hospital. She'd stopped by to see him here at the house a few days ago but he'd been asleep and she hadn't been back since. She had her own life. They'd texted, the usual banter between them, but he'd love to see her smiling face right now. And, if he was honest, check out that tattoo again.

Mind you, he'd make lousy company at the moment – he'd been cheerier in the hospital, maybe because the pain medication was stronger, who knew. But reality had hit since he left and it wasn't a reality he particularly liked.

By the time he went inside for dinner, he felt less tense. He let his mum take the crutches from him and sat at the table. Up until now, no matter what she did to help, all he could think was that it could never make up for the years she'd missed, but the night air had given him a bit of perspective. Because she was here now, she was trying.

'Thanks, Mum.' He picked up his cutlery to dig into the cottage pie she'd bought, heated up and served with a side salad.

'It's my pleasure,' she said.

Sitting next to her now, sharing a simple meal and conversation, he almost felt like a young boy. He and Marco hadn't had this, not in the latter parts of their childhood after their father walked out. But watching her now, sober, eating a proper meal and safe and warm in his home, made Gio realise that it wasn't only he and Marco who had suffered for so long. She had too. And didn't they all deserve a chance to heal?

* * *

The next morning, Gio had breakfast with Marianne before she went to work on the 10 a.m. until 7 p.m. shift. Just like with last night's dinner, it was good to sit at a table with her, watch her, know for himself that she was doing okay. But after a bowl of muesli and a couple of slices of toast, the conversation – or rather the questions about Marco and when he was next coming to visit – got too much and Gio excused himself for a shower.

'The physio will be here before 10 a.m. I need to make sure I'm ready,' he explained.

'I'll clear the dishes; you leave them to me.'

The hidden benefit of the tired downstairs shower room, which was more of a wet room, was that the shower didn't have a frame and so had all the space in the world in which to put the plastic chair to sit on while he washed himself the best he could. At this stage, it was better, easier and safer than trying to do it on the one leg he could weight-bear on and he kept repeating in his head that he needed to face his limitations. This was one of them. But it wouldn't be forever, right?

By the time he finished his shower, his mum had gone to work, so Gio got dressed and gave Marco a call.

'When are you coming here again?' he asked as soon as they got the hellos out of the way.

'I wasn't planning on it any time soon. Work, you know.'

'Well, I did...'

'Sorry, didn't mean to—'

'No, I apologise, that was unnecessarily touchy.'

'Mum doing your head in?'

'Kind of,' he sighed. The last thing he wanted to do was moan about her to Marco. He didn't want to put him off visiting even more than he already was. 'It's a bit full on, that's all, and I can't escape. And she's got two days off from tomorrow. You could come for the day, bring the kids; she'd love that.'

Marco didn't say anything.

'She's in a good place, Marco.'

'Yeah, but for how long?'

He couldn't argue with the logic. So many times, they'd thought she'd turned a corner but she'd always returned to the same street, the one she walked with booze and the loss of another part of herself.

'Is she in AA again?' Marco asked.

'She is.'

'She still has a job?'

'Yes.'

'Are you sure she's going there?' Gio had told him the truth about the pub job so it wasn't a surprise when he asked this question.

'I haven't followed her to make sure but she's out every day. She's been paid – I've seen the evidence in her bank account because she used my iPad.'

Switching his thinking had been hard for Gio but he got to see his mother's progress first hand; Marco didn't. And until he did, until he came to see for himself, Gio wasn't sure that Marco would ever believe that their mum was turning things around.

Gio was about to ask again when Marco could visit when the shrill fire station alarm in the background stopped their conversation in its tracks.

'You need to come some time, Marco,' he got in before his brother said goodbye and hung up the call so he could do his job. Gio imagined him pulling on his boots and his jacket, jumping onto the fire engine and heading off to a shout.

Gio would give anything to be doing the very same right now.

* * *

A little before lunchtime, Marianne called, but rather than it being to tell Gio she'd walked out on her job or that she couldn't stick it – he'd had those phone calls more times than he cared to remember and had braced himself – she called to tell him she'd seen a room advertised for rent. After she told him the price, she added, 'That's including bills so I don't have to worry about those on top, and it's furnished.'

Floored at how together she sounded, Gio quickly rallied and picked up his iPad. He wanted to check the place out online for himself.

She told him the approximate area where the house was. 'I can get the bus like I do now,' she explained.

It was a short bus trip to work at the moment; she reached the office of the cleaning firm in less than thirty minutes and from there, the cleaners went off as a team to their various jobs in a little van. She'd even talked the other night about one day getting her driver's licence – she'd never said anything like that before.

Looking at the area on a map, it was further than he'd thought. 'It'll be quite a trek to work.'

'Stop fussing. Be pleased for me, Gio.' With a huff, she pointed out, 'This is what you want, isn't it?'

'I want you to be safe and happy, Mum, that's all.' His voice came out small and she mellowed.

'It's really not that far.'

'No, I suppose not.' But it didn't stop him asking her for the exact address so he could find it online while she went back to work.

When the call ended, he let himself be happy that she was taking charge. He loved how elated she'd sounded – but then it reminded him of how she used to get that way after a couple of drinks. After two or three, she'd come alive, be good company, but then the really drunk Marianne showed up and it was another thing entirely.

Gio searched on the address and room to rent, found the advert online, and she was right; the price was reasonable. This would give his mum her independence back because it had to be hard having your son watching your every move. It would restore his sanity too, at least as much as it could return when he wasn't operating at full throttle with his wretched knee.

He looked on the map attached to the listing and zoomed in on where the house with the spare room was located and it was indeed near a bus stop so it could work even if the bus ride was longer. But on closer inspection, he spotted a couple of flies in the ointment – namely an off licence on the street corner and a pub at the other end of the road. He didn't want to be negative, but wasn't that tempting fate? One bad day could see her slipping into the off licence or into the pub and that would be that. Her sober days' total would be no more and she'd have to start all over again. And nobody wanted that.

With nothing much else to do, he kept his leg elevated and on his iPad searched for other rooms to rent, but they were all so expensive. At these prices she'd have no money for food and he was pretty sure that *bills included* didn't mean you ate for free.

By mid-afternoon, Gio was going stir crazy. He had to get outside again. He'd already done several rounds of the daily exercises his physio had shown him and now, he took the painkillers even though his knee didn't feel too bad. There wasn't much daylight left but he didn't care; he had to do this to keep his head straight. He'd go to the end of the path on those damn crutches, turn left and go round the block. He could walk it in fifteen minutes usually, run it in five, but he suspected it was going to take a heck of a lot longer than that this time.

He underestimated how long everything took when you were compromised. It wasn't just getting out and about. Putting on his coat should've been a five-second job, but he'd ended up having to sit down to do it when he stumbled. Putting on his shoes went in a similar vein. Then he'd forgotten a key, and getting from front door to kitchen took longer than usual, especially when his crutches caught on the coffee table and sent a mug flying. Luckily, it was empty.

Eventually, he opened the front door to the bracing December winds and set off down the path.

At the end of the street, he rested at the bench. Two young women walked past and he knew they were checking him out – he'd seen that same look from women when he was out on a job. They saw the uniform, they knew what was underneath – strength, stamina, bravery – all the things he hoped he still had, but right now, he felt as though he wanted to dress in a costume which was no longer custom-made for him. It didn't fit, and he hated that.

He carried on to the end of the road. He wished *Merry Christmas* to passers-by, and nodded to a guy who every year put a nativity scene on his front lawn for local kids to appreciate. Who was he kidding? Gio always stopped and gawped at the nativity scene for ages – it wasn't only for the kids. When he was four and Marco nine, they made their own nativity scene at home using a cardboard box, their Lego figures, and straw from the guinea pig hutch at the foot of the garden. He remembered it as a good Christmas, and the boys hadn't had that many.

Gio crossed the road, walked parallel with a field and acres of countryside beyond. Every now and then, he stopped, pretended to look across and admire the Christmas lights on houses, when really he was stopping because he was pushing himself more than he should.

But nothing good ever came from sitting back and doing nothing. He had to work hard at this.

There was no other choice.

12

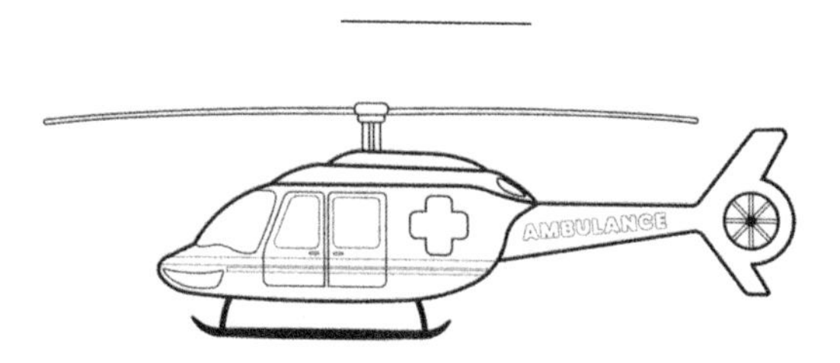

Bess had just come off shift. She'd finished late after a job and the paperwork it entailed. As she drove out of the airbase, the skies had taken on a rich cobalt blue and the air was crisp with a promise of the upcoming festive season.

Today had been busy – four jobs in Hilda and one in the rapid response vehicle to finish up with. But no lives had been lost so despite the exhaustion, she'd take it as a win.

Inside her bag, her phone bleeped. It would be her mum. Again. Since the day Bess had fled after overhearing her mum and Malcolm talking, she had come up with every excuse in the book to avoid seeing her mother – extra shifts at work, a Christmas party, a seasonal dinner with friends, a head cold, going to a Christmas light display. Because the truth was, she was embarrassed: embarrassed at having to ask for money, that Malcolm knew, and mortified at what her dad would say if he was here to see the mess she'd got herself into. Bess had used the £500 from her mum to cover a credit card payment and a payday loan repayment but as soon as one thing was dealt with, it seemed another appeared in its place, leaving her no closer to climbing out of the quagmire. Her debts continued to loom over her like the huge, threatening, black clouds that sometimes prevented The Skylarks from getting airborne to save lives.

As she drove away from the airbase, she wondered what Malcolm thought of her. Did he think she was a sponger? An adult acting like a kid when the chips were down? She didn't usually pay much attention to what other people thought of her personal life; she was forever telling others to do the same, that their personal life was their business and nobody else's. But in this situation, she was finding it nigh on impossible to take her own advice.

She stopped at the *Stop* sign before signalling and turning right. She approached the next junction but slowed as a person on crutches tried to cross to the other side the best they could. Which wasn't exactly quick.

When she saw the man's profile illuminated by a nearby house bedecked in what had to be hundreds if not thousands of fairy lights, she realised it was Gio. She must've been too focused on her own problems to recognise him at first.

She wound down her window. 'Gio!' she called out but he didn't stop and so she drove on and pulled in on the left where he was ambling along the pavement the best he could.

Crutches still fixed underarm, he stopped level with her car and bent his head so he could see in the passenger side to where she'd leaned across and opened the window.

'Good to see you on your feet,' she told him.

'I needed the fresh air. And I needed to move. I'm getting better with these.' He lifted one of the metal crutches ever so slightly.

'Want a lift the rest of the way home?'

'Now that would defeat the object of getting out for some exercise.'

As he shifted his weight, even his high-wattage smile didn't hide that he'd pushed it tonight and was trying not to admit defeat. It was the sort of smile she'd seen when they were sharing a house, when his mother had called him or he'd paid her a visit, a smile that said there was plenty going on in his life that he wasn't about to divulge.

'I'm thinking you've been out a while already, am I right?' Bess persisted.

'I did a lap around the block, first time.'

She flipped the catch on the passenger door to open it slightly.

Still he resisted. 'I'm quite capable of going the fifty metres or so that it is to my house; I'm not an invalid.'

She sighed. 'Would you put a sock in it, Gio, and let me help. We're friends; friends are there for each other. And besides, it'll make me feel good about myself.'

He gave up the protest when she climbed out to go around to the passenger side and help him negotiate getting in the car.

She was holding the crutches, their bodies almost touching, they were in such close proximity. He had one hand on the top of the car, the other on the door frame. And suddenly, he looked upwards to the sky.

'Breathtaking.' The single word made her look up too. 'I'm still getting used to the beauty of Dorset.'

'Told you you'd love it.' She followed his gaze to a cluster of sparkling stars. Bess had grown up in Dorset but even when she lived elsewhere for a while, she'd never forgotten the county's big, open skies, the incredible beauty of the scenery all around them.

'So have I made you feel good about yourself?' he asked her, still hovering between the car door and the pavement.

'You can't help yourself with the flirting, can you? We've been friends a long time; are you running out of women to try it with?'

He laughed. 'No, I'm being myself with you, that's all. So does it work?'

Bess was taken aback by him saying he was being himself. He'd never outwardly flirted with her, not for years anyway, because their friendship set unspoken rules neither of them had broken. But Bess knew her feelings for Gio had evolved since he'd come down to Dorset. She hadn't realised it at first; it had crept up on her until the day of his accident when seeing him there on the ground and in danger had made her heart constrict in a way that told her this might be more than friendship.

But the flirting remark stood. He'd always been a flirt and she'd seen him in action. Bess knew dating Gio would be fun – a whole lot of fun, in fact – but then what? It would crash and burn like all his relationships and their friendship would be left in tatters.

'Look, it's really cold out here,' she said, 'so if you don't just get in, I might drive away and forget to give these crutches back.'

'That would be cruel.' He was still leaning on top of the open passenger-side door, amused.

'Just get in.'

Once he was in and the crutches safely stowed, she drove to his.

She pulled up outside a home not too dissimilar to her cottage in age with a neatly kept front garden behind a low-slung gate.

'You want to come in for a coffee?' His smile faltered. 'I could really use the company.'

If he flirted with her again when they were inside, she wasn't sure she'd be able to stop the way her mind and body seemed to want to react. And that could only spell disaster for both of them.

'I can come in for a bit,' she said.

'Good. And I promise, no flirting.'

Had he read her mind?

'Unless you want me to,' he said.

Bess laughed it off as she got out of the car. Gio's personality was still intact and she wondered whether he was compensating, flirting with her to try to prove that he was the man he'd always been. Knowing Gio the way she did, being injured wasn't just physical for him. There was a whole lot of mental anguish wrapped up in it as well. Not being able to work would be devastating and she could understand what that must feel like for him. When she'd had her health scare, she'd had to take some time off to fit in her appointments; when her dad died, she took a lengthy leave for herself and to support her mum, but on some days, it had been a form of agony. That time away from work had been necessary, had helped in both cases, but equally, it had kept her away from doing what she loved. She knew even now that with her mounting debts, the days she went to work kept her sane, kept her perspective, gave her a form of support she could never do without.

As Gio turned in the passenger seat, Bess got out, retrieved the crutches and got around to his side of the car. He didn't have a driveway so she'd parked right outside his property, which was on a quiet road.

'Where's your mum?' she asked as she followed him slowly up the garden path. He was good on the crutches but wouldn't be winning any races just yet.

'She's at work; for once, she's managed to hold a job down.' Inside the house, he leant his crutches against the wall while he took off his coat. The house was warm, and he yanked his jumper over his head. 'Right, Bess, how do you want it?'

'Excuse me?'

'The coffee.' Crutches tucked beneath his armpits once again, he braced, the tendons in his forearms showing off the firefighter's physique. 'What did you think I meant?'

'Okay, enough innuendo, you're trying to make me embarrassed and you should know by now that it won't work.'

'Sorry, not being on the job means I have to do something for my amusement. Anything. Follow me, I'll get us the coffee. No more clever remarks, promise.'

She followed him into the kitchen. 'Black for me, no sugar.'

'Coming right up.'

He had a coffee machine like she did and busied himself making them each a cup. Bess loved her own coffee machine – she'd bought a posh one. But over the last week or so when she made a cup, it seemed to mock her from its position on the kitchen counter, because it had been yet another purchase she hadn't really been able to afford. It had made her feel good at the time, of course, but that was what had sent her down this destructive path in the first place.

'How is it having your mum staying with you in your space?' she asked as she thanked him for the mug he passed her. With their busy lives, they didn't catch up nearly as often as Bess would've liked and not seeing him when they crossed paths at work had made her miss his company all the more.

'Challenging.' He met her gaze. 'She's helpful – too helpful – and she fusses, which I suppose isn't a bad thing, but I kind of like living on my own. I'd rather hobble around or drag myself around some days than have someone waiting on me hand and foot. But...' He shrugged as if there might well be more to say. In all the time they'd known each other, Bess had got a handle on how complicated things were in his family, but he'd never really got down to the nitty-gritty details. Perhaps some of that was as a coping mechanism; the rest could be pride.

He indicated for her to go through to the lounge.

She knew what he was thinking: he was wondering how he could swat away her help and still get his mug to the lounge whilst on crutches. 'Just let me take it for you.'

'Fine.' He reluctantly let her pick up his coffee as well as hers.

'Sometimes, you've got to accept a little help.'

They settled in the lounge and he thanked her for staying. 'Company other than my mother's makes me feel semi-normal.'

'I see my mother often, she doesn't live that far away, but having a parent living with you must be a whole different ball game. How long is she staying for?'

'Not sure yet.' He took a tentative sip of hot coffee. 'Come on, give me some work talk.'

'You sound desperate.'

'I am, believe me. And you might be a critical care paramedic rather than a firefighter, but I'll take it. I need action talk. I want to hear about emergency scenarios, jobs, anything. The closest I've come to that is watching TV shows.'

Bess ran through today's emergency, the one where firefighters were on the scene. She gave her best descriptions; he was engaged, asked questions, and at the end, he leaned back against the soft sofa with a big smile.

'That better?' she asked, watching him close his eyes, satisfied with some shop talk. He was a handsome man with a chiselled jaw and a physique that was hard to look away from.

'Man, I miss the job.' He opened his eyes, looked at his leg.

'I'm not really cheering you up, am I? Maybe we should talk about something else.'

'You're doing better than you think you are.' When he locked eyes with her, she shifted a little. It was that same look he'd given her time and time again when they met at an emergency or when he showed up at the air ambulance base in support of The

Skylarks' fundraising events. The emergency services all tended to do that for each other – equally, she'd been to open days at the fire station and watched him do his demonstrations or talk about his job. The best times were when he had a group of kids to talk to. To look at him, you'd think he had no appeal to the younger audience but he came alive in a different way when kids showed up, as if he understood them and knew just how to get on their wavelength.

'Does the knee still hurt?' she asked.

'Only when I move it too much. And the brace helps, stops me twisting it the wrong way or knocking it.'

'And the walk before, when I picked you up, was that too much?'

'More on my arms using those crutches than anything else.'

His arms looked strong enough from where she was sitting, and she noticed his biceps, the way the sleeves of his T-shirt hugged them.

'Are you doing all the exercises they give you?'

'Religiously.'

'That's good.' And now she'd run out of things to say, aware that here she was sitting in close proximity to Gio and it felt different to all the times they'd done this before. They were still friends but her feelings had begun to spill over into more when they absolutely couldn't, not if she wanted to avoid making even more of a mess of her life than she already had. Gio wasn't the sort of man you went out with if you wanted a serious, stable future. He was fun, a right here, right now kind of guy, and she had enough recklessness with her finances. She didn't need to add it in to her personal life too.

'Bess—'

'This coffee is good.' She didn't want him to say anything that would make things between them complicated.

'I'm glad you like it. Could do with one of those brownies Nadia made to go with it.'

'Me too, they were good.'

'How about dinner?'

'Dinner?' She set her mug down on the coffee table. 'Now?'

'Not now, no. But dinner some time, me and you. We haven't met up for ages, not properly.'

'We're meeting up now.'

'We used to go for lunch frequently; we haven't done that in weeks.'

'Life is busy.' When he grunted, she cringed. 'Sorry, you're stuck here and not working, I didn't mean to rub your nose in it.'

'So help me out. Don't rub my nose in it; agree to letting me take you out for dinner.'

'You mean like a date?' Dinner together was one thing, but taking her out? 'Gio, I'm not sure—'

'You think it'll complicate things.'

'We're friends; we're on the job together.'

'We don't work together, not really. And yes, we're friends, but I'd say that's a good thing. So what other excuses have you got?'

She was all out. She did want to go on a date, she wanted nothing more than to say yes to him. She just knew that she shouldn't.

'I don't want to ruin things. I'm not in the right headspace to start something with anyone,' she said truthfully. 'And I don't think you are either.'

'I've hurt my knee, not my head or any other part of my anatomy.'

His voice was teasing and her mind went to the anatomy she knew lay beneath his clothes. She'd seen him enough times in action to know how strong he was and her imagination right now was running riot. She'd seen him around the house too, back when they shared a place with other people, when he'd sauntered downstairs for breakfast in nothing more than tracksuit pants hung low at the waist, the rest of his body on display. None of the housemates thought anything of walking around in their pyjamas; why would they when it was their home? But every time Gio had come into the room, Bess had felt uneasy, as if her gaze was constantly drawn in his direction. She should've known back then that if she was to admit it to herself, she thought about a lot more than friendship when it came to Gio Mayhan.

'When I get back on my feet, literally,' he said, 'I will take you to dinner.'

'Gio, I—'

'Try not to overthink it. We'll go to dinner, have a good time, what do you say?'

'We'll see.' The words were out before she really registered them.

He punched the air.

'I said, we'll see.' But she was laughing at his boyish enthusiasm.

'It's not a no; I'll take this as a good sign.'

She liked that he seemed a little happier, more upbeat.

But that changed when there was the sound of the front door opening.

Gio frowned. 'She's not supposed to be home yet.' And then he called out a little louder, 'You're home early.'

A voice hollered back, 'Mix-up with the jobs today so earlier finish and an earlier start in the morning.'

Gio's mum came into the lounge and when she spotted Bess, she beamed a smile her way. 'I didn't realise you had company, Gio.' She smoothed the front of the shirt she wore over faded jeans. 'And look at me, I'm in a state from work.'

'Don't apologise,' said Bess. 'I'm in my scruffs too.' She waved her hand down the sweatshirt and jeans she'd thrown on to make the trip from the airbase to home. 'It's good to see you again.'

'Same, love. Good to see you too.'

Gio eyed the carrier bags still hanging from each of her hands. 'Tonight's meal?'

'I have my uses.' She went into the kitchen and called back, 'Are you staying, Bess?'

'Thanks for the offer but I need to go,' Bess replied.

Gio leaned closer, his good leg almost touching hers. 'Wise choice. She'll be force feeding me meat pie, potatoes and peas.'

'That doesn't sound too bad to me.'

'It is when you've had it for the last four days straight.'

Bess laughed quietly, enjoying the proximity, trying to imagine how it might feel to go out with this man for dinner, whether it would be better than the other disastrous dates she'd had over the years. Would he turn out to be the guy she'd always assumed him to be? Or would he be this more laid-back, genuine soul who might just be hiding a bit of himself away from the rest of the world?

'Mum wasn't exactly one to be in the kitchen over the years,' Gio confided, 'so I think her repertoire is limited.'

'My mum is the opposite; she loves being in the kitchen.' He was still sitting so close to her that her pulse was racing. They'd been this close plenty of times over the years but never had it felt the way it did now.

'Home baking growing up?' he asked to the sound of clanging pots and pans coming from the kitchen. 'Lucky you.'

'She sounds like she's finding her way around the kitchen now.'

'Hmm…' His breath fell across her cheek when he called out, 'Need some help in there?'

Marianne came through with a head of broccoli in one hand. 'All under control. Just couldn't find your chopping board.'

'It's beside the microwave.'

She rolled her eyes. 'I had every cupboard out looking for it.'

'You should've—'

'Asked, I know.' She smiled in Bess's direction before heading back to the kitchen.

'Looks like you're having broccoli,' Bess told him. 'It's green, but it's not peas.'

'That's one of the things I love about you, Bess: your positivity.' His lips parted as if he might want to say more.

But Bess looked away quickly. 'I really should go.' When Marianne had asked whether she was staying for dinner, she had been kind of tempted and she knew Gio would've gone for it. But she'd been here longer than she'd intended already.

'Thanks for bringing me home,' he said as he manoeuvred the crutches under his arms to walk her to the door. 'And thanks for the company.' He stayed in the doorway after Bess got her coat on and stepped outside. 'I'll see you soon. We'll go for that dinner.'

She answered him with a smile. She couldn't manage much else.

Her phone beeped again with a message from her mum as she got into the car and then again when she got back home, so she plucked up the courage and called her, promising she'd be over to visit soon.

'You're out again this evening?' her mum asked.

'It's almost Christmas; Noah and Maya have organised drinks.'

'I was going to stop round; I haven't seen you in a while.'

'Another time, Mum. We'll do it soon.'

When she hung up, she fired off a text to Noah to say that she would join them this evening in the pub. It hadn't been a formal invite; it wasn't drinks for the entire team, just a casual suggestion if she had nothing else to do. And right now, she could do with the company. Otherwise, she wasn't too sure she wouldn't go back to see Gio. And whether that was a good thing or not remained to be seen.

Right now, she wanted easy friendship, banter, distraction, and the platonic side to Bess and Gio seemed to be long forgotten, especially for her.

And so she drove to the pub. She should be at home, saving the money, but she needed sanity, an escape. What was another tenner in the grand scheme of things?

It was a drop in the ocean.

13

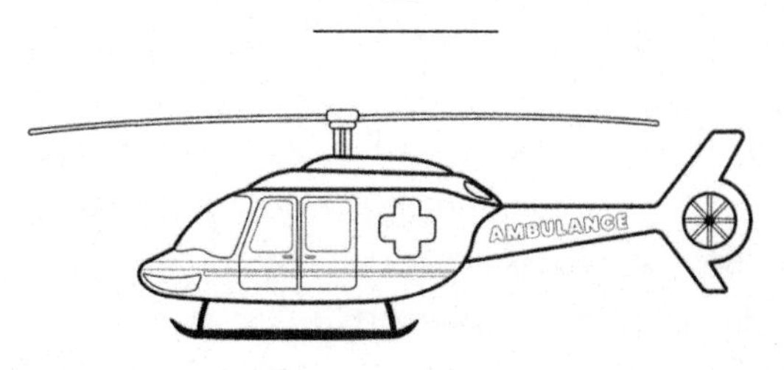

Gio could see the attraction of being a physiotherapist, putting patients through their paces, clocking their progress, encouraging them when they needed it, backing off when that was required.

In her late twenties, his physio Aysha was enthusiastic, he'd give her that, and she wasn't stuck in her ways; she didn't treat him like someone she had to fix but rather a person who was working alongside her to improve. It was an approach that kept her on his good side.

It might be December but he was wearing shorts, necessary for the session and for close inspection of his injury. They were in his small dining room, which had never had a table in and instead housed gym equipment including free weights, a rowing machine and a multi gym with its enormous stack of weights to take him through gruelling workouts to keep his fitness levels as they should be. He'd lost count of the number of times he'd looked over at it since he was injured, especially when he'd set up a camp bed in here when he was first discharged from hospital and unable to take the stairs. He'd looked at the apparatus from his horizontal position and longed to pound out a load of reps, work every inch of his body. He'd sat on the seat a couple of times as he began to improve, done what he could with his arms, the temptation to do the same with his legs almost getting the better of him, but he'd backed off at the thought of making his knee even worse and having a setback that would do him in.

'Are you still taking the painkillers as required?' Aysha felt his knee when he made a sound that went beyond an effort-filled groan after the last exercise.

'When I need them,' he answered.

Aysha finished examining his knee. 'The swelling and bruising have faded; everything is heading in the right direction.'

Vagueness. Nobody would give him a straight answer when it came to the question of how long it would be before he was back to himself. Gio was used to standing tall, strong, the fireman heading towards a crowd to save lives, put out fires, using his brute strength for the greater good. He wasn't a weak person, moaning at how his knee felt when he was sitting on his arse merely bending and straightening it.

'In the right direction,' he repeated. 'What does that even mean?'

'You know the answer to that.'

He did because they'd been through this many, many times before.

They spent the next hour going through a number of exercises – legs bending in different ways, creating flexion to the knee, knee extensions. They used bands, body positioning, he did some half wall squats, making sure the middle of his kneecap was in line with his middle toe.

He was so pleased with the session that he pushed himself and tried to go down into a full squat but the pain stopped him and Aysha was there hooking her arms under his shoulders until he pushed himself up to standing.

'Too much,' she said, although she didn't need to.

'I didn't think so,' he grumped.

'Your body says otherwise.' She hovered over him until he got the message and sat on the weights bench.

'What am I doing wrong?' He wanted to persist – perhaps he'd let his knee go off course, maybe if he focused again after a minute to rest, he'd get it in the bag.

Once upon a time, when something pissed him off, he'd pound the pavements to solve a problem, he'd bash out a workout with some of the heaviest weights he could lift, the blood would pump through his veins and make him feel alive. But right now, he was this weaker version of himself and he hated it. If Bess ever agreed to going to dinner with him, on a date, he wanted to be more than this. He wanted to be himself.

'You're not doing anything wrong.' Aysha's nose stud glinted beneath the light overhead. 'You pushed yourself a little too far and your body reminded you, that's all.'

'I feel like this body is the boss of me, not the other way round.'

'For now, it is. Be patient. One step at a time. It's the approach that will pay off in the end.'

Easy for her to say. She wasn't the one taking what felt like baby steps when all he wanted to do was make a giant leap, back to work, back to a normal life.

'I want to try again,' he said.

'Just half squats.'

'Let me try the full.'

She shook her head. 'Half squats and take it slow; stop the second it hurts. You know the difference between discomfort and pain?' He wasn't sure if it was a question or a reminder. 'Some discomfort is expected but pain is your body telling you to stop. There's a difference.'

Over at the wall, he easily got to half squat. He put everything he had into concentrating on the correct form but he hadn't moved much further down when the pain began again and no way could he disguise it.

Aysha had him sitting on the bench within seconds. 'We're done for today. Do not push it when I'm gone either.' She knew him too well. 'Promise me or you'll set yourself back and how annoyed will you be then?'

He reluctantly agreed but cursed.

Aysha obviously heard him. 'It's okay to be frustrated and if swearing helps, go for it.'

'It does help. But I shouldn't do it around you.'

'Hey, you could've gone a step further and, rather than swear at the universe or yourself, called me something terrible – patients have before, you know.'

That, for some reason, made him chuckle. 'You should claim for emotional stress on the job.'

'Sometimes, I'm tempted. Honestly, though, you're one of my easier patients.'

'Yeah?'

'Believe me, it's harder to work with someone who can't be bothered, who thinks this is their lot in life and the road to recovery is too hard to follow. When a person is in that mindset, my job is very hard.'

'You know what a buddy at work said to me when I was in hospital?'

She waited to hear.

'He said, listen to every single thing your physiotherapist says.'

She laughed. 'Good advice and at the same time, I listen to you; that's the way it works best.'

When they finished the session, he couldn't help asking the same question he delivered almost every time – even though every session, he told himself he wouldn't bring it up this time. 'Have you any idea when I'll be back on the job?'

She packed up her things. 'You and I both know the answer to that.'

He did and he didn't like it. *It'll take as long as it takes* wasn't a proper answer, neither was *every patient is individual.* They were fast becoming two of his least-favourite phrases.

'You're improving every day, remember that.' She shrugged on her coat. 'The work we're doing is restoring your joint range of motion, improving ankle, knee and hip strength. All of that takes time. And it's a process – we need to get you able to function in your everyday life before we even think about a work environment, especially the one you're used to.'

'But I'll get back there, right?'

'You know I wouldn't be doing my job if I made promises I couldn't keep. I've seen firefighters with far more extensive injuries make a full recovery, back at work inside six months. Others I've seen swap to desk duties.'

On his crutches to see her to the door, he still managed to lift his fist and put it to his heart before he got a grip on the walking aids again. 'The dreaded desk duties. Never seen myself as an office boy.'

'I hope we can get you to where you want to be, Gio.'

He didn't hope. He prayed. Not a religious person, he willed any God out there listening to do him a favour and come through on this.

* * *

Marianne hadn't given up looking for rooms to rent. Gio had had no choice but to explain why he was reticent about the one she'd been excited about and rather than make things awkward, it actually made it easier because she did the due diligence after that and looked at properties on a map, noted the surrounding area before she enquired any further.

Gio agreed to go and view another room with her, this time nowhere near a pub or an off licence.

'You need a second opinion, Mum,' he told her when she said yet again that she didn't need a babysitter as they made their way there in a taxi.

The taxi driver pulled up outside a Victorian terrace on the outskirts of Whistlestop River.

'It looks nice,' she said.

When they got out, Gio led the way up the path on his crutches. The property looked respectable and he had a good feeling about it. At least he did until the man with the room to rent opened up the front door and the focus was no longer the enormous bay window and the comfy-looking armchairs beyond; it was a beer belly exposed at the bottom of an ill-fitting shirt and the stains on the shirt that almost blended into the fabric.

'What do you want?' the man barked. He'd been expecting a woman, Gio realised, so stepped aside so the man could see his mum, who'd closed the gate behind them as Gio got a head start given his predicament.

'You must be Marianne.' The guy immediately tried to turn on the charm. *The smarmy git. Too late, mate.* Gio had already made his judgement and it didn't change when they were looking around the interior and Gio caught the man leering at his mother more than once, his eyes way south of her face.

'We'll let you know,' Gio said before his mother could say

anything when they got back to the front door after their little tour around. 'Thank you for your time.' He nodded for his mum to go out first.

As soon as they got to the front gate, he said, 'You are not moving in there.'

'But it was a lovely room. Reasonable rent too.'

'Didn't you notice the way the guy was looking at you?' He'd already gone onto his app to book the taxi when they were midway between the main bedroom and the shared bathroom but there were none available, so they made their way towards the bus stop.

'What do you mean, the way he was looking at me?'

'Like you could do some negotiating for a lower room price if you get my drift.'

'Well, it's nice to feel wanted at my age.' She seemed pleased rather than offended.

'Not with someone like that it isn't.'

Once they were on the bus, Gio felt his mum reach out to him and put her hand over his.

'Thank you for looking out for me.' She said it quietly enough that only he and nobody else could hear. 'I'll keep looking; something will turn up soon.'

'I'm sure it will.' And when they passed a house with a man out front looping Christmas lights around his front fence, Gio pushed the bell conveniently located right near their seats and got up gingerly. He knew where they were and what was close by.

'Where are we going?' Marianne asked.

'You'll see. Come on.'

Once they were off the bus, they walked about a hundred metres and when they turned into the next street, her face took on a warmth that was hard to look away from.

'It's the best street in Whistlestop River for Christmas lights,' said Gio. 'And you don't have to worry about me racing too fast and you not getting to see enough,' he added, noting the crutches.

'Oh, this is wonderful.' Her eyes lit up like she was a five-year-old waiting for Father Christmas. 'Look at this one, the polar bear, the penguins. Oh, Gio!'

They hovered outside every single house like that on the busy street with other people doing exactly the same. And the only thing that made Gio sad was that Marco wasn't here to share this with them.

And so when his mum was watching a moving Father Christmas climb up a ladder on a roof towards the chimney, a big sack slung over his shoulder, Gio sent his brother a message along with a photograph of Marianne, her face almost as bright as the lights, and told him again that this time, it was different. This time, she really had got herself together.

His brother's text came back in seconds:

We'll sort a date soon.

It was all Gio could ask for.

14

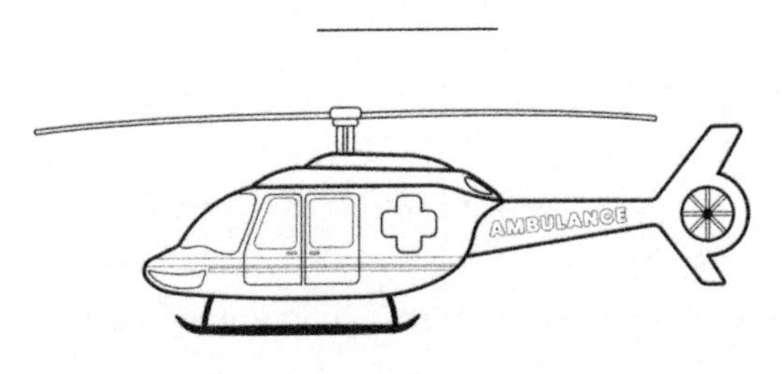

Bess had eaten a fish finger sandwich when she got home from the pub last night and when she came downstairs this morning, she cursed herself for having not rinsed her plate straight away because the smears of HP sauce were stuck fast and her dish-washer had gone on the blink, as if it wanted to have the last laugh at her finances. She was limiting the amount of time her hot water was on these days too, anything to save a bit more money, and it had already gone off. She put the plate to soak in cold water – who knew, maybe it would work – and made some toast to have quickly before Maya picked her up and took her to the pub car park to collect her car on the way to the airbase. As far as anyone at work knew, she was just rubbish at planning, hence the one beer last night turning into three as she relaxed and made the decision to leave her car. She shouldn't have been there at all with her lack of money but she'd wanted to block out her troubles, turn her back on them, just for the evening. And it was nearly Christmas, after all.

'Last night was good.' Maya beamed when Bess climbed into the passenger seat. 'I'm glad you came.'

'Me too.'

Maya pulled away from the kerb after Bess fixed her seatbelt. 'All right, out with it. Something is going on with you.' She was doing her best to both read Bess's expression and keep a good eye on the road, impossible multitasking even she couldn't manage.

'No, everything is fine, honest.' She'd thought she'd done a good job of hiding her problems. Obviously not.

'You know how I know it's not fine? When you say the word *honest* after the claim.'

Bess watched the wintry world go by out of the window. The pavements were slippery today; she'd come down the path very carefully when she heard Maya pull up. 'Thanks again for taking me to get my car this morning. I only intended to have one beer last night.'

'You're very welcome, but don't think I'll drop this, Bess. You wouldn't if you thought something was on my mind. So, we'll talk about it. It doesn't have to be now.'

The low-hanging winter sun had them both flipping their visors down as they turned the corner and pulled into the pub car park, where Bess thanked Maya again and rescued her car.

It was action stations soon after they arrived at the airbase and a call came in.

Maya had already brought the helicopter out of the hangar and onto the helipad, Bess had just taken delivery of bloods from one of the Whistlestop River Freewheelers and went to retrieve the cool box, and Noah got the details of the job.

Within minutes, The Skylarks were up in the air.

One of the parts of her job that Bess really loved was its unpredictability. They could be called out to roadside, by a river, near offices or residential homes or, as today, the beach.

'My favourite place to land,' Maya declared on the approach to the south coast sands. 'Even in the winter, the sea looks glorious.'

'Not if you're in it,' Noah said from the back. 'Do you know, Bess, this one wants me to try cold-water swimming?'

Bess spoke into her microphone attached to her headset. 'She tried to get me to do that last year but she's all yours now, I think you're going to have to take one for the team. And what happened to stand-up paddleboarding?'

'That's in the summer; I've been spared for now,' he laughed.

It was good to see Maya happy and trying new things. She'd lived so long under pressure from her ex-husband, she really was all in with her new relationship and Bess couldn't be happier for her friend.

Police had already cleared the beach, so The Skylarks updated HEMS on their arrival and within the next minute, clouds of sand billowed up as Maya set the helicopter down metres from the sea itself. With the stunning backdrop of the cliffs, this perfect stretch of golden sandy beach was a beauty spot for all seasons, except when there was an emergency like this one.

A young boy had been found on the beach not breathing. A quick-thinking, off-duty nurse had found the defibrillator nearby and used it. The patient was already in the recovery position, the nurse and the boy's sister both beside him. Thanks to the defibrillator, the boy's heart had been shocked back to life and, upon checking, he had a normal heart rhythm, but there was the worry he'd re-arrest because nobody knew why he'd collapsed in the first place. He was confused, which wasn't uncommon when a person had undergone hypoxia – a state of low oxygen – so Noah and Bess stabilised him and had him in the air ambulance as quickly as possible to take him to hospital for further treatment and investigations.

The wind didn't help their journey. It hadn't been too bad on the way here but it had increased by the time they left. It made for a shaky flight, something none of them wanted, and touching down on the hospital's helipad took longer than usual as Maya tried to hold the aircraft steady.

'Good job out there, team,' Noah declared when they were on the way back to base.

'Right back at you,' Bess smiled. The good thing about this job was that there was so much action, it blocked out any other noise in her head, although she did allow the odd thought of Gio. It was a type of therapy and instilled a sense of calm, which was new.

As soon as they were back at base and she'd put her helmet on the shelf ready to grab for the next job, Nadia leaned around the door jamb. 'Your mum is in reception to see you.'

And she would've seen the helicopter land so Bess couldn't even ask Nadia to say she was out on a job.

On the phone last night, Bess had said she'd see her mum soon. Her mum had probably got tired of waiting and knew that Bess's idea of *soon* was often different to hers.

She took a deep breath and headed for reception.

They hugged and when Fiona pulled back, she beamed. 'I saw your crew land just now; it never ceases to amaze me the work you all do.'

Bess led her over to the sofas at the far end of reception next to the Christmas tree. 'Thank you, Mum. My biggest fan.' When it came to work, yes; probably not so much when it came to her daughter's lack of ability to organise her own life.

Fiona came right out with it. 'Last night, you told me we'd

meet up soon but I decided I didn't want to wait any longer. You've been avoiding me.'

'I'm pretty busy. Talking of which—'

'I've been worried about you.'

Bess got the impression that today, there'd be no talking her way out of this. 'I didn't mean to cause you worry, Mum.'

'But you did.' She clasped her handbag on her lap. 'And that's how I know whatever is going on with you, it's very real. And I'm thinking the £500 I lent you doesn't even come close to sorting out your problems. Am I right?'

Bess said nothing. How could she? She was so ashamed.

'You don't come to me for help unless you really need it. You never did. You've always been determined to do things your way and on your own. But please, Bess, let me help you now.'

She looked down at her hands in her lap. 'I don't know where to start...' She broke off, glad there wasn't anyone else around them at this end of reception. 'If Dad were here, he'd be so disappointed.' She wasn't sure why the waters of the gene pool had muddied so much, she hadn't kept on top of her own finances the way her dad would have and the way her mum did despite losing him. Both of them had been capable; why wasn't she?

'Bess, how much trouble are you in? How much debt?'

She reiterated some of the details and, to be fair, her mum didn't let any shock show in her expression; she simply waited for Bess to finish.

'I can try to find you more money,' Fiona insisted. 'There has to be a way.'

'You shouldn't have to.'

'But that's why you came to me. For help.'

'And you did help.'

'Not enough.'

Bess hung her head. 'I hate that I took the money in the first place.'

'You didn't take it; I gave it. And I have more, some tied up in bonds, but I can get to the money eventually.'

'And pay a penalty? No way, Mum.'

'Love, your dad provided for us all; you know what he was like.'

'I do and he wouldn't want you to lose out. No, Mum. This is my mess. I have to be the one to sort it.'

And then came the worst question she could ask. 'Bess, how did you let it get this bad?'

Bess liked to think of herself as strong and capable; that was the way she was at work, certainly. She kept cool in a crisis, she could calm patients down, keep the stress out of a situation even when it seemed at its absolute worst. Last week, when they'd been called out to a near-drowning at a leisure centre after a patient dived in and hit their head, the parents had been in pieces, freaking out. It was Bess who took them aside, broke through their wails and barrage of questions to get them to a place where they could take in the information she was giving them. Noah and other first responders had all told her they weren't sure anyone could've handled it better. What was so wrong with her that she wasn't the same with her own life? Her mum was right; she'd let it get this bad, she hadn't talked herself out of all her stupid decisions along the way when she should have.

'I want to understand, Bess. I really do.'

'Dad always went on about how important it was to save, to put money aside, and from the day I got my very first part-time job, I did it. But when he died, all I saw was the unfairness of it all, the way he'd tried to futureproof himself, and for what?' She wasn't going to cry; she wasn't going to feel sorry for herself. Her hands balled into fists so tightly, she almost didn't feel her mum reach out her own hands to cover them.

Her fingers unfurled a little.

'Your dad was a great provider. For me. For you. That was just as important to him as making money for himself – more important, even.'

She thought about the first year after losing him, the first Christmas, the first birthdays, the myriad of occasions where his presence felt like a giant hole dug out of their lives.

'Is that why you started spending more money than you should?' Fiona asked. 'Because you didn't see the point in saving it in case something terrible happened?'

Bess nodded. 'It wasn't only losing Dad that did it.' Bess waited for Maya to put a file on the desk in reception before she went out back again. 'It was my health scare too. All the emotions it brought up: the worry, the relief when I got the all-clear. I hadn't got over my anger that Dad had been so careful and his life was cut short and then all of a sudden, I'd been given a reprieve. I felt I had to make the most of it. I booked holidays, I upgraded my car when I didn't need to, went on spa weekends, changed my sofa, splurged on whatever I wanted. I couldn't stop; it brought me comfort.

'Every time another bill landed on my doormat, I got more and more overwhelmed, and yet I didn't stop spending. I went into denial. I added those bills to the pile. The cost-of-living crisis didn't even deter me. I've been living my life to the full; that was how I saw it. I kept doing balance transfers to new credit cards as I realised I was short of money each month. And then I let interest get charged on those cards so the amounts on each card continued to climb even when I stopped spending. I could barely make the minimum payments.'

'I didn't see it happening, and I should have,' her mum said, as though any of this was her fault.

'Don't you dare blame yourself. This was me, all me.' She leaned in to her mum, who had got closer to her without Bess realising.

Fiona put an arm around her daughter's shoulders.

'I'll get it together,' Bess insisted. She had to. 'There are people out there with real problems, not things they brought on themselves.' She'd done this. She'd spent money to feel better and it had worked for a while; it worked even better when she buried the reality of it. Somewhere along the way, she'd stopped questioning whether she could really afford things.

Her mum asked again exactly how much Bess needed to get totally straight and reluctantly, Bess told the whole truth.

'That's quite some debt.'

'I know. And I'm out of options to fix this. I've drawn out cash on my credit cards too many times to pay bills; I've taken out a loan to pay off debts. What happens next – another loan to pay that loan and so on and so on? I haven't missed too many mortgage payments but I have missed one. And that terrifies me the most, because if I default regularly then I'm at risk of losing my home.'

'You won't, my darling. I'll go to the bank, see what I can do.'

'Absolutely not. And I will pay you back every single penny of the £500 as soon as I can. I mean it,' she added before her mum could try again to insist she took a financial hit for her daughter's benefit.

'No rush, no rush at all.' Tentatively, she asked, 'Have you thought about seeing someone for some proper advice?'

'That would cost money.'

'The Citizens Advice Bureau could be a good place to start; that'll be something at least.'

'I could try,' she said. 'You know if Dad were here and I could've brought myself to tell him the mess I was in, he would've been the perfect person to ask.'

'He really would.' She hesitated. 'I know someone else who might be able to help.'

'Who?'

'Malcolm. He's a retired financial advisor.'

Bess's body went rigid. 'No. I don't know him well enough; I really don't want him involved.'

Noah came into reception looking for her and she waved to indicate she'd be there in a minute.

'I have to go, Mum.'

'Mince pies,' Nadia announced as she was next to appear. She set a big platter onto the counter. 'Help yourselves.'

Fiona lowered her voice. 'I don't know why you won't talk to Malcolm; he could help. I know he's not your dad, but—'

'I heard you that day I came over.'

It dawned on Fiona what she meant. 'Is that why you've been avoiding me?' She stood up when Bess did, fastened the top button of her coat.

'He must think I'm a terrible person,' said Bess.

'Love, he doesn't. He saw you come to your mother for help. He has his own children; he'd do anything for them. He understands.'

'Mince pies!' Nadia urged again when nobody made a move to take one.

'I don't think you're going to get out of here without indulging.' Bess kissed her mum on the cheek and wrapped her in a hug. 'I really appreciate the loan; I'll call the Citizens Advice Bureau.' But she didn't mention Malcolm and neither did her mum this time. 'Now take a mince pie before Nadia loses it.'

And she did the same on her way out to join the others in the office.

They had four more jobs before end of shift and by the time Bess grabbed her things from her locker, she was exhausted. But not so tired she didn't notice Maya ushering Noah out of the locker room to leave the two of them alone.

'Subtle,' said Bess.

'Yeah, sorry about that. But I'm here, I have time to talk so hit me with it. Leave nothing out.'

'Maya, I'm fine, honestly.'

'No, no way. You are not leaving this room until you tell me.' She put her finger in the air as if she'd thought of something. 'It's Gio, isn't it? I heard from Noah who heard from a buddy of Gio's that you have been seeing him.'

Bess began to laugh. 'I haven't been seeing him. We're friends, remember.'

'So you say. But tell me this... has he asked you out?'

'He might have mentioned dinner.'

Maya was excited at the prospect. 'Well, good for him.'

Bess pulled her coat out of her locker but Maya hadn't finished. 'I want to ask you more about Gio but I know full well that isn't what is on your mind, at least not all of it.'

Bess thought about resisting it but instead, she sat down, coat on her lap, and spilled it all, every last bit of it: the spending, the bills, the credit cards, the loans.

'Shit, no wonder your mind has been all over the place. You need solutions, my girl. If I had enough money myself, I'd give you a loan.'

'No, I don't want to borrow off any friends.'

'Come on, back to my place with me. I'm cooking and we're going to talk this through.'

Bess picked up her bag. 'I don't want Noah—'

'He's at his tonight with Eva; I was having an early night. But I'd rather spend the evening with you.'

'I'm not a charity case.'

Maya gave her a look.

'All right, I need all the help I can get.'

Maya pulled her into a hug as they walked out of the locker room. 'We'll get you sorted.'

And for once Bess, having shared her problems with her mum and her very good friend, felt a glimmer of hope that perhaps everything was going to be okay.

15

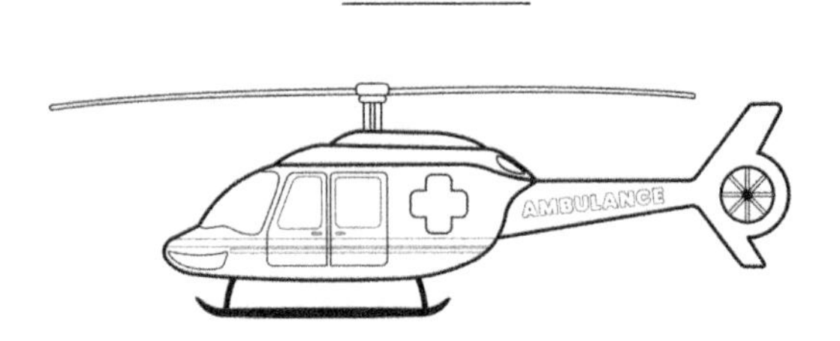

Gio hadn't been back to the fire station since his accident, but today he relented and popped his head in.

Along with using the crutches, he'd put his knee in the brace. He didn't want to risk getting it knocked when he was here, trying to do too much, because he knew in this environment, he would feel even more need to prove himself. And being careful and thoughtful had to be a good sign – he didn't want anything to stunt his progress, especially not denial of his injury or a too-much-too-soon approach.

His time at the fire station turned out to be less torturous than he'd expected. In fact, it ended up giving him a boost rather than putting him on more of a downer. He checked in with his crewmates, hung around as they made jokes, bantered back and forth, giving him faith that he'd be back there some day. But what really lifted his spirits was a visit from Stacey, the young woman he'd saved in the office fires, when she came in with a card and what looked suspiciously like a cake tin tucked under one arm.

'We knew you wouldn't want a fuss,' Norm whispered to Gio as Stacey spotted them and headed over.

So they'd known she was coming.

'And you got me here anyway,' Gio said to Norm.

'Smile, be polite.'

'I kind of like these visits,' he confessed. When people stopped by to say thank you, it meant the absolute world.

Gio opened the card, which thanked him for saving her, and he looked inside the cake tin when she passed it to him. 'This looks amazing.' It was a chocolate yule log with a sprig of edible holly on top – or at least it looked edible; maybe he'd let one of the other lads try it out to be sure.

'We don't eat Christmas cake in our family; we always have a yule log,' Stacey told him, but her smile fell away. 'How is your leg?'

'My knee is all repaired; I just need to learn how to use it properly again.' He felt terrible then because her eyes misted. 'Hey... don't make me bend down to talk to you.' She was looking at the floor to avoid his gaze. 'That'll set me back weeks on this leg.' When she looked up, he smiled. 'That's better. I'm doing fine. And I'm glad it wasn't you caught in the blast.'

'Me too, is that wrong?'

'Of course not.' He laughed.

The alarm he was so familiar with alerted the crew to a shout and Gio felt a tug, a pang that he wasn't a part of it. He and Stacey watched on as the crew pulled on kit, leapt into the engine, sirens blaring, and they took off.

All Gio could think of was to offer the girl a piece of cake which was helpfully already pre-sliced.

'This is good,' he declared. 'Did you make it?'

'No, I hate cooking. My dad made it.'

'Well, please pass on my thanks.' He had another mouthful before he asked, 'So, did you enjoy your internship?' And then he could've smacked himself. 'Sorry, probably not given the building was on fire and you were almost left inside. But did you at least enjoy the time as a personal assistant or whatever you were doing?'

But rather than be upset, she started to grin. 'Are you kidding? That was the best day. And it told me I need to toughen up.'

'Toughen up for office duties?'

'I have zip interest in being in an office for the rest of my life. I want to fight fires.'

Now that he hadn't expected.

He waited for her to finish her piece of cake. 'Come on, I'll give you a tour, tell you all about what it's really like.'

And when Gio left for home, he was still smiling.

Today was a good day.

But by the afternoon, Gio and Marianne were house-hunting, or rather room-hunting, and his good mood was starting to falter.

The first viewing was no good and neither was the second. And he was sick of climbing on and off the bus, the hassle of his crutches, the slowness of his movements compared to what they'd once been.

He couldn't face another ride on public transport so for the next viewing, he treated them both to a taxi. 'I'm getting full pay, Mum, don't stress,' he told her when she voiced her concern again.

In the back of the taxi, Marianne clutched the Post-it she'd scribbled the details onto after finding another spare room to look at. 'I've got a good feeling about this place.'

'You said that about the last.' He didn't mean to sound so despondent. That wouldn't help things for either of them. At least this next one was a female landlord, or should he say landlady? He was never sure. He wasn't sexist but the last three rooms they'd viewed had all been in homes owned by men and not one of those had been suitable. They'd called a fourth, a male landlord again, but there must be something in the water around here for men renting out their spare rooms because he was hard to understand on the phone and the only bit Gio comprehended as his mum used speakerphone so he could listen in was when the guy asked Marianne to send him a photograph for identity purposes. Gio had leaned across the arm of the sofa and hung up the house phone himself on that one, uttering the word, 'Pervert.' Before explaining that asking for photo ID at this stage was bullshit.

'I just need somewhere for a good three to six months and then I can get my own bedsit. I'd rather live on my own, Gio. I need that. You need it too.' She wiped her hand against the condensation on the back window so she could see out.

'I want to see you get a good place, Mum.'

'I know.' But she seemed to be losing hope the same way he was and with any downer for his mum came the risk she'd seek solace in the bottle. He knew that. And so did she.

'Cheers,' said Gio to the driver before paying the fare with his card when they reached their destination.

Kerbside, his mother was waiting in front of the pretty little house with a bottle-green front door that he was familiar with.

This couldn't be it.

'Are you sure you have the right address?' he asked after she handed him his crutches.

'Yes, of course.' And she was already on her way up the path to meet Elizabeth, the owner. The woman he knew as Bess.

Gio hovered next to his mum as Marianne lifted the door knocker and rapped twice, not too loud but firm enough to get attention and sure enough, it wasn't long before they heard the key turn in the lock.

'Hello, I'm Marianne,' his mother said brightly. She'd obviously rehearsed it to say the second the door was open because the words were out before she registered. 'Bess, it's Bess! Look, Gio, it's your friend.'

He grinned. 'So it is.'

Bess ushered them inside in the warm and it was obvious from her reaction that she'd suspected there weren't too many Mariannes looking to rent a spare room.

'What's with the name Elizabeth?' he asked once they were inside. 'Did you make that up?'

'Of course I didn't. It's my full name.'

'How did I never know that?'

She shrugged. 'Nobody ever, ever calls me that – think Dad did a few times when I was little and in trouble, but apart from official letters and documents, I'm Bess. You clearly weren't nosy enough when we shared a house.'

'You have a beautiful home,' Marianne told her, even though she hadn't seen much of it.

'Thank you.' Bess looked hesitant and he wondered whether that was because he was here too. But she must have expected it, surely, or was she remembering their conversation not so long ago and a none-too-subtle hint that his mum and jobs didn't always mix? If that was what she was thinking, that she was going to get a tenant who couldn't pay the rent, then this was all about to implode. But then why give Marianne the opportunity to come here if this wasn't going to work?

'Let me show you the room,' Bess smiled. Perhaps she'd forgotten all about their previous conversation and he was just being paranoid.

'I'll stay here.' Gio lifted the crutches as explanation while his mum took off her coat and shoes.

'Make yourself comfortable in the lounge,' Bess smiled to him.

He looked down at his feet.

'Don't worry about it; I'll make the exception for you this once.'

'Appreciate it.' Man, it was good to see her, sod the awkward circumstances.

He made sure he'd rubbed his shoes well against the mat before he went through to the lounge and settled on the sofa. He could hear the women's muffled voices from upstairs as the sound carried enough for him to deduce the room was adequate, as was the matching of landlady to tenant, given the sounds of laughter.

Bess came downstairs first. 'I told your mum to have a look in the bathroom without me and to check out the room again. I always think it's easier to be nosy when you're on your own.' But sure enough, she came out with it quickly: the real reason she'd come down first. 'I'm worried, Gio. Last time we spoke, you mentioned something about your mum keeping this job, for once. I remembered after I agreed to her coming over today but it worries me, I won't deny it.'

'I did say that. But she still has her job, she's still earning, still working hard. And I'll be her guarantor. That isn't a problem.'

'You will?'

He nodded. 'I don't think I'll be needed, but I'll jump in if there's any issue.' He stopped talking at the sound of footfall on the stairs.

'It's a lovely room.' His mum beamed when she came into the room but he could tell she suspected they'd been talking and most likely it had to do with her.

'There's plenty of storage for you,' Bess said brightly. 'I've cleared all my things out of there. That took a while; it's been a dumping ground.'

Marianne smiled but rather than following Bess into the kitchen to look around some more, she hovered in front of Gio.

Bess stopped in the doorway and turned back to them both. 'Is something wrong?'

'With the house? No,' said Marianne. 'But Gio has had a problem with everywhere we've viewed so far so I need his opinion. Gio, am I all right to keep looking round?'

Gio recapped to Bess some of the places or rather the supposed landlords they'd met so far.

'I can see why it's made you wary,' said Bess. 'And while I'm not doing this via an agent, I promise you I'm not a lech, I'm not a pervert, and I don't stare at women's chests unless in a medical capacity.'

'Good to know.' Marianne laughed but then stopped. 'Wait a minute. Did you two come up with this plan together?'

'No,' they said at the same time.

Gio took it from there. 'I promise we didn't. I was as surprised as you were when we came to this address. And I had no idea that Bess was an Elizabeth.' It felt like another intimate layer of her being revealed to him, a way of getting to know her more than he already did, even after so many years. He must've been so self-absorbed back when they shared a house not to know such a simple fact about the woman who'd become a friend, the woman he wanted to be more.

'I wasn't sure whether to put Bess on the room advertisement to sound more friendly,' Bess explained, her eyes drifting away from Gio back to Marianne, 'or Elizabeth to sound like I knew what I was doing.'

'Bess sounds softer,' said Marianne, 'Elizabeth very sensible.

So you really didn't come up with this to get me a place to stay?' Marianne looked between them both.

'We didn't,' said Bess.

One whiff of a pity party would've sent his mother marching out of here. She had her pride; she'd swallowed enough of it in the past, especially by asking Gio for help and a place to stay while she worked and got back on her feet, but even she had her limits.

'This is the first time I've rented out my spare room,' said Bess. 'The truth is... I really need the money.' Her gaze flitted his way but not for long before she looked at his mum again. 'Bills are sky high and I could use some help.'

The openness of her admission seemed to resonate with Marianne. 'You need help?'

'Yes, please. If you're willing to rent.' She put her hands together in prayer. She really did need this as much as his mum wanted it.

He wondered what sort of trouble Bess was in. Nothing she'd shared with him, even as a friend.

They briefly discussed the price and clarified that all bills except for the landline were included.

'I won't run up a phone bill,' Marianne told her. 'I have a mobile; the boys always had me carry one.' She smiled over the cup of tea Bess had made her before making her and Gio a coffee each. Sitting in the lounge, they did seem to be onto a winner; Marianne looked comfortable. 'And I won't take the mickey with utilities. I had a coin meter in my last place so it made me careful – lights off when I leave a room, layering up on clothes rather than bumping up a thermostat. I'll be a good tenant.'

'I want you to feel at home. I'm not going to be watching your every move,' said Bess.

Marianne chewed her bottom lip. 'Does this mean I can definitely have the room? Don't you want references first? I can get one from work.'

But Bess shook her head. 'I think given you're Gio's mother then I can go with his reference. I do have a lodger agreement; I'll need you to fill it out and I can show it to my mortgage provider, but it shouldn't be an issue. If they need further references, I'll let you know.'

Marianne nodded. 'It's better we have an agreement. It means it's official, no blurred lines, and it'll be better for me when I find a place of my own eventually.'

Marco wouldn't believe it if he could see their mum now – together, in control, decisive. Those were qualities that had done a bunk when her husband left her and their boys.

Bess patiently went through the lodger agreement with Marianne while Gio finished his coffee. Gio was happy to add his details as guarantor and by the time they were ready to leave, he could've kissed Bess for the way she'd handled his mum, for her admission that she needed help, which probably made his mum feel as though she wasn't the only one who struggled.

'I'll see you in a few days.' Marianne smiled. She pulled Bess into a hug but immediately released her. 'I'm sorry, that wasn't very professional.'

Bess laughed. 'Doesn't have to be – I want you to feel comfortable around me. In truth, I put up the advert and dreaded interviewing people because sharing my space is something I'm not used to. But I have a feeling you and I are going to get along just fine.'

Marianne crossed her fingers on both hands. 'I think so too.'

Gio was about to call a taxi for them both when Bess offered to give them a lift home. And all the while she was driving, Marianne couldn't stop chatting. It was a good sign.

While Marianne went inside first because she was desperate

to use the loo, Gio hovered on the pavement, leaning the best he could towards Bess's open driver's side window.

'Thanks for this, Bess.'

'Saves you the challenge of the bus or a taxi fare.'

'It does.' He smiled. 'But also it's a thank you for the room, for giving Mum a chance.'

'Mutual benefit – I need the money.'

'She'll be in for Christmas; is that okay?'

'The sooner, the better.'

His eyes locked with hers and he sensed this was more than needing a little bit of extra cash but Bess, confident and bubbly, wasn't about to let it show. 'Anything I need to know?' he asked.

'I'd say it's probably none of your business.' And although she said it with a little laugh, he had a suspicion she meant it.

'I shouldn't have asked.'

She groaned. 'I'm doing it again, snapping at you.'

'You're going to have to apologise to me you know. You could do it by letting me take you to dinner?'

'We'll see.' It wasn't a no but the window closed, putting a partition between them again, and he waved his goodbyes.

'She's wonderful, isn't she?' said his mum as Gio stepped inside out of the cold.

All he could do was agree that yes, she really was.

But selfishly, he hoped his mum wouldn't do something to mess this up because if she did, it could ruin his chances with Bess for good. He'd always held back from making a move, but since his accident, he'd begun to flirt around her. She thought it was him, it was the way he was with every woman, and she'd be right in some ways. But not with this. He was interested in Bess properly, as if all the dating up until now had been a practice run.

And to be honest, feeling that way scared the hell out of him.

16

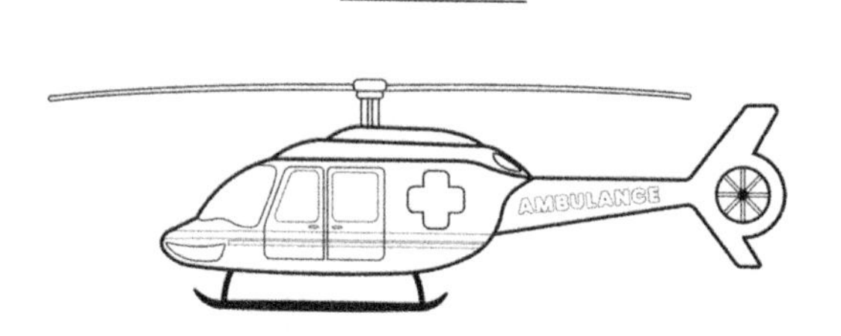

Bess told herself she'd get used to it, having someone in her home. She told herself to think of the money because with the extra pounds coming in, she could allay some of the worry.

She'd made the decision to rent out her spare room after talking it through with Maya the evening Maya insisted they go to her place and wouldn't take no for an answer.

'I've been thinking...' Maya had said as she served up the pasta dish. 'Isaac struggled to find a student house for this academic year and we were almost at the point of renting a spare room, anywhere, in a family home, whatever it took.' Isaac was Maya's son, who was at university in Scotland.

'Are you suggesting I take in a lodger?'

'Why not? You have a lovely spare room – I should know; I've stayed in it a couple of times after the pub. And you don't have many guests as your friends and your mum are local. You wouldn't have to do it forever, but you could make a few hundred quid a month, enough to top up your income and get you on top of things.'

That day, Bess's initial reaction was *no way* but then an image of those bills piled one on top of the other had come into her head and she'd changed her mind.

But now Marianne had only been living here for just over a week and Bess was struggling. It didn't help that Bess's shifts had been confined to days, which meant that she only had an hour of quiet before Marianne got home.

It wasn't Marianne herself that was the problem; it was more that Bess liked a bit of space. As sociable as she was at work, even she needed her alone time and she missed it. Which made her feel terrible because Marianne was trying her best.

And so was Gio. He called his mum every day; Bess often caught the tail end of conversations and had to admit she was beginning to see a deeper side to him, a man with heart, a man with soul.

Marianne's humming carried down the stairs as Bess cooked dinner but she bit back the temptation to call up to ask her to be quiet. Tolerance was something she had to learn and Marianne was pulling her weight in the house. This morning, she'd cleaned the bathroom and done a way better job than Bess ever had, and before Bess could stop her, she'd vacuumed the hallway, stairs and then the landing. She'd claimed she could do cleaning in half the time of anyone else given it was her profession.

And so Bess had insisted she cook for them both this evening seeing as it was Christmas Eve and neither of them had other plans. She pulled out ingredients and before too long, Marianne joined her in the kitchen. Beyond the window, they had what looked like very fine snowfall that had no hope of settling but looked inviting nevertheless.

'I've left my mobile at Gio's,' Marianne grumbled. 'He'll drop it over in a few hours, he said. If that's all right?'

'Of course it is. You don't need to ask.' She was sure her voice had gone up an octave, giving away her not-so-platonic feelings towards him, but if it had, Marianne hadn't noticed.

Marianne leaned up against the counter as Bess washed a big handful of green beans. 'May I ask a personal question?' She paused. 'It might be none of my business...'

'But...'

'I wondered whether maybe you're Jewish or a Jehovah's Witness.'

Bess dropped the beans into the colander in the sink. 'Neither.'

'But you don't have a Christmas tree.'

And now she felt like a crap landlady. 'I'm sorry, I didn't think. I don't usually bother because my mum has a tree and I'm usually with her, or I'm at work where they have loads of festive cheer.'

'You sound like Gio; he always says he's either working or can enjoy a tree at the pub or elsewhere.'

Bess felt terrible. 'I apologise, Marianne.'

'No, it's fine. I don't usually have one either. I was just curious.'

Bess turned on the tap and showered the green beans, rinsing them off.

And then she stopped the flow of water, dried her hands, threw down the tea towel. 'Come on.' She picked up her car keys.

'What are you doing?'

'Let's go see if we can find a tree.'

'But it's Christmas Eve,' said Marianne with a hint of child-like mischief that suggested she was all in with this.

And both of them lit up with glee when they nabbed the very last Fraser fir, reduced in price but no less stunning, from outside the nearest supermarket.

* * *

'Dinner first, we'll decorate later,' Bess instructed as soon as they got back to the house. They'd hauled the tree out of the car and left it in the lounge in the stand it had been sold in. Later, they would crown it in its full Christmas glory.

'Good idea, I'm hungry.'

Marianne set the table while Bess continued the prep for the meal and got going with the cooking.

'Can't believe we got the last tree.' Bess grinned, suddenly glad she had one. 'What a stroke of luck.'

'It's a stunner for sure. Now it feels more like Christmas; I can smell it from here, even with the dinner cooking.'

As Marianne folded over a couple of napkins, she told Bess that Gio was making the Christmas dinner tomorrow. 'He'll do a better job than I ever did, I'm sure.'

Gio cooked? He hadn't done much of that in their shared house. But Gio Mayhan was going up in Bess's estimations all the time and the thought tickled her. 'Lucky you.'

The lamb cutlets were soon sizzling in the pan, the potatoes simmering, the greens waiting to be plunged into water.

'I had hoped Marco and my grandkids might come for Christmas but Marco has to work,' Marianne went on. 'He's a firefighter too.'

Bess stirred the mint sauce she'd prepared and set it on the table. 'It's a job much like mine that continues 365 days of the year. I had today off but I'll be back in tomorrow, Boxing Day and the day after.'

'Don't you hate it? Lord knows I didn't give enough of myself over the years on a day that is supposed to be for family, but I want to now. Don't you wish you could be with yours?'

'Actually, I don't mind working over Christmas, as strange as it may sound. It feels good to be there for others.' And Christmas had never been the same since her dad died anyway. This year, knowing Bess was working, her mum had Malcolm coming over but had promised Bess that the pair of them would do a belated Christmas Day with all the trimmings once Bess had time off.

Bess served the lamb cutlets along with buttery, herbed new potatoes and fresh greens and took the plates over to the table. But she soon leapt up again.

'I almost forgot! It's Christmas Eve, so... what do you fancy? I have red wine to go perfectly with cutlets.' She pulled open the cupboard where it was kept before moving on to another. 'Or... I think I have a bottle of Prosecco at the back of this cupboard...' She reached in and standing on tiptoes, managed to grab a hold of the glass bottle's body.

'I'll pop this in the freezer,' she said. 'It won't take long to chill.'

Bess had had both bottles of alcohol for a while; she didn't often drink at home. Her drinks usually happened at the pub when what she was craving more than a beverage was the company.

Marianne picked up the jug of mint sauce and added some to her plate, eyes not leaving the dinner. 'Not for me, thank you.'

'You sure?'

'Completely sure.'

Bess shrugged. She considered pouring herself a glass but drinking alone wasn't quite as attractive as having company, so she left the Prosecco and the bottle of red where they were. 'I won't either. Probably better seeing as I have work tomorrow.'

'I admire you all, you know. You, Gio, Marco. You all do such a wonderful job, saving lives, putting your own at risk.'

'Gio is missing it a lot.' She sliced into a piece of lamb. 'He's like a bear with a sore head some days.'

'I don't doubt it.'

'This lamb is so tender; it's delicious.' Marianne speared another piece onto her fork. 'You're a good cook. I'm terrible.'

'Not true, you've been cooking dinners for Gio, I hear.'

'Basic stuff any moron could plonk in the oven or in a pan.'

'You're selling yourself short.'

'You know what I'd really like to do?' Marianne asked between mouthfuls. 'I'd like to cook my boys a belated Christmas dinner. When Marco and my grandkids finally come to visit, I want to do the boys and them a turkey, the full works.'

'That sounds like a lovely idea. I'd be happy to give you some tips if you need me to.'

'Could you teach me how to do a Christmas dinner? I've done a few over the years but not for some time; I'm not the best.'

'I'd love to help you out. I'm working for a few days, I'll need to see when I'm at Mum's for our belated Christmas, but we'll definitely pick a day and do some cooking.'

It felt good to help, it mattered, and Bess knew it was partly her burgeoning friendship with Marianne but also how much she wanted things to go right for Gio.

They chatted over their meal, the constant conversation something else Bess was getting used to. She was a talker in her own right but sometimes, she yearned to zone out and hadn't realised how much she needed to until she had someone living with her. She'd come to realise the best place to zone out was in her bedroom. Marianne seemed to respect the boundaries of the bedroom door and likewise, Bess did the same. It took Bess back to her student days: your bedroom your only sanctuary and everywhere else sheer bedlam with noise and bodies lazing about everywhere.

Marianne caught sight of some of the items pinned to Bess's pinboard behind the counter. She pointed to the photo of Bess taken next to some stunning, ultramodern architecture. 'Where's that?'

'Dubai.'

'It looks hot.'

Bess had a long-sleeved, floaty dress on, her curls pinned up, her cheeks pink. 'It was. I'd give anything for a bit of hot weather right now.'

'I love the sunshine too. Never been as far as Dubai, mind you, but I'm not a winter person.'

'I actually love the seasons. And winter has its perks, like when the frost glistens on the rooftops, when you're all bundled up beneath clear blue skies and the sun is so bright, it bounces off the ground.'

Marianne smiled. 'A friend of mine went to Lapland once, saw Santa. She says that was for her daughter's benefit but I'm no fool.'

'I'd love it too. It wouldn't matter whether I was five or fifty. I'd try snow shoeing, or ride on the back of a sled pulled by huskies. Can you imagine?'

'I think I've a long way to go before I have enough money for anything quite as fancy.'

And crashing back to reality, Bess realised she probably did too.

'When the boys were young, we'd take them to Norfolk.' Marianne smiled with her whole face. 'We'd head right up the coast. The boys would swim in the sea, eat fish and chip suppers, exhaust themselves. I remember the salty tingle on my skin and theirs.' She gulped and Bess didn't miss the enthusiasm wane. 'I miss those days.'

'What was Gio like as a boy?'

'Cheeky.' Bess laughed at that. He hadn't changed. 'Sensitive too, although he hid it well. His brother Marco was much the same; they're rather similar.' She met Bess's gaze. 'I've made some mistakes as their mother; I have a lot of regrets.'

'Gio seems to want you around.'

'He was always more lenient on me compared to Marco. Can't blame Marco, though; he was the parent to Gio for years when neither me nor the boys' father were capable.'

Bess didn't pry, she didn't ask for details. Given her friendship with Gio, it felt like a betrayal to find anything out about his past unless it came from him.

Gio showed up while Bess and Marianne were upstairs finding the Christmas ornaments stashed in the very top of the wardrobe in Bess's bedroom. Shoved right to the back, they had easily been forgotten about.

When he handed over Marianne's phone, Bess urged him to come in.

'You sure?' A car was waiting for him at the kerb.

'Of course.'

'I'll tell my mate.'

'I'll do it,' said Marianne, zipping past them and out to the car.

Gio gave the driver a wave. 'A mate from the station came to see me and offered me a lift round to save me the taxi fare or trying to get myself on and off a bus.'

When he stepped inside, his gaze didn't leave Bess's, his eyes watching her every move. 'Something smells good.'

'All Bess,' Marianne announced before recounting exactly what she'd served up tonight. She made it sound more like cordon bleu cooking than a simple meal for two.

'Fancy helping us with the Christmas tree?' Bess beamed at him if only to break the tension between them. There was definitely more than friendship in the air tonight.

'You've left it late.' The teasing note in his voice did little to defuse the crackle of intimacy Bess was beginning to yearn for every time they were close.

'We picked it up a couple of hours ago.'

They barely heard Marianne say that she'd leave them to it while she cleared up the kitchen.

'Come on then,' he said and when her eyes fell to his knee, added, 'I'm not useless. I can hobble around a tree and put a few ornaments on.'

'We'll start with the lights.'

He pulled a face. 'I should've pretended I couldn't manage. Hate doing the lights.'

But between them, the lights were strung in no time.

'You need a break.' She spotted his discomfort after they'd circled the tree a few times and he'd bent down to flip the switch to illuminate the tree, making it easier to make adjustments to ensure that the twinkling was evenly spaced.

'Yes, ma'am.'

'We'll carry on in a bit. Let me see if I can help your mum finish the cleaning up.' She'd shooed her out of the kitchen twice already and told Bess she was happy to do it all.

Bess came back to the lounge with two cans of Coke and handed one over to Gio.

'Don't tell me, she told you to go away again?' He grinned.

'She's in her element in there.'

'You could be right.' He clinked his open can of drink against hers. 'I took her to see the Christmas lights, you know.'

'She mentioned it; she told me how she often took you boys when you were little.'

'We loved it, every year we went. Until it stopped.'

'Whistlestop River puts on a good display.' Bess didn't want him to dwell on any unhappy times. Not right now. 'It looks even better from high up in the sky. Flying at night is different, prettier looking down at the town all lit up and when it's Christmas time, it's brilliant. All those lights, shapes and patterns are insane – makes it a little difficult to identify the flashing blue lights at an emergency scene sometimes, though.'

'I'll bet it does.'

She set down her can: time to finish the tree. 'You can sit a while longer.'

'No need.'

She began to hang the first of the baubles. 'It must be hard to sit back and watch when you're injured.'

'It's a few Christmas decorations, Bess. Don't write me off yet.' He was up again and they were so close, she thought for a moment he might tip his head down and kiss her. A couple of months ago, she would've freaked out at the prospect, and perhaps she still should, but she wasn't.

As they continued to hang ornaments, their fingers collided between branches. As they reached for different sections to ensure the decorations were evenly spread, their bodies danced around each other.

But he must've overdone it, not rested his leg long enough, because after he put the star at the top of the tree, he lost his footing and stumbled to his right, catching the pile of papers beneath an artificial pot plant. She'd started to go through the collection of bills and demands earlier when Marianne was cleaning but had been waylaid by the postman delivering a parcel, then by a cold-call telemarketer, then she'd been interrupted when Marianne came downstairs for some bleach, and in the end, she'd shuffled them all out of the way again, ready to look at before dinner. She'd planned to hide them in her bedroom after that, but she'd never got the chance what with dinner prep and going out to buy a tree.

'In case you hadn't noticed,' he said, 'I've become a bit of a klutz. Wasn't this way at work; think they'd have fired me long ago if I was.' He was trying to bend down but Bess moved to get in there first, scrabbling to get the pieces of paper that had scattered. She hoped he hadn't seen the red words *final demand* or any of the wording about court threats or debt collectors.

But when she pushed the paper edges together into a neat pile and put them back where they were, she knew he'd seen something. Although what probably gave it away were her flushed cheeks, her anxiousness to hide the papers as quickly as possible. She didn't exactly have much of a poker face.

'Everything all right?' His deep tone, gentle enough to give off sympathy, or pity, almost undid her.

'Everything is fine.'

And when Marianne came in to help, they laughed, they talked, but the mood had partly died and it was almost a relief when Gio left.

'Cup of tea?' Bess offered Marianne as soon as his taxi departed from the kerb.

'Definitely.'

Bess put the kettle on and as it came to the boil, she pulled a box of doughnuts she'd picked up from town after shift finished from the very back of the food cupboard. 'Dessert.' She flipped up the lid to reveal the mouth-watering, festive, glazed doughnuts, each with a Rudolph face on them. She'd forgotten all about them until now.

'I won't say no.' Marianne grinned.

Neither of them needed to share their life story. Not right now. For the moment, this was enough, and Bess had a feeling that both of them needed this new living arrangement, more than either of them had realised.

17

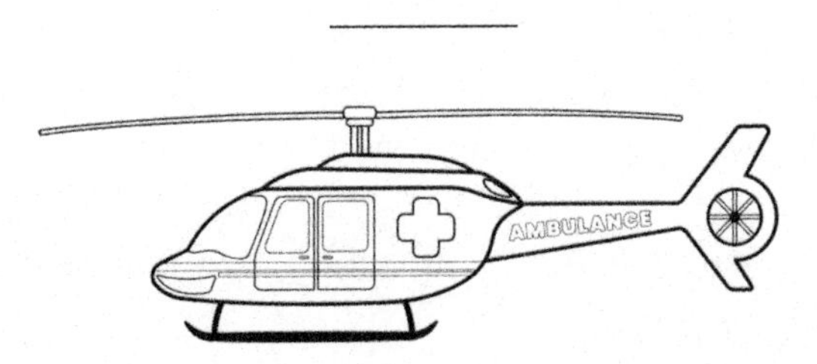

The highlight of his Christmas had to be seeing Bess unexpectedly last night. He'd thought he was dropping over his mum's phone; he hadn't expected to be invited in. And he'd never expected to be decorating a tree with Bess, getting so close, he'd brushed against her – not on purpose, and she'd got just as close to him – hopefully intentionally if he was honest – more than once. It was a shame the evening hit a sour note when he knocked the paperwork off the side. It was none of his business but he wasn't stupid; he'd seen more than a few bills and it didn't take a genius to put two and two together. That had to be why she needed a lodger. Good for her, getting herself out of a tight situation. He only hoped it wouldn't affect his mother, although he didn't see how it could. Perhaps he was worrying unnecessarily.

Now, on Christmas Day, he put the potatoes into the oven on the shelf below what – even if he did say so himself – was a beautifully browning turkey.

He called Marco over FaceTime while their mum was out for a stroll around the block so he could get a word in before she joined. But first, Billy and Matilda wanted to tell him all about Father Christmas and what he'd brought them this year.

After Gio had had the full run-down of presents, Billy's face came a little closer on the screen. 'Do you have an apron on, Uncle Gio?'

Matilda giggled behind her brother.

But they lost interest quickly enough and ran off to play with their toys which were far more appealing than adult conversation.

'You're taking charge of dinner,' Marco chipped in. 'Not surprised.'

'Mum offered to help but I wanted to do it. Probably the only time I ever will.' When was Marco going to stop being so hard on her?

'Unless you settle down one day, little brother.'

'Don't hold your breath.' Although if Bess changed her mind and took a chance on him, you never knew.

Marco broke off to yell something to the kids and then came back on camera. 'They're putting on their wellies ready to go out in the back garden.'

'Is it snowing?'

'Trying to, but I don't think it'll settle.'

'Remember the year it snowed so much, we built an igloo?'

'Yeah, you were rushing it; you didn't want to take your time and get it right.'

'Of course I didn't, I wanted to play in it.'

'And then you wanted to demolish it.'

'All part of the fun.'

'Where is Mum, by the way?'

'Out for a walk, thought I'd start the call while she's still out, give us a chance to talk. You know she thinks you either begged to work or that you're not really working at all.'

Once Christmases with his mother had become a thing of the past, Gio had often volunteered to work over the major holiday. Others in his crew had wives, kids, parents to spend it with. It always felt selfish to him to take the time off when he wasn't going to do anything in particular.

Over the years, Gio had had a couple of Christmases with Marco and Saffy. They had the proper family Christmas the brothers had long forgotten about: the one with both parents, nobody wasted and unable to function properly, the one where the only yells were from over-excited children or from the television as an all-action movie took centre stage. The year Saffy was pregnant with Billy, Gio had taken charge of making the Christmas dinner at their place so Marco, Saffy and Matilda could have some time together. That was the year the boys' mother had been living it up in her bedsit where a few of the other tenants from the building organised a big Christmas dinner of their own. The boys plus Saffy and the kids had been invited but they'd politely declined – they could only imagine the ruckus, the chaos, the misfits their mother hung out with celebrating together.

'I really am working,' said Marco. 'That's why we've eaten the roast already. Saffy's family are coming over later on and I'll be going to the station.'

'Mum wishes you'd brought the kids here.'

His brother put a hand to the back of his neck, a sure sign he was irritated. 'I'm a long way from trusting her with my kids.'

'I know. But she's doing well. Give her a chance.'

Marco's silence confirmed he was thinking exactly what Gio was as those words left his mouth – they'd given her a lot of chances along the way. There was the summer when Gio turned sixteen and he'd had a birthday party planned at the house. Their mother had organised it all – she would be around but not present; she'd let Gio have until midnight with his buddies playing as many computer games as they liked, eating pizza and drinking cola. She hadn't stayed in the background at all; she'd got pissed on a bottle of wine in her bedroom and cranked up the music as the clock rolled towards midnight, dancing in the lounge where everyone could witness Gio's humiliation. Then there was the winter Marco passed his driving test. He'd been driving with a full licence a total of a day before she called him to pick her up because she'd missed the last bus home. Not only had he had to collect her from a pub; he'd literally had to pick her up from the pavement when he found her lying on the slabs outside the establishment, probably five minutes away from getting scooped up by the police.

She'd been unreliable for as long as the boys could remember and it was hard to push her from that mould. She hadn't been a mum but rather someone they had to look out for, be embarrassed by, hoping she wouldn't do anything illegal or anything that got any of them into strife. At least she kept a roof over their heads but it was Marco who kept the household going after their dad left and she turned to alcohol to numb her feelings. It had started out just at the weekends, and the boys put it down to her way of coping after a week at work. She was waiting tables at the time but she soon lost that job. She found another and another after that but none of them lasted. And the more time she had off in between, the more she drank. She had boyfriend after boyfriend; none of them hung around, thankfully. They were as bad as she was.

As soon as Marco turned twenty-two and Gio was seventeen, Marco moved out, but it wasn't long before the family home was repossessed and Marianne and Gio were out of there too. Gio lived with his mum in one grotty place after another, he worked part time, finished his education, completed his training to become a firefighter and then he left for good. He'd stayed in the area at first, moved into the house share where he met Bess, helped his mother out when he could. He'd continued to support Marianne over the years until finally, in his forties, he'd seen his chance for a totally fresh start.

'We've given her a lot of chances,' said Gio to Marco, 'but I've seen it for myself this time. She's here in Whistlestop River, this is the longest she's been living near enough to either of us that we know what she's like from day to day, and I'm telling you, she's turned a corner. Just think about a visit. I didn't even see you when you visited me in hospital.'

'You were pretty out of it.'

'So will you come?'

There was a significant pause but eventually, he said, 'I've got time off a few days after New Year. How about then?'

Gio would've leapt in the air if it was safe with his knee. 'Look forward to it.' But he wouldn't tell their mother yet. The last thing he wanted was to get her hopes up, have her disappointed and spiralling into a melancholy that could be catastrophic for someone like Marianne with her addiction. He supposed at some point, he'd have to stop being so protective but for now, he was keeping his guard up.

'How's that knee of yours anyway?' Marco asked.

Gio shared his progress, his frustrations, the way he missed work and when Gio heard the front door, Marco went to beckon the kids inside so they could chat with their grandma.

It was probably easier for Marco than trying to talk to his mum on his own.

Marianne enjoyed the FaceTime catch-up and Gio could tell how desperate she was to see them all in person.

'It was good to see them on the screen,' she said as they got ready to sit down to lunch. Gio had just put a bottle of Appletiser in the centre of the table and he poured two glasses while his mum brought over the gravy boat.

'I don't expect you to avoid alcohol for my sake,' she said, watching the fizz settle in the glass he'd just poured.

'I'm not fussed, Mum.' He was lying and she probably knew it. Christmas Day with no work was usually a definite excuse for a few drinks, maybe even a visit to the pub, but he wouldn't do that to her. She was in control of her life and decisions but he sure as hell wasn't going to be the one to derail that, so he went with a small white lie. 'I took pain meds after my walk anyway – not a good idea to drink on those.'

They chatted their way through dinner and she reminded him that *The Wizard of Oz* was on the television.

'I remember watching that as a kid.' He went for yet another few slices of turkey and several roast potatoes he probably – definitely – didn't really need. 'We'd be allowed to put our pyjamas on, demolish our selection boxes.'

'I worried you'd make yourselves sick with all that sugar.'

Back then, she had very much been a mother. Things had been different.

They cleared the table together, and even that, Gio treasured. Because with the simple task of clearing up came normality and Gio didn't think he'd felt so close to his mum in years.

Earlier that day, they'd exchanged small gifts and as they walked off their Christmas lunch, Marianne rolled up her coat sleeve to look again at the silver knot bracelet with an emerald stone he'd given her. Gio was wearing the gloves she'd given him, welcome in the cold when he couldn't shove his hands in his coat pockets because he had to keep hold of the crutches. He was getting better on them, though – faster, less clumsy.

Back at his place, they played a few games of cards, by which time, his mum was shattered and wanted to go back to Bess's where she planned to watch an old black and white movie and enjoy some time on her own. Gio had planned to have a quiet night in alone himself but he'd had a text from Jeremy at the fire station to say that the crew members who were single and, in their words, weren't *whipped* and under instruction to get home straight after shift had decided to congregate at the pub on Christmas night.

When Gio walked into the Whistlestop River Inn, he felt a sense of relief, the sense of belonging he was missing these days.

'Glad you came.' Jeremy, a probationary firefighter, was shouting the beers next and included Gio.

Gio thanked him for the beer. The first sip was the best; he needed this today. 'You settling in all right?'

'I think so. Unless you heard different.'

'Not at all.'

It felt great to be in their company. He'd been slightly worried putting his mum in the taxi back to Bess's in case the festivities of the day were making her crave a drink more than ever, but he had to stop obsessing for both their sakes.

He fidgeted in his chair at a table in front of Jeremy, stretched his leg out a bit better.

'Your knee still painful?' Jeremy swigged from his bottle.

'On and off, which is better than constant like it was at the start.'

'You gonna get back on the job, though, right?'

'Of course.' He wasn't about to admit that there were no guarantees. It was bad enough reminding himself of that fact, let alone anyone else.

Gio managed one game of darts but holding yourself steady while leaning on a crutch and with one foot off the floor was such a challenge that the lads, who'd sunk way more beers than him, had decided they should have the same encumbrance.

It was amusing to watch. Jeremy tried first – a crutch beneath one arm, the opposite foot off the floor. The dart missed the board entirely. It was Jock's turn next and his first dart did well, so did the second, but the third fell south of the board by a good metre when he lost his balance.

Gio got his crutches and had just hobbled back from the bathroom when he spotted a familiar, curly-haired beauty at the bar.

He scanned the crowd to see whether his mum had come in here with her. But it seemed Bess was with the crew of The Skylarks.

'You're handling the crutches like a pro,' she said as he sat on the high stool next to her, ideal seating for someone with his injury.

'You've been watching me?'

Her glass hovered in front of her lips. 'How was your Christmas Day?'

'Good. Managed not to incinerate the turkey at least. How's the tree?'

'Still standing.'

'Joint effort,' he smiled.

'Totally.'

'How was work today? Busy shift?' He'd spotted some mistletoe at the top of the archway leading through to the eating area but there was no sign of any near the bar now. Pity.

'Not too bad at all: only three calls, no fatalities, all patients likely to fully recover. And people are lovely at Christmas, no matter what predicament they're in, and so thankful.'

People were always grateful but something about Christmas gave them a whole new appreciation when you showed up as if it was any other day. Which to them on shift it was.

'Is that Hudson over there?' Through the crowd, Gio spotted

the patient and family liaison nurse laughing loudly with a couple of others from the Whistlestop River Air Ambulance.

Bess frowned. 'It is. I've no idea what's going on with him. I thought he'd be home with the kids the second he finished work. Maybe his other half has taken them away.'

It was Gio's turn for a round so he ordered bottles of Budweiser for himself and the others. 'Can I get you another?' he asked Bess when the landlord saw to the first part of the order.

'No, I'm good, thanks.'

'What are you drinking anyway?' It looked like a soft drink to him.

'It's a Coke. I'm saving money so I've allowed myself this and then I'll go home. If I want some wine, I've got a bottle in the cupboard. Or there's Prosecco in the fridge. It is Christmas Day, after all.'

He winced, knowing his mum was in the house, probably alone right now, with temptation in her path when she opened the fridge door. He wasn't sure why in all the time he'd known Bess, he'd never told her his mother had a problem with alcohol. She'd been aware for a long time that his family life was difficult but if Gio had told anyone the details, it would have made it all the more painful. Instead, he'd dealt with whatever came up, and then tried to return to his own life and block some of the bad stuff out.

He fought the urge to order a taxi and go via Bess's place to check up on Marianne – he decided he'd call her in a bit instead. He'd be able to tell when he heard his mother's voice whether she'd had a drink; they didn't need to be face to face.

'So this is the first time you've rented out your spare room?' he asked in an effort to deter his mind from going places it was probably best not to.

'It is, and it's going really well. Your mum is a model lodger. I could've got someone terrible but we get on, we talk, she's nice.'

'I'm glad you think so.' He wondered what they talked about – was it deep or just the minutiae of daily life?

'She says she's no good at cooking.'

'She's not terrible but she's not great either – remember that time you were over and I told you about the meat pie, potato and pea dinners?'

'I do. And when she first moved in with me, she really only ate beans on toast or pie with a side of potato but a few nights ago, she made chicken pasta in a sauce; tomorrow, she's doing a pork stir fry.'

'I'm impressed.'

'Didn't she help you with the Christmas lunch?' Bess asked.

'She offered but I told her to relax. She headed out for a walk instead.' He watched her; she was holding something back. 'What's wrong?'

'It's not my place to say.'

When it came to his mother, he really needed people to share what they could; he needed as many clues as he could get. 'Bess, what is it?'

She hooked a stray corkscrew curl behind her ear. She had her hair down today – it was always tied back at work. It was so thick, he wondered what it might be like to run his fingers through it. 'She wants to make you and your brother and his kids a proper Christmas dinner one day. I get the feeling it's really important to her.'

'So I should have let her help, that's what you're saying?'

She shrugged. 'I just thought you should know.'

'Christmas dinners were usually down to Marco and me. For a long time. Not the best memories, I'm afraid.'

'You mentioned Christmas a few times over the years: how it wasn't always a happy occasion.'

He'd said that? He'd thought he'd kept it well and truly close to his chest.

'Actually, I've offered to teach her how to make a roast in a few days once I'm freed up from work.'

'That's incredibly generous.' He wanted to reach out and run his hand across her cheeks, the cheeks that rosied up when she smiled.

'It's no bother; I enjoy the fact that I'm considered someone who can cook. I'm pretty sure I've never been described in that way before.'

Jeremy appeared at his side, citing his extreme thirst and blaming the delayed delivery of beers. 'Come on, you're up next.'

Gio grabbed his crutches. 'I'd better oblige and get back over there. It's making me feel better at least – turns out that when they have to use a crutch and not put a foot on the floor, they're way worse at darts than I am.'

She laughed. 'Good to see you, Gio.'

'Likewise. You hanging around?'

'I'll be off home soon.'

'Early night with work in the morning?'

'Something like that. I might even have a couple of glasses of wine first to relax before I go to bed.'

His heart sank again. The thought of his mother around alcohol in any capacity sent a shot of terror right through him. He'd known that if his mum was a lodger with anyone, there might be this issue; it was one of the reasons – among the many others – why the second place they looked at was a terrible idea. The guy had a bar in the lounge downstairs. Gio had had a long talk with Marianne that night, suggested she might want to explain her sobriety to a landlord, but she'd point-blank refused.

'Then they'll never rent me the room,' she'd said. 'And I'll never get my independence.'

'Do yourself a favour, Bess. Don't open the wine; get an early night.'

Her beautiful face adopted a frown, as well it might. It was a weird thing to say and he wanted to shoot himself in his good knee for saying it. But instead, he went back over to the lads and the next time he looked towards the bar, she was gone.

Gio called his mum before he got into another game of darts. They chatted for a couple of minutes, enough for him to be satisfied that she was stone-cold sober, and he was even happier when she said her movie had finished a while ago and that she was already in bed. With any luck, she wouldn't even go downstairs when Bess got home so if Bess did have a glass or two of wine, she wouldn't be offering it around and about to shake the foundations Marianne had so carefully begun to build.

All it would take was one little drink to ruin everything.

18

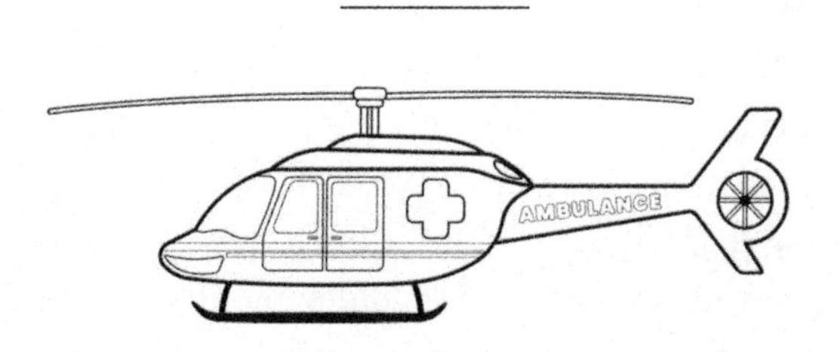

Bess and her mum had planned to have their delayed Christmas lunch once Bess wasn't working, but Fiona had come down with a heavy cold and so New Year was almost upon them before they got the opportunity. Fiona had had the big lunch Christmas Day and so had Bess with The Skylarks at the airbase courtesy of Maya and Noah cooking up a festive feast with the works that, for once, they got to finish. That almost never happened.

Malcolm answered the front door at her mother's. Not only had Fiona and Bess decided that they'd have a regular lunch because they were both a bit over the festivities, they'd decided that Malcolm would join them. In fact, Bess had suggested it because she so wanted to support her mum.

'She's got her hands full making the dumplings,' Malcolm announced as the waft of her mum's beef stew snaked its way through the air towards her. And on a cold, wintry day, her mum's beef stew with dumplings recipe was the epitome of warmth and comfort.

'Mum's speciality.' Bess hung her coat on the peg in the hallway and went through to the kitchen.

Bess hugged her mum the best she could as Fiona shaped a dumpling between her palms. 'How are you feeling?'

'Much better, love. And this morning, I had a bath with some of the luxuries in the hamper you gave me for Christmas. I feel thoroughly spoilt.' Her hands were covered with flour as she set down the dumpling and made the next.

'You deserve it. And I feel thoroughly spoilt having dumplings for lunch. One of my favourites,' Bess smiled.

'Malcolm's favourite too.'

Knowing that felt oddly comforting to Bess – it had been her dad's most-loved dish when the colder months set in. 'I hated dumplings when I was a little girl,' she told Malcolm, who'd sat at the table and looked about as uncomfortable as he had the first time they'd met here in the same kitchen. Her mum was now too busy with the meal prep and it was just the two of them talking.

When Bess sat down, Malcolm seemed to relax a little bit. 'My kids loved them. Their mother made them as soon as winter hit; she'd refuse to make them in summer, though. Too heavy, she said.'

She already knew he was a widower but hearing him directly share with her a part of his private life softened Bess even more in her approach. 'Your kids must miss their mum.'

'They do. But we get through, with each other.'

When Liquorice put a paw up beneath the low-hung branch of the Christmas tree over by the front doors, Bess went to save the day. 'Oh no you don't!' She scooped him into her arms before he could pluck the little nutcracker ornament.

'He's a rascal.' Fiona laughed, briefly turning from her position at the bench.

'He's gorgeous.' Bess buried her face in his fur. 'Have you made your donation yet, Mum? For the tree collection.' This year, The Skylarks had organised to collect real Christmas trees across town in exchange for a donation to the Whistlestop River Air Ambulance. Once a donation was made, a label with The Skylarks logo was sent out to fix to the tree, ready for collection day in January.

'Already done,' said Fiona. 'The leaflet came through my door well before Christmas. I donated there and then so I didn't forget.' She took the lid off the Le Creuset pot and the smell of the stew filled every corner of the kitchen as she plopped the dumplings in one by one, submerging each beneath the liquid before she slotted the pot back into the oven for the dumplings to cook.

They continued their chatter as Liquorice settled on Bess's lap for a fuss. Perhaps attacking the Christmas tree – apparently for the first time in days – had been the cat's ploy to get some attention.

As they talked, Bess watched her mum relax. This was hard for her too, hard for both of them, all of them even. It must be difficult to introduce a new partner to your children – it was like being a teen waiting for your parents' approval.

The beef stew was wonderful, the thick liquid rich and flavoursome, the dumplings light and fluffy. The company was pleasant – Malcolm turned out to be easy to talk to – and when he insisted he did the washing up while the women settled in the lounge for a natter, she and her mum talked more about Malcolm, the coach trip he and Fiona had planned to Hengistbury Head. Her mum was happy and it filled Bess with more joy than she'd thought possible.

Before it was time to go, her mum asked briefly about her money troubles.

'How is it all going?'

Bess didn't have the heart to say it was getting worse. She

didn't want her problems to become her mother's. Not when she seemed happy again at last. 'I'm okay. Thank you for lending me that money. I will pay every single penny back.' She'd said it before but she wanted her mum to know she meant it.

'I get the feeling you're holding back.'

'Mum...'

'I'm worried.'

'Please, don't be. I'll sort it.'

But her words felt hollow. Her mum was right not to believe a single word.

Bess's debts were no closer to diminishing. In fact, they were only getting worse. And no matter what she seemed to do, she couldn't get on top of them.

She had to keep trying. But was that really ever going to be enough?

* * *

On the second day of the new year, Bess and Marianne finally had a day off at the same time. Bess had done her best to get another shift, to earn some extra money, but she wasn't needed. And so for now she put thoughts of her debts aside and focused on something pleasurable.

Usually, Bess relished her alone time, and liked the way their shifts didn't always line up, but today it felt good to do something for Marianne and give her that cooking lesson she'd promised. She'd found a turkey joint in the freezer section at the supermarket – the last one, with a huge discount – and they'd been in the kitchen for a few hours now.

Marianne had had moments of panic but also moments where she relaxed into it and enjoyed the cooking. She wasn't anywhere near as bad as she claimed.

When it was almost ready, she turned to Bess. 'This is a big ask, but… would you mind if I called Gio, got him to come over? It's just… well, I've never made a dinner quite like this.'

'Sure.' But a flutter of nerves took hold and no way would she be staying in the tracksuit pants she'd pulled on, nor would she answer the door until she'd put a half-decent top on. 'Prepare a few more carrots and sprouts; we've got a load of potatoes, it's all good. He's very welcome.'

And while Marianne called him and took care of the vegetables, Bess sneaked upstairs to make herself more presentable.

When he arrived a short while later, Bess answered the door and tried to act as though she hadn't just checked her hair for the umpteenth time.

'Here…' He handed her a bottle of sparkling non-alcoholic wine. 'I thought you might be working; this way, you can indulge too.'

'That's very thoughtful. Thank you.' Although Marianne was so thrilled this was working that Bess had already decided she was going to get the chilled Prosecco out when it was time to eat. It was cause for celebration, surely; Marianne had wanted to make a Christmas dinner so badly and assumed she wouldn't be able to do it.

'Does it smell good?' Marianne asked the second Gio got into the kitchen.

He watched her, apron on, oven mitts adorning her hands. 'It does.'

While Marianne took the turkey joint out of the oven, Gio lowered his voice and said, 'I wanted to take you to dinner, but this will do.' And then he looked over at his mum. 'Is she doing okay?'

Bess liked the way he wasn't all out for himself. He was thinking about her and dinner but his family was more pressing and she liked witnessing the loyalty, the concern. 'She's doing better than okay. I hope you're hungry.' She went and got the glasses out ready for drinks.

Bess looked across at Marianne, who still needed a few prompts. 'Marianne...' She nodded to the carrots waiting on the board.

'Right, yes, carrots. How much olive oil?'

'A drizzle.' She watched her. 'Bit more... that's plenty.'

When it came time to serve, Marianne was even more excited and Bess knew it was a combination of the meal she'd prepared and having her son here to witness it. She piled the plates with the meat, pigs in blankets, roast potatoes, vegetables.

Bess pulled the Prosecco from the fridge and took it to the table with a flourish. 'I'm not working, none of us are; perhaps we make this a real celebration.'

But her suggestion was met with a hard no from both of them.

'Oh... I just thought...' She turned to put it back in the fridge. 'Never mind.'

'Let's just enjoy the food,' Marianne chirruped, still sounding excited.

Bess sat back down as Gio poured the non-alcoholic beverage and they settled into the lunch and chitchat.

The meal was a resounding success.

'No way are you washing up, Mum,' said Gio when Marianne automatically went over to the sink to make a start.

'You're not doing it with an iffy knee either,' said Bess. 'I'll do it.'

'You do realise I take walks, I get myself up and down stairs at home now. Oh, and I helped decorate a tree, so plenty of time on my feet.' His gaze settled on Bess, reminding her of the proximity of their bodies the day they'd done that.

'You're like a pair of children,' Marianne scolded, making them both laugh. 'I'll clear up because I'm so pleased this went well that I'm too jittery to do anything else.'

Gio looked confused. 'Why aren't you using the dishwasher?'

'She needs to get it fixed,' said Marianne. 'Gio, you're good with fiddly things, why don't you take a look at it?'

'Mum, I'm no dishwasher expert.' He rolled his eyes, turning to Bess to say, 'Better to get the professionals or it will end up costing more when they have to fix whatever I've made a whole lot worse. I happen to have the number of one; I can pass it to you.'

'It's fine, I've got one lined up, always use the same guy; he just has a waiting list,' she lied. So did her finances: one thing at a time.

Bess loved his company, the way he was with his mum, the way he was with her.

And she would have gone to bed with a smile on her face if the evening had ended there.

Except it didn't.

Gio left, Marianne went to bed, and Bess locked up. She drew the thick, velvet curtain across and that was when she found the brown envelope that must have tumbled through the letterbox and somehow got hidden beneath the curtain, undiscovered until now.

She opened it up. And then sank down on the bottom stair, the tree and the lights taunting her from their position in the lounge.

This was it. Her life had gone pear-shaped and she had no idea what she was going to do now.

19

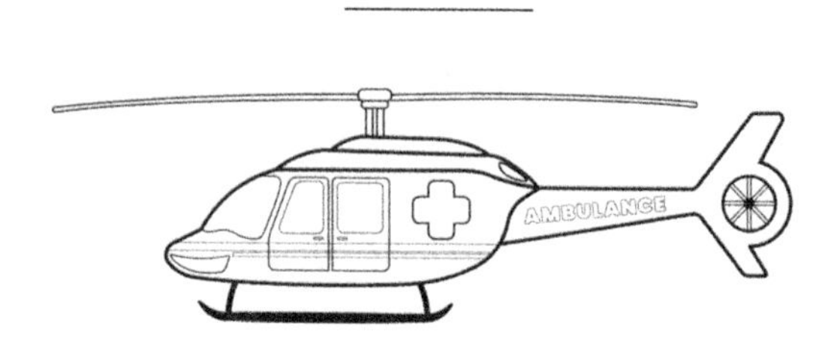

The howling winds of early January did their best to rattle their way into the house through the windowpanes but the winter gloom couldn't dampen Gio's spirits. Not today.

His physiotherapist gave him a sideways glance when he was part way through a set of leg raises. 'You're in a good mood.'

'What's wrong with that?' His thigh muscles tightened as he lifted his leg off the floor.

'Nothing.' But Aysha's suspicions lingered. 'It's making me uneasy; I'm used to you being a bit sulky.'

He burst out laughing.

'It's most disconcerting.' But he saw the glimpse of amusement behind her reprimand.

He'd managed to hobble around with just a stick rather than crutches this morning. Aysha had observed him to make sure he was ready and it had her seal of approval. It felt like another step in the right direction – no pun intended – and boosted his mood no end. But it wasn't just that. It was the dinner with his mum and Bess yesterday evening. It had gone so well. And he hadn't imagined it. He'd caught Bess watching him more than once.

The only uncomfortable part of the turkey dinner had come when Bess brandished the bottle of plonk. It had had him on tenterhooks and, he suspected, his mother too.

Seeing that bottle had reminded him of the sound of the popping cork on one of their worst Christmases as boys.

'Oh, relax,' Marianne had told her teenage boys when she came into the lounge that particular Christmas. The boys had been clearing out the grate. 'Haven't you heard of people having a Buck's Fizz on Christmas Day? It's tradition! I don't know who started it but I say bottoms up to whoever did.' And she proceeded to down the drink from her champagne flute that was likely to be 80 per cent alcohol, 20 per cent juice at best.

Marco whispered, 'How many of those do you reckon she'll have before lunch?'

'I'd say that bottle doesn't stand a chance.'

As they laid another fire and watched *The Terminator*, their mum insisted she didn't need help with the lunch; she was in total control. And so they left her to her singing, warbling the Christmas music at a volume the neighbours could probably hear without opening their windows.

On the dot of 2 p.m., she hollered that lunch was ready and although she was slurring her words, given she'd polished off the champagne and was already on the wine, both boys sat down to what looked set to be their most civilised lunch since their dad had walked out on the three of them. She'd even remembered to buy Christmas crackers and that day, Gio had felt as though maybe their family was hanging together okay.

But when he cut into the second piece of turkey, it wasn't cooked. 'Mum...' He showed her the piece and he hoped he hadn't polished off any that colour already. The thought made him feel like he was going to puke.

Marianne leaned over, speared the piece of offending turkey

and dumped it on a napkin in the middle of the table before telling him, 'The rest is fine.'

But his stomach churned at the thought of eating what could be a dinner teeming with bacteria. And the remaining turkey wasn't much better so instead, he focused on the less-than-crispy roast potatoes and the vegetables which were almost pureed, they'd been on so long. It was as though their mother had dropped the brussels sprouts into the boiling water as the same time as the potatoes had gone into the oven.

His mother had been happy in herself at the dinner table but the second she noticed her boys, particularly Marco, shifting pieces of food around their plates and avoiding the meat, she started to cry.

'You both think I'm useless.'

'Mum…' Gio tried to stop her rant in its tracks because past experience told him that once she got going, it would be next to impossible to come back from.

But she had already worked herself up.

'You're both acting as though I've served you something poisonous.'

'You have.' Marco forked a piece of the meat on his plate and lifted it up to show how pink it was inside. 'I offered to cook.' His comment did nothing to defuse the situation.

She thumped her fist on the table. 'Why do you never trust me, why do you always assume I can't do anything?' The wailing started again.

'Because you can't,' Marco snapped before getting up from the table, the crackers unpulled, no paper hats to be seen nor a joke from the scraps of paper inside to be heard between them.

He was right; she was pretty bad when it came to cooking, because she was usually half-cut when she did it.

Gio cleared the rest of the table and left her to wallow.

'Why can't you be a normal mum?' Marco raged as Gio scraped the remains of his dinner into the bin.

'I am doing my best! Your father walked out, the bastard! Why is everything my sodding fault?' And with that, she came back into the kitchen, grabbed a fresh bottle of wine from the fridge, and retreated to her bedroom.

And Gio and Marco did what they usually did; they retreated too. And that was that. Both boys went to bed and wished for the whole thing to be over.

Last night at Bess's, when she'd got that bottle out, Gio's head had been right back there on his mother's worst days. But the evening had turned into one of the best and spending all that time with Bess was something he'd fallen asleep thinking about and woken up smiling about too.

'Gio, are you listening?' Aysha prompted. 'You're not, you're really not. Are you tired, is that it?'

'Nope. Not too tired. Wall squats next?'

'Right then, let's go. Whatever has put you in this mindset today, I like it. But—'

'Don't push it, I know.'

Over at the wall, he placed his feet hip-width apart and at the distance away Aysha had indicated before he slowly slid his back down the wall. His knees were almost at a 45-degree angle, he held for five seconds, his quads burned but it felt good to be strengthening his body again.

'You've turned a corner, Gio.'

'I've been progressing for ages.'

'I'm not talking about physically,' she said when they were done with the squats. 'I'm talking about mentally.'

Aysha called him her star pupil after they finished up another couple of exercises and he felt ridiculously happy with the praise. He felt like today, he was getting to see a glimpse of the man he'd been. And he liked what he saw.

On a high, Gio decided the exercises and the short walk earlier was enough for the day. He didn't want any setbacks and so he made some dinner and parked himself in front of a movie.

He was beginning to drift off when his phone rang beside him. He'd started to dream about Bess, not something he wanted to be disturbed from, but he reluctantly answered the call and mumbled a hello.

It was his mother. He put a finger in his opposite ear. 'Mum, speak up, I can't hear you. Where are you? Is Bess having a party or something?' That or her television was on so loud, it sounded like they were.

He got fragmented pieces of speech – 'Gio... with Bess... pub... no money... taxi.'

All he heard in that spiel was the word 'pub' and he closed his eyes. This couldn't be happening.

'Gio... sorry...'

And then came a crashing sound, an *Oh my God!*, followed by a lot of laughing.

She was off her face.

A male voice took the call and Gio realised it was the landlord. 'Look, mate, she's wasted, needs to be picked up. Neither of them have any more money or cards on them.' He sounded unimpressed. It was one thing to drink in his pub, another thing entirely to cause trouble and hassle.

Gio thought about putting the phone down, washing his hands of it all. But he wouldn't be the man he was if he did that. 'Get them a cab or whatever. Take them to Bess's place and I'll make my way there to pay the fare.' If he left now, he'd arrive around about the same time if they got a lift in the next ten minutes.

He felt like putting his fist through a wall. Why? Why had she done this to them again?

He pulled on his coat, picked up his walking stick, but immediately swapped it for the crutches. Funny how you got used to something you'd once resented. They'd get him there a lot quicker than the stick.

He couldn't bear the thought of Bess being angry at him, that this could interfere with their friendship or anything that might have had a chance to develop between them. She'd taken his mother in as a lodger, he'd assured Bess that she would make the rent. He hadn't thought he'd have to also explain her addiction and that it could cause no end of problems. Bess didn't deserve this.

Marco was going to say *I told you so*, and not only that, he wouldn't be bringing himself and his kids here to visit any time soon either.

The cold air whipped at his cheeks as he made his way to Bess's. He thought about the dinner they'd shared, his mother's face radiating joy, the pride practically bursting out of her.

But tonight, she'd ruined everything. Again.

And this time, Gio wasn't sure even he could manage to be so gracious as to give her another chance.

20

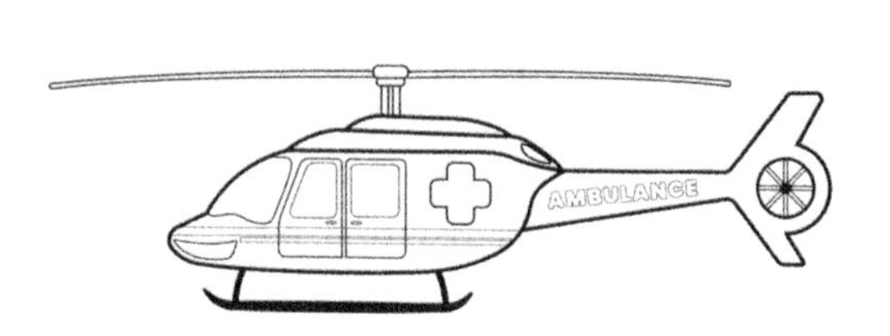

Bess woke up bleary-eyed the morning after the pub. And right away, she remembered the contents of the brown envelope that had been lying in wait for her before she headed up to bed the night of her dinner with Marianne and Gio.

The letter was the most frightening one yet.

Bess had thought she was on top of it all, at least as much as she could be for now. Her mortgage payment had gone out of her account, she'd paid her electricity bill, the amount owing on the payday loan, and she'd worked out she could afford to pay the minimum amounts for two credit cards as well. What she'd failed to realise the significance of was the missed council tax payment. Somehow in the haze of so much debt, she'd not registered the urgency of the demands she'd been getting, and she'd let it go a step too far.

The letter that had been lurking on her doormat obscured at the edges of the thick curtain she'd drawn across her front door was a court summons. Going by the date, the saving grace was that it had only been there since that morning. But it was small comfort when she opened it to read that she was being taken to court! There would be additional court costs, she would have to find the full amount to cover the council tax bill for the entire year. And the only way to avoid court was by paying that amount before the deadline.

Which was impossible.

She'd dropped the letter at her feet and sobbed her heart out before taking her troubles up to bed.

She hadn't slept a wink, she got through work the next day on autopilot and as she let herself into the house after shift, her problems engulfed her yet again. And that was why when Nadia's text came through to ask whether she'd make up the numbers on the pub quiz team, she'd accepted straight away.

She wanted to forget everything, if only for a moment. One more night out and then she'd have to take action, maybe start selling some of the contents of her house to pay her debts – her television could go, her furniture. Maybe the car would have to be sold, although she needed some form of transport for work. Whatever she did, it had to get her out of this mess that scared her deep to her core.

Bess drove to the pub and Nadia was at the bar when she arrived. She was buying a round and Bess had asked for a Coke but changed her mind last minute and ordered a beer. After a few sips, Bess felt herself relax. And she knew then that she wouldn't be driving home. She knew then that forgetting her troubles was going to take a lot more than a single beer.

The quiz wasn't easy but they came a very respectable second. Bess had been able to answer the two medical questions that came up, leaving her team members glad she'd joined them. They won a fifty quid voucher for behind the bar and had all decided that there was no time like the present to enjoy their prize.

By the bottom of her fifth beer, Bess was unsteady on her

feet. Nadia had left and offered to take Bess home as she was driving, but the music had drawn Bess in to dance near the pool table with the rest of the town who'd come in here to escape the January blues. Just like her. Hudson showed up and he seemed to be in the mood for partying so they danced for a while before he was summoned home by his other half.

When unsteadiness hit, she found a stool at the bar. She ordered a shot of tequila, then a second, a third. She was usually sensible with her drink but tonight, obliteration was the name of the game.

'Obliteration!' she called out, holding up the little shot glass in the landlord's direction before knocking it back in one. And then, because most people had peeled off, she'd pulled her phone from her rear pocket and called Marianne. 'Get yourself down here! I need the company, please, don't be a killjoy. Come on.' For every *no*, Bess put in another argument and when she still didn't get anywhere, she started to sob. She couldn't speak. In the end, she hung up the call.

What the hell was happening to her? She wasn't this person.

Marianne came into the pub almost an hour later.

Bess brightened when she saw her and wiped her tears. 'Marianne!' She beckoned her over. 'Everyone, meet Marianne! My lodger!' She wasn't talking to anyone in particular.

Bess looked to the landlord. 'Drinks, please! Marianne, what's it to be?'

'I think you've had enough,' Marianne said gently.

'Oh, I've definitely had enough.' She waved her card in the air. 'But not of the drinks.' She ordered another tequila but her card was rejected.

'Well, that's just great.' Bess groaned and slumped her arms and upper chest onto the bar counter. And when she sat up again, Marianne looked as though she'd rather be anywhere else than here.

Bess cringed. 'I'm embarrassing you. And myself. I'm useless. I'm a waste of space.'

'Why don't I take you home?' Marianne said so softly, she almost didn't hear her. 'We'll have to walk, I'm afraid. I don't have money to spend on a taxi.'

'You walked here?'

'Bus. But that was the last one tonight.'

Bess pulled her car keys from her small bag and handed them to Marianne. 'Our chariot awaits,' she slurred. 'Out in the car park.'

'I can't drive you, Bess; I don't have a licence.'

'I could teach you!' she gushed.

'Not today. We need to get you home. Can you even walk?' Marianne and the landlord exchanged a glance. 'I'm going to call Gio.'

Marianne dialled a number and Bess got up to dance to another song.

But her foot got caught on the bottom of her stool and she fell forwards onto the carpet with a whack and she heard Marianne yell, 'Oh my God!'

'I'm fine,' Bess giggled as Marianne scooped her up from the floor. 'I think I bounced.' But she lost the smile when she was upright because the landlord had taken the phone and as he talked into it, he looked even more unimpressed at her behaviour.

The next thing Bess knew, she was being led outside, the fresh air slapping her in the face. She stumbled down the kerb and reached out to save herself by grabbing Marianne, who she took down with her.

Marianne was up first and tried to haul Bess to her feet.

Bess gasped when she saw Marianne struggle to put her weight on one foot. 'You're hurt.'

'It's fine.'

'No…' And then she started to cry. 'This is all my fault. I'm a terrible person. You should hate me. I'm sorry. I'm really sorry.'

'It's all right, Bess. Come on, here's our taxi.' She waved an arm to flag it down.

'Taxi? But we have no money,' Bess groaned.

'Just get in.'

Bess got into the taxi, leaned her head on her lodger's shoulder on the way home, and then stumbled out of the vehicle at the other end.

'Gio!' Bess hollered when she saw him coming towards them. 'You're getting good on those crutches. Here, let me have a go.' She tried to stand up straight.

He ignored her request.

'What are you doing here? Are you here to take me out to dinner? Because I'd go, you know. On a date.'

He hesitated but only briefly. 'Not tonight, Bess.' His kind smile was nowhere to be seen. 'I'm here to bail my mother and by the looks of things, you, out of a situation.' Angry puffs of air that came with every word he uttered had her giggling.

'Uh-oh… Marianne, I think we're in trouble!'

Gio took out his wallet and sorted payment for the driver. All Bess could hear was Marianne trying to get her son's attention as she attempted to get out of the back of the taxi.

'You might need to help her,' Bess laughed. 'She hurt herself when she fell over.'

Gio shoved his wallet deep into his coat pocket – it took some skill doing that on crutches; Bess was impressed.

'I'm done helping her,' he said.

'He's very angry,' said Bess in what she thought might be a

whisper but judging by Gio's reaction was loud and clear. 'Marianne, your son is maaaaaaaaaaad!' She dragged out the last word on her lips before turning to stagger up the path.

She spun around when she heard Marianne, who had managed to get out of the taxi by now, calling after him, her son's name taken away on the cold wind. She was yelling to him, something about not drinking. What was she, a teenager justifying a trip to the pub to her son?

Weird.

Gio used to be fun.

Bess fumbled with her keys and eventually found the right angle and the correct key to open up.

She fell inside, by which time, Marianne had given up on Gio.

'What's his problem?' Bess was slumped on the floor in the hallway and attempted to yank off her boots. 'You're allowed a bit of fun.'

'He'll cool off; I'll talk to him.'

'He's hot-blooded... Hot-headed? Or is it both? I don't know.'

Marianne took her other boot off for her before heading to the kitchen with the declaration that Bess needed water and plenty of it.

Bess dragged herself onto the bottom stair. Right now, it felt a long way up to bed.

A glass of water was thrust in front of her and she reluctantly took it and began to drink. She watched Marianne lock up before removing her own coat and scarf. She took Bess's scarf from around her neck and held the half-empty water glass while Bess wrestled off her coat, the sitting on the bottom stair not exactly making it easy.

Marianne fetched another glass of water when she finished the first and then helped Bess up the stairs to bed.

'I'm sorry,' Bess cried as Marianne tucked the duvet around her. She felt like she was a teenager all over again, at her mum's house, her parents there for her when something went wrong – a break-up, trouble at work, any little thing – and all that was needed to mend it was a night at the family home and magically, it all went away.

But that wasn't going to happen this time, was it?

Bess remembered all of it now, the morning after the pub, in technicolour. The clock ticked its way towards midday as she emerged from the bedroom and before she did anything else, she cleaned her teeth. She knew she was lucky not to have been sick last night. Thank goodness she'd left the pub when she did.

Gio must think she was a terrible person. In the house share, they'd seen each other drunk plenty of times, they'd gone out drinking together, but it was one thing doing that in your twenties, quite another in your forties. And she was mortified at how she'd behaved last night.

And had Gio been angry?

She spotted her creased forehead in the bathroom mirror as she frowned. Yes, he had been furious from memory.

She gingerly took the stairs down to the hallway and went into the lounge, where Marianne was on her phone but ended the call when Bess went in.

'He's not answering,' she said.

'Gio?'

'He's angry, probably upset. I need to get round there but I don't think he'll answer the door.'

Bess felt terrible. 'I'm really sorry. About everything. Last night. Gio.' She sank into the sofa's cushions, wishing they could wrap her in their comfort forever.

'You don't need to apologise.'

Bess would've sat up straighter if she could. 'I do. I acted very badly, irresponsibly. And it's my fault Gio is angry with you. I'm not this person, Marianne, I'm really not.' And then she suddenly remembered stumbling outside the pub. 'And you hurt yourself, your ankle, because of me.'

What a total mess. Last night. Her life.

'My ankle is a little bit tender but much better today.' Marianne sat down next to Bess. 'You say you're not this person and I know that already. Last night was out of character – so what was it all about?'

Bess's head pounded and she winced, so much so that Marianne went and got a glass of water and a couple of paracetamol. She waited until Bess had taken them before she spoke again.

'We had a lovely dinner the night before last, you were happy, then the next thing I know, you're calling me from the pub and you're completely the other end of the scale.'

Bess hugged a cushion on her lap, her focus on the tassels, the few that had tied themselves in knots.

'Bess, I'm a good listener. I haven't always been. In fact, my boys will tell you I was the opposite when they were younger, but I've learned a lot over the years. And it hasn't always been easy.' She paused. 'You don't have to tell me if you don't want to but sometimes, talking about things can help.'

'I think I'm too much of a mess to be helped.' She leaned her head back against the sofa and closed her eyes.

'I very much doubt that.'

'I'm ashamed of the mess I'm in.'

'I've been there myself, believe me.'

Bess opened her eyes. 'Is that why you came here, to Whistlestop River?'

'I need to make amends with my boys, both of them. Gio is the easier one to start with.' Bess waited for her to go on but she didn't elaborate on that; all she said was, 'Please remember that the answers to your problems are never going to be found in the bottom of a glass.'

'It made me forget for a while, though.'

'It's temporary, but that feeling of escape doesn't last. Believe me, I've tried it.'

Bess drew her knees up against her chest, curled into the corner of the sofa. 'You drank a lot?'

'You could say that.' She met Bess's gaze. 'I've been in Alcoholics Anonymous for a while now.'

Bess tried to process the revelation. She gasped. 'I offered you a drink! I've got alcohol in my fridge! Right there under your nose!' She shook her head because now, thinking back to Christmas night in the pub when she'd seen Gio and told him she was going home to enjoy a glass of wine or two, it made sense. He had told her not to open the wine. He hadn't wanted her to do it in front of his mum.

Marianne nodded. 'I won't lie, it's been a test.'

Bess sat upright and then wished she hadn't because her head rushed in a way that sent her slinking back again. 'I made you come to a pub, for crying out loud. How could I be so stupid?'

'You're not stupid; you were inviting me out and that was a nice thing to do. And nobody *made* me come to the pub. You called and the more I said no to joining you, the more upset you got. And then, well, it reminded me of the pain that alcoholics like me have, the pain they're trying to block out with a few drinks and then a few more. Maybe I imagined it partly, but I couldn't ignore it because it reminded me of myself on some of my darkest days.'

Bess put a hand to her tummy.

Marianne was up like a shot. 'Are you going to be sick?'

'I don't think so. I think I'm hungry.'

'You stay put. I'll make you some crumpets and a cup of tea.'

Her hangover had kicked in when she first woke up but it was as though it was onto round two already.

The first bite of crumpet was heaven, the second even better and when she'd finished and drunk half of the tea, Marianne came back in from the hallway where she'd gone to try calling Gio again.

'I'm pretty sure the pub isn't a place recommended at your AA meetings,' Bess said sheepishly.

'No,' Marianne smiled. 'And it wasn't easy to walk inside. But my focus was different last night. I wasn't there looking for a good time; I'd gone to get you.' She shrugged as if embarrassed. 'I may have overstepped. You're my landlady, after all. Tell me if I'm interfering.'

'Don't say landlady; you make me feel old.' Bess hoped that the humour would take away any guilt for Marianne that she absolutely should not be feeling. 'And thank you for coming to help. I don't think I was doing much for my reputation getting so drunk; I bet it was noticed and I could be the talk of the town today.'

'Actually, there were hardly any people left by that point; all saving their pennies in January.'

'Which is precisely what I should've been doing. That's what got me into all this trouble.'

'You've got money worries?'

'You could say that.' It would be easy to deny that anything too major was going on, simple to skate over it like she'd done with Maya for such a long time. But Marianne had come out with it, disclosed that she was an alcoholic, and that was huge. She hadn't had to make the admission; she'd done it to explain and perhaps to help Bess realise that all alcohol would do was mask problems she couldn't ignore.

'I'm in trouble, Marianne. Big trouble.'

'A girl like you, with a great job, friends, a wonderful home?'

'I've kept up a front, hidden it from most people, but the shit has really hit the fan.'

'Well, the shit hit the fan several times for me over the years. Nobody gets it quite like I do, my girl. But I also know that the truth can set us free. If we admit to our mistakes, our problems, it might be how we turn them around.'

Bess didn't say anything for a few minutes, neither of them did until Bess said, 'I'd like to tell you about what's been going on if you're willing to listen?'

And Marianne relaxed back against the sofa too. 'Lovie, I'm all ears.'

21

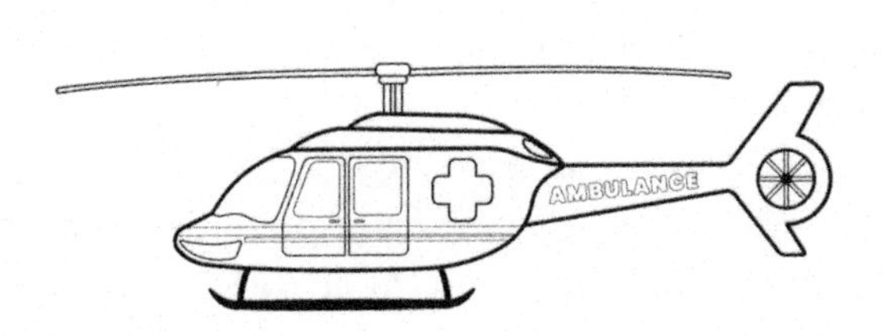

Gio yelped in pain when he did a squat against the wall that took his knees to 45 degrees and he held it so long that by the time he pushed himself to standing, he knew he'd taken it too far.

'All right, rest time.' Aysha would have had a chair under him and pushed him down on it if he hadn't taken a seat on the weights bench of his own accord.

'You're trying to do too much too soon,' she told him. 'It's a risky approach.'

He'd called her over for a session today even though he wasn't due another just yet. He had the exercises to do, he was working through them, but he wanted pushing to the next level. He needed it. To get his head to a different place.

'What's going on with you?' she asked.

'Nothing.'

'Crap.'

His lips curled into a smile. 'Just having a bad day, that's all. I want to get back to work, you know how it is.' No way was he admitting the truth: that his mother had gone back to her old ways and he'd been the sucker who trusted her that this time was different.

Marianne had been calling him all morning and he'd declined every single call. She'd be showing up here any second, he had no doubt about that, but he wouldn't be letting her inside.

He wasn't particularly happy at Bess either for being with his mum, at a pub. But then again, she had no idea, did she? It wasn't like either of them had been transparent with Bess and for that, he felt guilty. So maybe they were even.

As predicted, he was showing Aysha out the front door when his mother came walking up the front path. He said nothing, waited for Aysha to go and with the front door still open asked, 'What do you want, Mum?'

'To explain.'

He leaned closer.

'What are you doing?'

'Trying to sniff out whether you've had a hair of the dog or not.'

She wrapped her arms tighter around herself. It was bloody freezing out here and he wasn't far off closing the door in her face.

'I didn't drink last night, Gio. I haven't broken my sobriety.'

But he wasn't buying it, not this time. And now he was shivering, which made his knee feel worse.

'Can I come in? Just for a bit, so we can talk.'

'I don't think so.'

'Gio, please.'

'I've had a gutful, Mum. I've given you chance after chance and I can't do it any more. And you don't need to keep up the pretence for Marco and the kids because when I tell him what's happened, he won't want to come within a hundred metres of you.'

He felt terrible when he saw her gulp back tears but he couldn't ignore what she'd done. Not this time.

For once, instead of bawling her eyes out and apologising, she kept talking. 'Please, hear me out, five minutes and if you're not happy with what I've got to say, I'll leave. You never have to see me again.'

Something about the finality of her words had him opening the door wider. 'You'd better come in then.'

He didn't go through to the lounge to make her feel welcome; he did it so he could sit down after his gruelling physio session, which had been harder than usual because he'd pushed himself to the edge.

'I promise you I did not touch a drop last night, Gio.'

'You were in a pub. Bess was wasted.'

'Yes... Bess *was* wasted.'

'So were you when you called.'

Her brows knitted together. 'How do you work that out? I barely spoke to you before the landlord took the phone when Bess fell over.'

'I heard it in your voice.' Her asking the question had him remembering nothing more than a fragmented call from his mother. But that still didn't change the fact she'd been in the pub. 'How's the ankle?'

'I think I twisted it a bit last night. Bess pulled me over outside the pub. I was careful today when I walked, took it slowly, it seems okay.'

'You walked here?'

'I can't afford a taxi, Gio. And I missed the bus and didn't want to wait for the next.'

He harrumphed. The sooner this conversation was over, the better.

'I called you last night because I don't have a credit card, I'm down to my last fifteen pounds in my bank account until my pay comes in, and I didn't know what else to do. Bess had no money, her card was refused, I had to get her home safely.'

'So you need more money?'

'What? No. I don't need you to give me money.'

'Then what do you want?'

'I told you, I need to explain the events of last night because you think I fell off the wagon and I didn't. Gio, this time you are wrong. I didn't go to the pub *with* Bess last night; I went to get her. She called me, she was drunk, she wanted me to go and join her. I said no but then she got upset.'

'So you're a saint, is that what you're telling me?'

She stood up then, the most miffed he'd seen her in a long time. 'You know what, Gio? Getting sober was the hardest thing I've ever done and I could really use the support. Okay, so my track record is dire, but I swear to you this is it, no going back. Do you realise how hard it was to go into a pub of all places?'

He raised eyebrows. He couldn't think of what to say because whatever words he came out with would no doubt be sarcastic. He still wasn't sure he believed her claims, although to be fair, she didn't look remotely hungover and even with her professional drinking status in the past, she'd never been able to hide that telltale morning-after look.

'Talk me through what happened again then, Mum. Give me every last detail.' A few more minutes and he'd know whether she was telling the truth or not, he was sure of it.

She went back to the start, right from Bess's phone call to finding Bess at the pub, her falling off the stool, the landlord none too happy as she was getting lairy, leaving the pub and Bess stumbling and saving herself by pulling Marianne over.

'That must've been quite some test,' he said, still unable to look at her. 'Going into a pub. You couldn't do it for the cleaning job.'

'This felt a bit more important.' She let the moment settle. 'I've been on the phone to my sponsor this morning in between trying to get a hold of you. I needed to talk to her and I need to get to another meeting. There's one tonight.' She waited for Gio to look at her. 'I'll always be an alcoholic, I'll always have temptation, I'll go through hard times when I'll want a drink more than ever, like now, because you don't believe me. You doubting me makes me wonder why I don't just give in, have a drink and be done with it.'

'Are you saying this is my fault?'

'That wasn't what I meant. Please listen to me, Gio. I know that's asking a lot given my past behaviour, but I need you to put your faith in me. I haven't let you down again. Do you know what really made me change this time, apart from wanting you boys in my life? It was what they call rock bottom.'

Yes, and he was sure she'd spent time there before. It had never changed things.

'I ended up in hospital, had to have my stomach pumped. And the doctors warned me I might not be so lucky if it happened again, if I kept going the way I was.'

'You never told me.' As much as he'd hated those sorts of phone calls, he'd taken every one, dealt with them as they came.

'I didn't want you boys contacted – the nurse had seen a photo of you two in my purse, I told her you both lived overseas, and then I discharged myself as soon as I was able. I went to an AA meeting, figured it was the same as usual, that I'd lose interest but on my very first session, I made a friend. Sara. She has two daughters, she was in a similar situation to me twelve months previously: neither of them had wanted anything to do with her. But when one of them had a baby, she knew that she would never be a part of her grandchild's life if she didn't sort herself out. She'd been at those meetings for over a year and she showed me a text message from her daughter inviting her over to her house to meet her grandbaby. It made me think that if it happened for her, then why not me? Why couldn't I work just as hard and find a way back to you boys?'

He hesitated, waited for her to look directly at him. 'You really didn't touch a drop last night?'

'I really didn't.'

He rubbed his chest. 'I need a coffee.'

She leapt up to make it before he could, which at least gave him some space.

When Marianne brought his mug through to him, he asked, 'What's going on with Bess? Why was she so wasted?'

But his mum gave nothing away. She hid behind a sip of her own coffee.

'Getting that drunk isn't like Bess. I saw her drunk when we were in the shared house but never since. With her job, she's responsible, respected around here.'

'She is.' She chose her words carefully. 'Bess has confided in me what's going on with her but I can't break that confidence.'

'I wouldn't ask you to.' He had a bad feeling about this. Maybe Bess's house hadn't been such a good idea after all if she had big problems and was using alcohol to deal with them. She was his friend, he'd wanted more for a while, but right now, his worries had to be with his mum, who'd come so far.

'I want to help her,' Marianne went on. 'I had people in AA to help me; it made all the difference. I think Bess just needs to know there's a way out of her situation.' She smiled. 'I think I've started to be a much better listener.'

After the last twenty-four hours, thinking the worst of her, his voice caught when he admitted, 'I'm proud of you, you know.'

Her eyes filled with tears. 'You are proud of me?'

'I wasn't before we had this chat, believe me. But hearing what you've done and want to do for Bess, to help her, that's nice. And... well, I'm starting to believe that this time, you really have turned yourself around.' He almost told her that Marco, Saffy and the kids were due to visit soon but he still didn't want to jinx it. He couldn't see her overjoyed and then be the one to take that away from her.

'I promise you I have. There's always the threat that I'll fall off the wagon and it'll hang over me for the rest of my life. But I'll carry on battling it, I swear to you. And Gio? Don't be too angry with Bess for putting me in temptation's way.'

She knew him better than he realised – she had the ability to read how he was feeling when he didn't come out with it. Perhaps his memories had only held onto the bad stuff of his childhood and teenage years, her absences, both physical and emotional. Maybe he hadn't let himself see that she had still been his mother in ways she simply wasn't able to express back then.

He sighed. 'I seriously thought it was you who was wasted when you called.'

'I know you did and I'm sorry for that.'

'No, Mum. I'm the one who's sorry. I shouldn't have made assumptions.'

'You had every reason.'

'Maybe we should have told Bess your situation before you moved in.'

'I considered it, but I knew there was a chance I'd be refused the room and I'm sober now. I need to build my life again and part of that was moving out of here. I want to be close enough to you to prove myself but not so close we fall out.'

He smiled. 'I think we love each other better from a distance.'

'Maybe, but a short distance.' When she laughed, it wasn't the haunting sound it had once been, the sound he associated with her drunken state so many times. Now, it was a welcome sound, one that told him they were approaching a new type of normality.

'I'm good with that, Mum.' And as he reached out to give her a hug, this one felt genuine, like both of them meant it, like it was a line under the past and they were looking to the future.

22

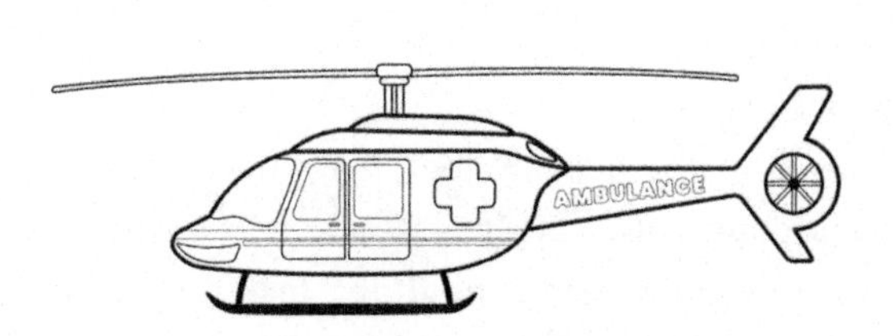

Bess opened the door to Gio. 'Your mum is at work.'

'Good, because it's you I came to see.'

She had a suspicion that was the case but wishful thinking and all that.

She stood back, let him inside and closed the door. *Here goes*, she thought, waiting for him to lose it with her, to yell at her for getting his alcoholic mother to go to a pub of all places and, worse, have to deal with a drunk person who was trying to push drinks on her until she knocked her off her feet. The night could've easily been so much worse.

They looked at one another for what felt like ages until eventually, Bess said, 'Go on, hit me with it. I can take it.'

'Hit you with it?'

'Given your reaction last night, I'm waiting for you to hit me with your worst... insults, yelling, whatever it may be.'

'I'm not going to do any of that.'

She looked up at him. 'You're not? But what I did...'

'What you did was call your lodger to come and join you at

the pub. Sounds a pretty normal thing to do. And you weren't to know about Mum.'

'I offered her alcohol here, in the house where she lives.' She cringed again at the memory.

'She'll have to deal with people offering her drinks or drinking in front of her for the rest of her life.'

'So, you're not worried?'

'Didn't say that.'

They stood in the hallway looking at each other. She hated that he was concerned, likely still a bit annoyed, even if he claimed not to be. Because if he didn't feel any strong emotion about the situation, he wouldn't be here right now, would he?

'You're not leaning on your stick much.' She noted he didn't have the crutches this time.

'I'm getting stronger, trying to remember my current limits. I can put some weight on the leg obviously, but not for too long.'

'Come in, sit down.' Hovering in someone's hallway was probably classed as pushing it a bit when he had been weight-bearing to get around. She tilted her head in the direction of the lounge. 'Can I get you a coffee?'

'Go for it, warm me up a bit.' He followed her through the lounge and into the kitchen.

She took mugs down from the cupboard. 'You're doing well to have walked here. Assuming you did?'

'I could pretend, be all macho, but no, I got a lift from a mate and got out at the end of the road.'

'In case I saw you and didn't answer the door?'

He laughed at that. 'Didn't even cross my mind.'

She heaped coffee granules into the awaiting mugs.

'Coffee machine not working?' He nodded to the gleaming contraption tucked in the corner.

'Something like that.' Marianne hadn't asked why she'd

suddenly bought instant coffee; she sensed she was a woman who knew that not everything was always as it seemed. In fact, they both knew that, given the revelations this morning.

Bess took the coffees into the lounge and when Gio settled in the armchair, she took the sofa.

Both of them spoke over the other before Bess insisted Gio talk first.

'When Mum called me from the pub, I assumed... wrongly, I now know, that she was drinking again. I came over to pay the taxi and I was so furious, I was never going to listen to what she had to say. I'd heard it all before, too many times than I care to remember.'

'She was frantic this morning when I got up, trying to call you every few minutes.'

'I feel bad about that now. I know I need to trust her more but I think it's going to take time. For the both of us.'

He looked her in the eye and it made her quiver; how did he have the ability to do that? 'Are you going to suggest she moves out?' Bess asked.

'Do you think I need to?'

'No.'

'But you see where I'm coming from?'

'Of course.' She hated that her voice wavered. 'I had no idea she was an alcoholic. You never said, even after all this time.'

'It was a detail of my life that I didn't want to admit to. I'd moved out of home when I went to the shared house, I'd escaped a lot of the hassles and the shit that went down in our family. I still had it going on in the background but I avoided rehashing it to anyone.'

'I wish you'd confided in me. If I'd known, I never would've offered her alcohol, I never would've called her from the pub. You have to believe me when I say that.'

'I do.' But the muscle in his jaw that twitched suggested the night at the pub had instilled enough worry in him that this wouldn't be easy to move on from.

'I enjoy having her here.'

He waited a beat. 'Even the humming?'

'Well, that I could do without on some days, but it's harmless.'

'Are you sure you want her here knowing what problems she has?'

'She's sober.'

'Yes, and she's one drink away from destroying that. It wouldn't take much at all. You have to realise that as much as she says, and I hope, she won't drink again, it's a possibility. I'm worried, Bess... I don't know what's going on with you, but my concern is that whatever it is, whatever drove you to get that wasted and need my mother to get you from the pub, will affect her.'

He was protective, looking out for his family. It hurt that he thought she might be a threat to his mother's sobriety, but could she blame him?

She needed to be honest, because she had thought about what would happen should Marianne start drinking, now she knew she was an alcoholic. 'What do I do if she does have a drink? I'm hoping she doesn't, but what if—'

'Then you call me. It's not for you to have to deal with.'

'That's an enormous burden to carry, Gio.'

'I've been carrying it for a long time.'

'How long was she drinking for, before she got sober this time?'

'Since I was a boy; my brother was more of a parent than she was.'

'I'm sorry... I don't know what to say.'

'Marco copped the worst deal, I reckon.'

'She talks about both of you, a lot.'

'Life has been tough on all of us. You know my dad walked out when we were young. It broke Mum. But there must be other women that has happened to, other men whose wives have left. Not everyone turns into an alcoholic and loses all sense of themselves.' He put his head in his hands.

Bess almost stretched across to comfort him. 'I'd be angry too.'

'I'm not angry with her.' But he paused when he looked up. 'All right, I am. I'm angry she couldn't hold it together and be a real mother. And I'm even angrier that she and Marco butt heads so much, my own brother puts off visits. He's supposed to be visiting soon but I haven't told her yet because I'm waiting for her to do something that results in him being a no-show.'

'For what it's worth, I think your mum is really trying to make amends.'

'Isn't that one of the AA steps?'

'I think so, but even if it's not, she wants to. I think she needs you and your brother in her life; she wouldn't have turned up in Whistlestop River and got a job here otherwise.'

'A job she's actually keeping hold of for once.' He tipped his head back to get the last of his coffee and then set his mug down on the side table. 'What's the deal with your coffee machine? You said *something like that* when I asked if it was broken. Come to think of it, isn't your dishwasher on the blink too?'

She put her own mug down, put her hands on her thighs. 'It's one thing in a list of items I can't really afford, should never have bought.' She looked right at him. 'I'm in a bit of trouble. Didn't your mum tell you?'

He moved as if he was going to sit forward but thought better of it, either because he decided not to or because his knee was making it difficult these days. 'What sort of trouble?'

'The money kind. Your mum really didn't say?'

'Look, she's been a crappy mother over the years but she's fiercely loyal. You tell her something in confidence, she won't break it.'

Bess wouldn't cry; she wouldn't let herself. She'd never looked weak in front of this man, both of them capable in their jobs, strong, to be relied on, not shadows of their former selves. 'I'm in financial trouble, big trouble. It started after my dad died, continued with a health scare—'

'You never told me you had a health scare.'

'We were in touch but it's not the sort of thing you call up a friend about and say hey, Gio, guess what has just happened to me.'

'Actually, that's exactly what you should do. What happened, Bess? Tell me.'

She swallowed hard. 'I thought I might have breast cancer.' She immediately added, 'The lump was benign; I had it removed.'

'I wish you'd told me.'

'It was too personal to share. And I suppose I found it easier to keep it mostly to myself apart from Mum and a couple of close girlfriends. It let me carry on leading my life without those questions being asked; it allowed me to be the same person I'd always been.'

'And you're okay now?'

'I'm fine.' She smiled. She liked that he cared, loved that he seemed relieved to hear it. 'I have had check-ups since and there's no sign of another lump.'

'Good.' The corners of his mouth lifted into the smile she

knew and recognised. 'Otherwise, how will we ever go out on a date?'

'You said you wanted to take me to dinner and I'm okay with that.'

'But not if it's a date,' he said.

'Maybe we're better as friends.' She never wanted to lose that.

He shrugged. 'We'll see.'

His flirting, his implication that they should be more than friends, made her feel better and gave her a lift but she had to get this all out now she'd started.

'When Dad died, I kept telling myself I had to live each day like it was my last.' She paused. 'And that escalated after the health scare.'

'I can understand why.'

'Yes, and while that's all great in theory, it turns out it's not so good when you have a house, a car, bills to pay. I don't even know how I got in such a damn mess.'

'It happens.'

She swiped angrily at the tear that dared to creep out of the corner of her eye. 'Not to me it doesn't. I have a responsible job that I love, a home I adore. This isn't like me; it just spiralled out of control. I've been living in denial.' Her lips trembled with the admission.

'Listen, you don't have to tell me anything more unless you want to, but I've not got to get to work so I've plenty of time. It seems we could've both confided in each other over the years and saved ourselves a whole lot of heartache.'

For a moment, his words comforted her until she felt the cloak of misery and hopelessness settle around her shoulders again.

He waited a beat before he asked, 'Why don't you tell me

what got you so upset that you went on a totally-out-of-character bender?'

'Haven't drunk that much since my twenties. Remember that night Louis made us do shots to commiserate with him failing an end-of-year exam?'

'My head hurts just thinking about it.' He laughed.

The memory was funny, the present not so much as she filled him in more. 'I missed paying a few bills, maxed out credit cards, defaulted on loan payments, I got final demands left, right and centre, took out a ridiculously high interest loan. I've borrowed some money from my mother, which I hated doing, I have the threat of court looming over me for the council tax I haven't managed to pay.' She looked across at him. 'See, told you I'm in a mess.'

'I could lend you some money, although I'm not flush with cash at the moment and I need to be careful because I won't be on full pay forever.' She hated the frown that creased his forehead. 'I hope I'm back to work soon but there's no guarantee.'

'I can't take your money, Gio, even if you had plenty. This isn't like borrowing twenty quid for a takeaway. I have a lot of debt.' She gulped. 'You must think I'm a total idiot.'

'I think we both know I don't think that, Bess.'

'Renting out my spare room eases things a little, it tops up my income, but I'm still not sure where to go from here.'

The only solution Bess could see right now was to go to her mum and ask her to take money from one of the bonds or whatever she had, use that and Bess would have to pay it back plus the money her mother had forfeited for getting to the money sooner than she should. She hated that this was the only thing she could do, she'd even entertained the idea of another payday loan if that were possible, but whatever she was going to do, she only had a few days to decide.

Without using his stick, Gio took both mugs out to the kitchen, moving slowly but so much better. She didn't mind the rear view either.

'Thank you for being honest with me,' he said when he came back.

So where did that leave them? Where did it leave the tenancy arrangement which they had an agreement for but a very flexible one? She couldn't blame him for worrying, wouldn't blame him if he got his mother to pack her things and move back in with him.

And where did it leave their friendship? Where did it leave the potential for more?

Would he want to take her for dinner as he'd suggested before or was that totally off the table now she'd revealed the truth?

'I'm sorry again, for the pub,' she said as they made their way towards the front door.

'I'm sure things aren't easy for you.' He pulled on his coat, zipped it up, without the usual flirtatious smile or another attempt to ask her out on a date. All that flirting had irritated her at times, she'd kept her distance, but now she missed it more than anything. Because she'd disappointed him and it was a weird feeling to have when it came to Gio.

His shoulders immediately hunched up against the cold when he stepped outside. He turned back to face her as she stood in the warmth of the hallway. 'Are you really happy for Mum to stay on as your lodger?'

'If you're happy for her to be here then for now I don't see a reason to change anything.'

But he was clearly having a tough time answering that, which was probably why he gave a simple nod, said nothing else, and walked away down the path without another backwards glance.

And Bess felt unbelievably sad when she climbed the stairs to bed.

23

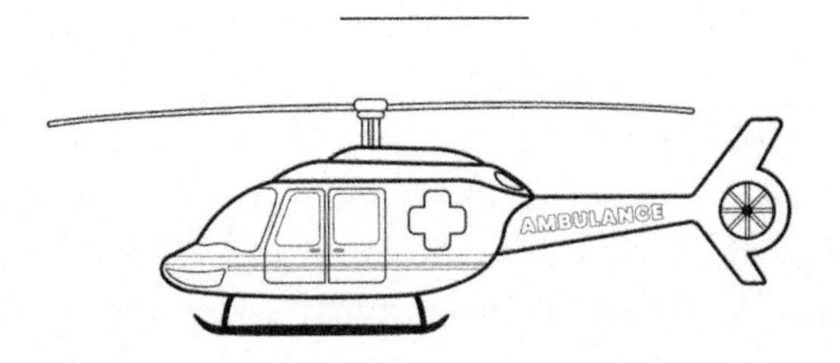

Once they'd settled in to the 4 p.m. shift, and as the skies grew dark, Maya, Bess and Noah finally packed away the Christmas paraphernalia at the airbase for another year. The decorations had already been taken down from the walls, the ornaments and lights had been removed from the trees, but with interruptions from jobs taking precedence, returning the boxes to where they came from was still on the to-do list. They stored the boxes at the top of the cupboards in the room upstairs with a few small beds should anyone need to sleep on shift when they were quiet. It rarely happened, mostly they all stayed awake, but if you ever did a double shift, those beds were a godsend.

Back down in the office, the Christmas tree looked as sorry for itself as the one that had stood in reception until they'd moved it outside. Stripped of all its merriment, needles littered the floor of the office due to the tree drying out. Bess and Marianne had taken their tree down at home already and left it on the grass verge in front of their house with the label displaying the logo of The Skylarks. Bess hoped it would be a gentle reminder for anyone else in the street to do the same if they'd already made a donation and got a label, or that it might prompt anyone who wasn't aware of the tree collection to support their local air ambulance and get rid of their tree at the same time.

Bess thought again about Gio and how he hadn't stopped by since he came to see her about the pub incident. Marianne was still her lodger, but Bess felt as though she was on her last chance; if she did anything else to rock the boat, she sensed Gio would have his mother out of there. It made her feel terrible about herself and yet she totally understood his reasoning.

Bess and Maya carried the airbase's tree outside and rested it against the side of the building next to the other one, where they wouldn't be tripped over in the dark.

'Should've worn our coats.' Maya rubbed her arms when they went back inside to the warmth of the office.

'It's getting colder for sure.'

'When will the chipper arrive?' Bess asked.

Noah confirmed it was due in two days, in time for the trees the crews would round up and bring here.

'What do we call this time between New Year and Christmas?' Maya asked. She got nothing but confused looks. 'I was thinking, if the time between Christmas and New Year is known as Twixmas then there might be a name for this time period too.'

Noah just laughed. 'I'd call it time to appreciate the rest of the days in between.'

'He has a point,' Bess grinned.

'Hey, talking of Twixmas.' Noah spun around in his chair. 'I could murder a Twix right now.'

Bess bent down to get something from the bottom drawer and threw it to him. 'Catch!'

He began to laugh at the gold-wrapped bar that had just landed in his hand. 'How did you conjure that up so quickly?'

'Mum gave me a selection box for Christmas, an enormous

selection box. Thought I'd share it around a bit; can't eat it all myself.' One look from Noah and she admitted, 'All right, I easily could, I just don't think I should. Maya, can I interest you in a packet of Rolos? Crunchie? Double decker?'

'Not for me, thanks, still full from my sandwich.'

The phone let out its shrill sound to notify them of a job and the crew snapped into action. Unlike a daytime job, it wasn't a case of getting the helicopter started and leaving within a few minutes. At nighttime, they were required to do a lot more preparations prior to leaving the base.

Armed with maps in the office, the team identified potential landing sights. There had been a road traffic collision involving a bus that had veered off the road and into a ditch. Most of the passengers were unharmed, but an elderly man was trapped at the front of the bus and the fire brigade were on the way to assist.

'Landing on the road isn't an option,' Bess confirmed. 'Too narrow and winding.' Those sorts of roads were beautiful to look at, to drive along in the height of summer with the windows down, but hazardous in the winter, especially for a bus. Unfortunately, those types of roads were the only way to get to certain places. 'There's a farmer's field on our left as we approach. It looks big enough.'

'There's a second field the other side of the road too,' Noah added. 'Plus, there's a car park, which is a trek but it's an option should the first two not be good enough.'

'All right then,' said Maya. 'Let's go. I'll get Hilda ready.'

Maya left, Bess got the cool box of blood and plasma, and Noah collected the drugs, and with helmets and jackets on, it was time to go.

'Is it rain or sleet?' Maya wondered once she lifted the helicopter into the air and they set off for the job thirty miles north from the airbase.

'I've no idea.' Bess couldn't tell which it was either.

Night-vision goggles guided them towards their destination along with a powerful white light underneath the helicopter which illuminated the ground.

Bess thought about Gio, how as horrid as the circumstances were, she wouldn't have minded seeing him there tonight. He'd been pleasant enough when he'd come to the house and seemed to understand what she was going through but she hated thinking she'd plummeted in his estimations since the stunt she'd pulled at the pub. She wished more than anything that she hadn't done it now, that she and Gio were just as they'd been before.

'You think it'll snow?' Noah's voice came over the microphone. The weather conditions were hazardous and right now, out on a job, they all hoped it wouldn't get any worse.

'Maybe,' said Bess as what she'd deduced as sleet carried on.

'Eva will love snow when she sees it.' Maya, who seemed to enjoy being a part of the little family, beamed. She and Noah were getting serious.

'She sure will,' came Noah's voice from the back of the helicopter. 'I can't wait to build a snowman with her.'

Maya laughed. 'You're a big kid; don't pretend it's all about Eva.'

'Okay, I admit, I want snow. Doesn't happen very often in Dorset but we can hope for some.'

They were almost at the scene and general chitchat, which was always interspersed with work talk, reverted to work-only. They couldn't land in the first field; it had farm machinery on the perimeter which made it difficult to get access to the road. The other field was too sloped, the car park became their best bet and Hilda set down safely in no time at all.

Maya stayed with the helicopter and Noah and Bess made their way to the scene lugging the heavy bags.

A firefighter updated them on approach. The elderly gentleman was talking, but he had severe leg injuries.

Noah and Bess attended to the patient. To stabilise him, they administered a blood transfusion on scene.

With the patient on the scoop, Norm, the strapping, blond, Scandinavian-looking firefighter, was on hand to help. The muscles to lift the patient, who was on the heavy side, were welcome as he and Noah took charge of the scoop and Bess picked up the rest of the equipment.

As they paced towards the helicopter, Norm mentioned Gio to Bess. 'The whole crew is rooting for him.'

'I'm sure you are.'

'It's killing him that it might not happen.'

Bess's wet curls stuck to the side of her face. With this crappy weather, it was impossible to keep a hood up, to stay dry. Hazard of the job but the sleet was particularly brutal tonight. 'What do you mean, "it might not happen"?'

'Spoke to him earlier. He had a visit with the doc,' Norm called above the noise of the wind and everything else around them. 'He's not sure whether he'll ever get back on the job.'

That couldn't be right. He was recovering well, getting his strength back. 'Surely it's a matter of time.'

'Time... patience... luck. And in this job, it's physically demanding even on a slow day. You know how it is.'

He was right. There was recovery for a person with a regular job and then there was recovery for a person who climbed ladders, jumped on and off engines, hauled around heavy equipment.

Once at the helicopter, Norm left them to it and Bess and Noah transferred the patient to the litter inside.

The sleet carried on once Bess was in position as technical crew member next to Maya. It grew heavier as they reached the hospital's helipad, and the entire crew gave a sigh of relief when they got back to base.

Marianne hadn't mentioned anything about Gio seeing the doctor and being given bad news, which had Bess wondering whether Gio hadn't told her because he didn't want anything to rock her emotionally. He had to be hurting, though. It would be torture to a man like Gio to not be able to do the job he loved, be who he was before, full of strength and able to do anything when it came to saving a life.

And as Bess headed inside the hangar and out of the fat flakes of snow that had begun to come down in place of the sleet, much to Noah and Maya's excitement, Bess wasn't just preoccupied with her own issues; Gio's problems were on her mind too.

Which meant she cared. More than she'd ever thought she would.

24

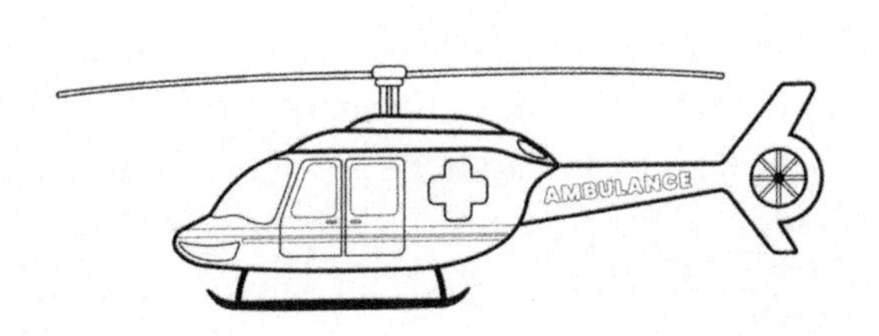

Gio didn't feel any joy today. Not even when he looked out of the window at the blanket of snow covering the ground and weighing down the branches of the trees, muffling everything around. The world seemed so quiet – his head was anything but. He couldn't get his thoughts in a good place at all. He was a grumpy sod.

The fact that he couldn't even enjoy the snow felt like yet another setback to him. And it didn't help that local kids were whizzing by outside on foot, dragging sledges behind them. Schools must be closed; it would've been declared a snow day today.

He knew where they were going. There was a steep slope not far from here in a public meadow; he'd been walking through it last year as the rain came down and he talked to his brother on the phone. His brother had had snow where he lived and Gio had looked at the slope and thought how much of a thrill it would be to go down it if they had snow in Whistlestop River.

He took his plate into the kitchen and dropped it into the

water in the sink, already brown from the baking tray he'd shoved a meat pie on. It had been left over from the stocks his mum had bought when she was staying here. It hadn't tasted great – didn't help that he'd burnt it – but he was in the sort of mood where thinking about anything other than getting food from freezer to oven to plate was too much.

As he let the plate sink into the murky depths of the washing-up water, he thought back to his doctor's appointment the other day, the way he'd gone in with hope and an air of positivity and left feeling crap.

It was his fault. He'd pushed for straight talk, for blunt answers and facts, and he'd got them.

'Gio, come in, sorry to keep you,' the doc had apologised after keeping him waiting almost fifty minutes. 'How are you?'

Gio recapped the physio regime he'd been following, they talked about painkiller use, the doc examined his knee and took him through exercises as if to prove his claims.

Gio pulled his jeans back on, sure his quad muscle on the bad side was half the size of the other. He'd have to work on that.

'When can I go back to work then, doc?' He had a smile on his face until he saw the doctor's hesitation. He knew that expression – it was the one they used when they weren't sure how to answer a question, the look which said they were buying time while the words churned over inside their head and would hopefully come out the right way.

'You know I can't give cast-iron guarantees on outcomes.'

They couldn't, but surely by now, they knew more than they had at the start.

'Ballpark,' he pushed. 'One month, three, six—' The doc held up his hand and Gio filled in the blank for himself. 'You don't know.'

'I'm not trying to make you feel worse or take away any hope but if I tell you six months and you're not back at work, you'll be gunning for me. And your knee is a bit swollen again.'

It was ridiculous but part of him had hoped the swelling wouldn't be noticed. He'd overdone it, he'd pushed himself trying to go up and down the stairs at home a few times rather than only going up and down to the bedroom. He'd thought of it as training, although he hadn't cleared it with the physio and would be unlikely to admit how many times he'd done it if she asked him at his next session.

'I was doing stairs, to help strengthen it.'

'That's good. You need to move,' said the doc, 'but you've pushed it too far if there's swelling. And it's hard for me to know if that'll happen every time or not. Injuries like this vary from person to person.'

'I know some firefighters with similar injuries who were back within six months.' Gio had done his research, hadn't cared whether the articles he read were evidence based; he'd wanted the assurance and belief that it could happen for him too.

'As I said, with this level of swelling, I'd recommend pulling back a bit for now. Use the crutches again, let the swelling really go down, then let's start from there.'

Start? That word felt as though he'd been thrown right back to the day of the injury when the whole of his recovery was lying in wait for him.

'Have a talk with your superiors, see whether you could return to work in a different capacity for a while?'

'An office job, you mean.'

The doc came round to Gio's side of the desk and perched his behind on the corner, hands clasped on his lap. 'A job that doesn't mean you're twisting, jerking or doing anything unpredictable with this knee for a while. Getting from A to B on your feet is a lot different to the demands of a firefighter. You don't need me to tell you that. The only other thing you have control over is patience and not pushing it too soon and re-injuring yourself. Let's look after that knee joint, reassess in a month or so. In the meantime—'

'Get back on my crutches and start accepting I'll be at a desk for the foreseeable.'

'Until we know more,' the doc tactfully corrected.

Not returning to a fully functioning firefighter was his worst nightmare. It was all he wanted to do, all he could imagine doing. *Until we know more* wasn't what he wanted to hear. It wasn't what he'd expected to hear either. He had a sudden vision of sitting at a desk at the fire station, the alert of the alarm sounding, listening to the thud of footfall on the stairs as the crew raced to get ready for a shout, the blare of the sirens as they roared out of the fire-station doors, leaving him behind. And the highlight for him might have been taking the call in the first place if he was lucky.

No, that couldn't happen.

He couldn't let this be taken away from him.

And yet he had a sinking feeling he had little choice in the matter. He'd given physiotherapy his all, he'd never backed off once, and still it hadn't been enough.

Gio had left that appointment feeling as if all the positivity had been sucked out of him.

He stood at the front window of his house, watched another couple of kids run on past, one of them dragging a red, plastic sledge behind her.

If he didn't get outside soon, he'd be certifiable.

He wanted to feel alive, he needed to feel like himself.

He wanted to feel the slap of cold against his skin, the raw bite of winter that had the town in its grasp.

He put on a jumper, his coat, grabbed the crutches and

opened the door to a bright day that would be beautiful if he could enjoy it properly.

He didn't know where he was going. He didn't care if he fell.

What was the point of anything when a return to the person he really was still felt so far out of his reach?

25

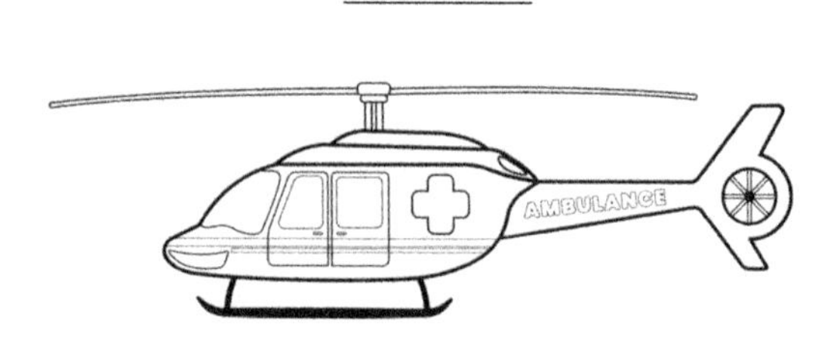

Bess crunched her way through freshly fallen snow on her way to the gym. She'd tried calling them to cancel her membership but she was locked into a direct debit agreement and they wouldn't listen. It was so black and white to whoever had answered her call – you signed up for a year so it didn't matter whether anything else came your way, that was that. She was on the premier membership too, which made it worse, and the most galling thing was that she barely used it. She'd signed up determined she would, but then like so many others they probably had on their books, she'd just become a contributor to their profits, getting nothing back for herself. It was her own fault, but she was getting more and more desperate and this seemed an easy thing to get rid of if only they'd hear her out. And that was why she was heading there now – it got her out of the house on a day off and perhaps if she spoke to them face to face, she might have better luck pleading her case.

She was almost at the gym when her phone rang. It was Nadia. The Skylarks were desperate for a fill-in after Kate on the blue team had gone home sick.

The gym would have to wait. Bess doubled back home and got her things, picked up her car keys and carefully drove to the airbase. The roads closest to town had at least been ploughed and gritted so weren't packed with snow like the pavements, but Bess knew from news reports and social media that a lot of roads in this part of Dorset remained impassable.

Vik and Brad were in the office when she reached the airbase but it wasn't long before The Skylarks were called out on a job.

Bess took the call from the HEMS desk and while they didn't have much to go on, they did know that there had been a sledging accident at Wildacre Meadow, renowned for its steep slope that in summer, kids often slid down on steel trays, which was a bit like sledging except without the snow. Bess remembered it as a kid, the thrilling speeds you could reach.

But before Bess hung up the call, she had to ask the person on the other end to repeat the name she'd just given her. 'Are you talking about Gio Mayhan?' Because the woman had said Gio, right?

'I just have the name Gio. The caller wasn't very clear, I'm afraid, but we got the location, sounds like a leg injury and then the call cut out.'

As Bess went through the motions of getting her helmet while Brad gathered together the drugs and the bloods, she couldn't help her head from going there – Gio had had a doctor's appointment that didn't go as expected, his goal of getting back to work to do the job he'd been trained for was slipping further away. Had he thrown himself down the steep hill on purpose? To somehow prove that he was just like everyone else and didn't have an injury?

It was a short distance to Wildacre Meadow but as soon as they'd heard the location, Vik had gone out to the helipad to get Hilda ready. The surrounding roads would be impassable, the roads stretching beyond the same, meaning a road ambulance wouldn't be able to reach the patient or get them to the help they needed.

The Skylarks flew over Whistlestop River. Visibility wasn't great but at least it was daylight and Vik was experienced in landing in all types of conditions so fully understood the implications of flying and setting down a helicopter in ice and snow.

The good thing about Wildacre Meadow was that it had the steep incline but a nice level area as you reached the bottom of it. They'd needed that as kids, sliding down it on trays; Bess wasn't sure she would've dared to do it otherwise. And today, it worked out well for the helicopter because there was plenty of space to land and a couple of helpful adults at ground level had kept the kids back and out of the way so that The Skylarks could keep everyone safe.

Bess had her mind on the job but knowing it was Gio in trouble changed things. She was more anxious, her heart was pounding, but she was together as much as she needed to be.

There were too many people at the bottom of the slope to see their patient. But soon, they were clear to leave the aircraft. They had kit bags and the scoop, all of which weighed so much more when you had to trudge through the snow, which was deeper in some parts than others. Bess made sure she had the specially designed thermal blanket with the rest of the kit. The air ambulance played a key role in a patient's chances of survival – the job of The Skylarks would be to intervene on scene and prevent further deterioration of the patient until they could get them the further help they needed. Bess knew that in these temperatures, providing thermal management with the blanket was critical to maintain the patient's core body temperature and prevent hypothermia and any further heat loss.

As they drew nearer to the crowd, they were waved over to

one side near a tree. A tree that if hit at high speed, could be catastrophic.

Bess felt as though she was seeing things as they got to the patient and realised that it wasn't Gio but a young boy, next to whom Gio was kneeling.

'Thank God you're here.'

Bess kept a level head. Gio wasn't the patient. Gio wasn't seriously hurt, at least not any more than he had been before today.

The boy's name was Lionel, Gio told them as Brad reassured the boy that help had arrived. He was crying so much, terrified Bess suspected, but perhaps not as cold as he might be had Gio not covered him in his coat.

'Gio, you must be freezing.' Bess picked on someone in the crowd and asked them to run over to the helicopter. 'Vik is the pilot, ask him for an extra blanket and bring it right back here.' They'd use the thermal blanket on Lionel but even when Gio got his coat back, he'd probably need a bit of extra help to warm up.

Lionel likely had a broken ankle, a fractured wrist and some bruising. Brad had him sucking on a mouthpiece for gas and air to relieve some of the pain while he and Bess got him on the scoop ready for transfer.

'It really hurts,' Lionel sobbed when he let the mouthpiece fall from his lips.

'I know, mate,' said Gio, at his side.

'Do you know him?' Bess asked.

'No, we met today, didn't we, Lionel?'

Lionel managed a ghost of a smile. 'He wanted to use my sledge.' He registered The Skylarks' logo on Bess's jacket. 'Am I going in a helicopter?'

'You sure are,' said Brad.

Before they'd got him on the scoop, Bess had radioed to find out the status of contacting the parents. Hudson had managed to reach them. They weren't nearby, both were at work and closer to the hospital where they'd airlift Lionel to, so it was agreed they'd meet them there. As a result, it was suggested that Gio come in the helicopter so he didn't have to navigate his way back up the hill on crutches. Lionel, at his age, height and build meant it could be done; they could take the extra weight.

Bess thought he was going to refuse but it was a big hill and when Gio looked back at it, he must've seen what a nightmare it was going to be.

Now that the pain relief was helping, Lionel chattered away, asking what their jobs were, who flew the aircraft, and then he asked Gio if he was a paramedic too.

'No, not me,' he answered.

'He's a fireman,' Bess piped up because she had a sneaky suspicion Gio wasn't going to say it.

Lionel's eyes widened. 'A real one?'

'Yes, a real one. But I'm injured at the moment.'

'Did you fall off a ladder?' Lionel asked. Distraction – and in this case the gas and air – meant they didn't have a scared little boy any more; they had one with a curiosity about the world.

'There was an explosion. I was knocked off my feet,' Gio replied as they lifted the scoop up ready to head back to Hilda.

'You flew into the air?' Lionel's eyes were as wide as saucers.

'Something like that,' said Gio.

Vik had run over from the helicopter, and he and Brad took charge of the scoop and upped their pace back to the aircraft.

'How does it feel?' Bess asked as she picked up the extra kit bags to follow Vik and Brad, staying at Gio's side as they walked.

'My knee? Bit rubbish, I knelt beside him for a while.' He wasn't bad on the crutches even in the snow, until they got to the deeper bit which slowed him down further.

'I meant how does it feel to have helped?'

The familiar smile appeared. 'It wasn't the same as being back at work, but man, it felt good. I felt alive again doing something useful today.'

'I thought it was you when we got the call. I thought you were hurt.'

'Me? You thought I was stupid enough to go sledging?' He laughed when she didn't answer. 'I was out for a walk. I was pissed off. I walked all the way here and yes I was stupid enough to ask to borrow Lionel's sledge like he said. But he was using it. I watched him go off at a terrifying speed. The next thing I knew, he'd come off and the screaming had everyone else's attention.'

'How did you get down the hill?'

'I didn't have any choice but to grab the sledge next to me. I needed to get to him, to help. I kept my bad leg up and on it, used my other one to steer, brake, whatever I needed to get down there. The girl whose sledge it was came down with my crutches soon after. Anyway, I knew we needed help when I saw him lying there. I got his friend to call the emergency services and tell them we were at the bottom of Wildacre Meadow – there isn't much coverage here and it was better for him to do it than have me trying to hobble anywhere. He must have dropped my name in the conversation and I assume he was panicking, which meant he confused you all.'

Bess said nothing but she knew he was watching her while trying his best to keep up.

'You were worried about me,' he said.

The others had reached the helicopter and were transferring Lionel onto the litter.

'You wish.' But this time, there wasn't anywhere near as much denial behind her words before she hurried her pace to reach Hilda.

Up in the air, Bess was in the front seat, so couldn't see Gio in the back but she was acutely aware of his presence, so close, his voice every now and then reaching her as he and Brad kept Lionel's spirits up on the way to the hospital.

Bess and Brad managed the handover to the staff on the helipad at the hospital, away from the snow up here, but the view reminded them that at ground level, it was a different story. Hilda had, once again, allowed The Skylarks to get their patient medical attention which otherwise would've been next to impossible via road.

Back at the airbase, Vik and Gio made their way inside while Brad and Bess unloaded everything. Bess had wondered whether Gio might have left by the time she went inside via the hangar. But he was sitting in the kitchen with Nadia, a steaming mug of tea in front of him and one of her shortbread biscuits.

'For the shock,' he smiled as Bess picked up her mug of tea.

'Help yourself to more,' Nadia prompted him and pushed the tin of shortbread his way before she left the kitchen.

Vik came in for a mug of tea and took his and Brad's and after Bess said she'd join them soon and catch up on paperwork, she sat opposite Gio.

'Lionel will be fine, thanks to you.'

He'd put his crutches in the corner, leaning up against the side of the fridge. 'I'm glad I could help. I didn't think about my injury so much when I saw the young boy was hurt; I grabbed a sledge and knew I had to get to him. I was in a terrible mood before that but I kind of forgot all my own problems for a moment.' He met her gaze. 'I needed that.'

'Norm told me you went to the doctor and it didn't go so well.'

'He's got a big mouth.' But he smiled as he said it. 'A big, caring mouth. It's not his job but he likes to think he keeps the team going and motivates us all.'

'They all want you back.'

'I want to go back.'

'You're doing everything you can, Gio.'

'I know... except being patient. I was gutted after the doctor visit. Annoyed that nobody will ever say for sure that I'll go back to full duties. But nobody has said that I won't and after today, I don't know, maybe my head is in a better space.' He turned down the offer of more shortbread when she pushed the tin closer to him. 'Nadia has already made me have a few of those, no more.'

'They're good.'

'They are.' And he locked her gaze. 'So, you were worried about me.'

'I was. What? Why are you smiling?'

He shrugged. 'It's nice to have someone worry about me, that's all.'

'Your mum worries.'

'I know she does.'

'Are you still worried about her living with me?'

'It's not you I have a problem with, Bess, not really. It's trusting Mum. And I know I have to, but it's going to take time. The pub was a shock, that's all; it's not like I've been teetotal all my life so I shouldn't be judging you. How's it all going anyway?'

'The debt?' She smiled. 'Still there. Overtime helps.'

'This shift is overtime?'

'Yup. And I'd better get on and finish up my paperwork before the next job comes through. Are you going to call a taxi? I would offer to take you home but I won't finish for a while yet.'

'No need for a taxi.' Hudson came into the kitchen and went straight for the shortbread tin, plucking a couple of pieces. 'Nadia has a lot to answer for.' He closed his eyes as he bit into a piece. 'I'll take you home, Gio. Assuming you're local?'

Gio reeled off the name of his street.

'Great. I'm leaving in about ten minutes as I have to get home for the kids. And I've got my four-wheel drive so that snow doesn't stand a chance. Meet you in reception?'

'Cheers, appreciate it.'

Bess looked out of the window, the white landscape beyond, when it was just the two of them. 'I don't think we'll get any more but it could take a while to melt.'

Gio positioned his crutches under his arms ready to go. 'I'll see you soon then?'

Bess smiled. 'See you soon.'

And as she walked into the office to do her paperwork, she couldn't stop thinking about the man who wasn't just that little boy's hero today; he was beginning to feel like he could be hers too.

26

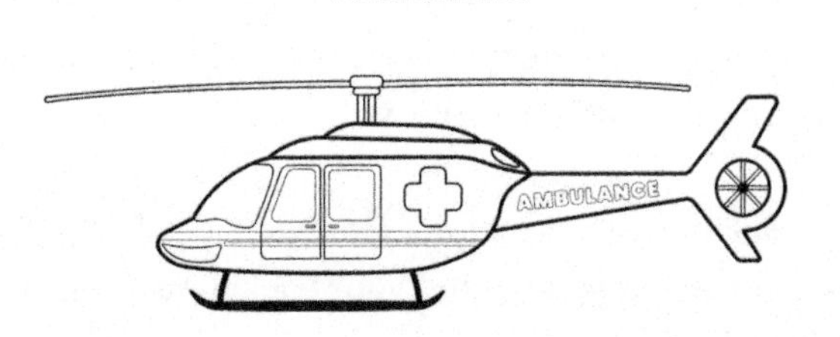

Bess finished up in the shower and got herself dressed. Marianne was out at a cleaning job and it felt good to have a bit of quiet time on her day off. She planned to call the Citizen's Advice Bureau today – she'd been putting it off long enough. Hopefully, whoever she talked with could perhaps help her steer her way out of the mess she was in with money.

She drew her bedroom curtains and looked out at the wintry scene. The snow was lingering enough that it still looked like a winter wonderland, but they hadn't had a fresh fall and it was on track to melt over the next day or so. Bess hated the slush they got after a pretty layer of snow and always hoped a downpour would wash it all away quickly, but it didn't always happen like that.

When someone knocked at the front door, Bess assumed it was the neighbour come to pick up a parcel Bess had taken in for safekeeping.

But it wasn't the post lady.

She was so stunned to see Malcolm, without her mother at

his side, that she stood there letting the cold wind blow its way inside and her bare feet already felt the chill.

'Hello, Bess. Would it be all right if I came in?'

She snapped to attention. 'Of course.' She closed the door behind him.

Malcolm pulled off the woolly hat, the static sending a few strands of grey hair comically into the air. 'I'll come out with it right away. I'd like to help you, Bess.'

'Help me?'

'With your current situation.' He held up a hand. 'I haven't been gossiping about you behind your back; I just want to help.'

'Malcolm, I—'

His voice didn't have its usual steadiness when he told her, 'This morning, your mother gave me your information so I could make a transfer, into your account. It's a loan, she's sent you an email about it, sent it after I left the house, but I thought I'd come and explain myself.'

Bess was pretty sure she'd been standing with her mouth hanging open.

'Why would you do that?' she eventually stammered. 'Why would you loan me money?'

'I care about your mother, Bess. And, if I'm allowed, I'd like to care a bit about you too because you are your mother's whole world.'

Tears pricked her eyes and she turned round to head to the kitchen. 'Cup of tea?' she trilled over her shoulder. She didn't know what to feel, or think, she just knew she wanted to do something as what he told her sank in.

When he appeared in the kitchen, where she'd taken out the mugs, he'd taken off his coat and hung it on the back of a chair.

'Sugar?' she asked, unable to meet his eye yet.

'Not for me, thank you.' He cleared his throat. 'I understand you don't find this easy. Accepting help, especially from me.'

She looked at him now. 'It's not that I don't like you, or that I resent you being with Mum.'

'I know that. But I lost my dad when I was only twenty-one. Nobody would have ever replaced him. I promise that is not what I'm trying to do here.'

No preamble, just like that, he'd addressed what she'd found so hard about this aside from her mum sharing her financial problems. 'I'm sorry you lost your dad so young.' She turned her focus back to the mugs and poured the boiling water onto the tea bags.

She passed Malcolm one of the mugs when she was done. 'You're incredibly generous lending me money, but I really can't take it. It wouldn't be right.'

'You're not taking it; you're borrowing it.'

Bess sat at the table and gingerly, he sat down next to her as though he still wasn't sure about how she might react.

He cleared his throat again; maybe he did it when he was nervous. 'In exchange for loaning you the money to pay off some of what you owe, I want you to do something for me.'

Bess's heart sank. This was where she found out he was a dodgy dealer, someone she didn't want in her mother's life, a criminal, about to bribe her and ask for goodness knew what.

But when he spoke, it proved he was none of those things. 'I want you to sit here with me and make a proper plan.'

'A plan?'

'One that sorts out your finances, gets you out of this mess.'

'That's it?'

'It'll take us time, I won't lie.'

He wanted to help. She'd doubted him, she hadn't been overly welcoming and yet he was still here.

'Okay.'

Malcolm beamed as though she was the one doing him the favour, not the other way round.

'I have my own condition, though…' Bess said.

'And what's that?'

'If it's going to take time, then we need a decent packet of biscuits.'

He reached down to the leather bag he'd brought with him. He took out a laptop and then a carrier bag which he passed her. 'Your mother knows you well.'

And when she peeked inside, she saw a supply of some of her favourites. 'Then I guess we should get started.'

The surface of the kitchen table was soon covered in paperwork – statements, bills, loan information, correspondence. The first thing he had Bess do was pay the council tax bill in its entirety, which removed the threat of being taken to court. And once that was done, Bess felt as though it was a giant leap in the direction she needed to go in.

They got through almost a whole packet of custard creams and what felt like a gallon of tea. Malcolm went through all her paperwork with her and slowly, the shame every time he picked up another piece of paper gave way to a calm that came with dealing with something she'd put off and then been befuddled by for too long.

Malcolm talked through the finances succinctly and so kindly, Bess found herself thinking how similar he was to her dad in many ways. Her dad had always listened, he'd rarely got irate, he was always looking for solutions rather than throwing his hands up in the air when things got too hard. Malcolm explained the concept of a debt consolidation loan but recommended other routes instead, given those loans came with high interest rates and might also be difficult to obtain. 'Your credit history so far, from what you tell me, isn't awful.'

Her eyebrows raised. 'It's terrible!'

'Not from what I've seen and what we've talked about. Yes, there are missed payments, late payments and a lot of only paying the minimum on your credit card each month. Believe me, it could be a whole lot worse.'

'It might have been if you weren't helping.'

'Then I'm glad I could.' He cleared his throat again, perhaps emotional rather than nervous this time. 'Now, going by your credit card statements, you haven't made a habit of frequently withdrawing cash on your cards, which doesn't build a very good credit history. I think we've caught this in time and if we get on top of it, you shouldn't have too much trouble building up your credit score again.'

Between them, they came up with a plan. They took it one step at a time, the phone red hot all afternoon as Bess sorted her finances out. She cancelled cards, secured a better deal for car insurance, reducing her monthly direct debit, she got better deals for internet and on her mobile phone, she dropped unnecessary subscriptions including extra channels on the television. She got another person on the end of the phone when she called the gym again and this time, they listened and eventually agreed to end the contract early. She and Malcolm talked about simple measures like fewer takeaways, more planning before supermarket shopping, not splashing out on holidays unless she could really afford to. He also advised using credit cards only in emergencies or when she knew she could pay off the entire balance before it incurred interest. All of these things were basic common sense, it was just that Bess had been blinkered, living in her own world for so long, she hadn't known how to do any different.

When Malcolm first sat down with her he'd asked her to find all of her physical credit cards along with their statements. She had a few. She'd been drawn in with zero interest on balance transfers and ended up with more cards than any one person should have and of course she'd soon been restricted to paying off the bare minimum and had got herself further into debt as time went on. With the money Malcolm had put into her account, Bess paid the final payment for her car, which meant she owned it now. And then one by one, she paid off the balances of her credit cards.

The whole time they were taking steps to get on top of her finances, Malcolm kept saying 'we'. *We've* caught this early, *we've* got on top of this, *we'll* get your credit score back up.

He might be a relative stranger but as she watched him diligently go through the mountain of paperwork, one thing at a time, dealing with each, it struck her that he really was a very good man. And she needed her mother to know that. She deserved to be happy. She'd lost the love of her life and nobody would ever replace him but that didn't mean she couldn't find a second love. It would just be different, that was all.

They looked at Bess's payslips next and came up with a structure for her to repay Malcolm's loan as well as the money Fiona had given her. It was very doable, if she made the changes they'd discussed and if she kept her head and changed some of her behaviours. She really wanted to, she had to, she wanted to be Bess, sensible and fun Bess, the homeowner who had a bit of an idea how the real world worked. Not the Bess who had been burying her head in the sand and living life like each day was her last.

Malcolm picked up the pile of credit cards, the stack of six pieces of plastic that had played their part in getting her into trouble. He held one apart from the rest. 'This is the only one I didn't get you to cancel. It's got the best record of payments looking through your statements, you've had it a long time and you've made more than the minimum payment several times over the last eight months. It also gets you points with your bank, which gets you vouchers. So, use it wisely and any points earned will help you too.'

'What happens with the rest?'

He went over to the knife block and pulled out the big kitchen scissors.

'I should cut them up?'

'Yes.'

'But I cancelled them all.'

'Call it symbolic.' He handed her the scissors.

And he was right. As he held up each in turn and she sliced through every one, each chop was a slice of victory at getting on top of things once and for all.

'And this one?' He held up the one remaining card they hadn't cancelled. 'This one needs to be used correctly and it'll help build up that credit history of yours again.'

She took the card. 'I can do it. I can keep that in my purse and I know after all of this, after all this panic and shame at how I've let this get out of control, that I won't be silly with it.'

Malcolm smiled. 'I believe you, girl.'

She put the credit card safely in her purse before turning back to Malcolm, who was putting all the bank statements back into the manilla folder. 'My dad would've liked you, you know.'

He closed the folder. 'I think I would've liked him too. He sounds like a wonderful man.'

He was and Bess hoped that if he was looking down on her today, he might be proud of what they'd accomplished and proud that she was letting someone new into their lives.

27

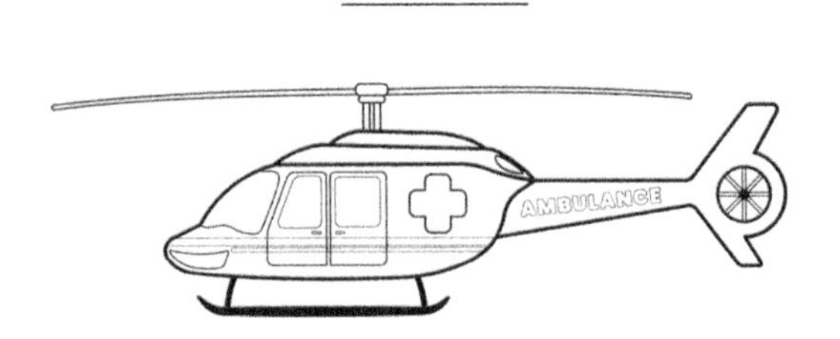

Gio came to the end of another physio session and rather than be pissed off and gung-ho in completing every exercise and every repetition more than he needed to – either to make a point or speed up his recovery – he felt as though his approach had settled.

Aysha had even commented on it as she packed her equipment away, ready to leave.

'You're in a good headspace, Gio. It's good to see. And you must have been careful enough getting to the young boy; your knee doesn't seem any worse.'

Hearing that felt good. He'd told her about the sledging: the way he'd bolted out of the house, angry with himself and the world; the way he'd come home in an entirely different mood. He knew his mood would likely dip again but for the first time, he saw that that might well be normal, that a dip was okay and he could bring himself up again. Helping Lionel seemed to have opened up a part of his soul he'd been protecting since his injury. He loved being a firefighter for a lot of reasons – the adrenaline, the physical exertion, but he also did it to help people. And he'd helped Lionel yesterday. It might not have been rescuing him from a fire, but it was a rescue nonetheless, a rescue he'd played a part in. And boy, did it feel good.

But it wasn't only Lionel; it was seeing Bess at the scene too. He'd watched her attend to the patient, he'd seen her concentration, her skilled approach, all the while thinking about the look on her face when she realised he wasn't the victim. Her reaction showed she cared and that had done more for him than he'd ever thought possible.

Since the night at the pub, he'd been worrying about his mum, but he'd also felt a part of his sympathy going to Bess after she told him the whole truth about why she got so wasted. He'd gone over to her house to make sure she knew how serious this was with Marianne, that he didn't want her to have a slip and start drinking again. But he'd left discombobulated because watching Bess struggle to tell him what she'd been hiding, the mess she'd got herself into, he'd realised he wasn't only worried about his mum; he was worried about her. And that meant he was falling for her on a much deeper level than simply finding her attractive and wanting to take her out to dinner. And it was scary. He didn't do relationships. He asked women out; they never lasted very long – sometimes they ended it or he did when it ran its course. He got the feeling that if Bess ever let him take her out on a date, it would work very differently for both of them.

Gio had only just closed the door on Aysha when his phone chimed with an incoming FaceTime call. It was his brother.

'You're smiling,' Marco noted. He'd been busy for a couple of days with work, the kids, and the last contact Gio had had was a brief text to say they'd talk soon. And that had been in response to a rather long rant via voice message.

'What's wrong with that?'

'Going by your voice message the other day, I expected you to be crying. Good to see you're accepting the doctor's appointment for what it was – not great but not shite either.'

'You've such a way with words.'

'Look, it wasn't a flat out no about ever returning to full duties, and sometimes that is the case.'

'So I should count myself lucky?'

'You're allowed to be angry, frustrated, but try to keep positive as well.'

'I'm trying, but it's hard sometimes.'

'I know.'

The fact he did the same job made Gio feel more like he was missing out on some days when he heard his brother talk about the fire station, a shout they'd been on. But on the flip side, Marco understood his pain better than anyone, even the doctors. Marco understood what Gio's job meant to him.

Gio recapped on the sledging incident, the rescue of the young boy.

'How did it feel?' Marco asked.

'Bloody fantastic to be outside in the fresh air.'

'I didn't mean that, I meant helping the young boy.'

'Why do you think I'm not moaning so much right now? It felt good to help, good to not feel entirely useless.'

'So dramatic,' Marco laughed.

'What if I'm confined to a desk forever? I'm not sure I could take it.'

'Like I said... dramatic.' But the ribbing didn't last. 'Remember when I broke my arm and was on desk duty for a month?'

'I'd forgotten. I bet you hated it.'

'Of course I did. I'm not gonna lie. I was bored out of my skull.'

'Not helping me, bro. Did you call hoping to cheer me up?'

'I called to tell you to buck up. Grow a pair. Whatever.'

He knew he had to, but knowing he should and actually doing it were different things.

'I did admin when I was desk bound,' Marco went on. 'But there are other things. Training new recruits, for a start. One of the crew here had an op on his ankle; he's part of the recruitment and training process now.'

'Watching other guys gear up to do the job I want to do is hardly therapy,' Gio grumbled.

Marco didn't speak straight away, but when he did, he told it how he saw it. 'Gio, you can either feel sorry for yourself and become that guy that is so miserable, nobody wants to be around him or you can find a distraction for a while. Sounds like you did that yesterday. I wouldn't recommend hurling yourself down any more steep inclines on a sledge but sitting at home all day every day will drive you batshit crazy.'

They talked for almost an hour. Gio tentatively brought Marianne into the conversation threads, despite Marco's reservations about trusting her again. And by the time he ended the call to answer the door, Gio had to admit that he was beginning to see the light, albeit one that wasn't quite glowing yet.

And his mood improved another notch when he found Bess standing on his doorstep.

'Come in.' He almost leapt in to ask whether this was about Marianne, but he held off.

'I'm here to collect an iPad. Does that make sense?'

'Oh, yes, I'll go grab it.' It was in the kitchen with its charger and he brought it through to Bess. 'I got her a reconditioned one; her phone is basic rather than a smartphone so this will be good for her. She insists on paying for it but please remind her there's no rush.'

'She'll want to pay for it; it gives her a sense of achievement.'

He smiled. 'I like that she tells you things.'

'She's been really good to talk to about my own problems.'

'I'm glad.'

'You are?'

'Of course. And being at your place has been good for her.' He didn't miss the relief on her face. 'I mean it.'

'She's working very hard, picking up extra shifts.'

'She's a new woman.' He put a finger against his own forehead. 'You've got a bit of dirt right here.' He hadn't noticed it until she hooked her hair off her face and behind her ear.

She swiped at it with her hand, rubbed until he let her know it had all gone. 'Thought I'd got it all. I've been helping a couple of the elderly residents on my street, dragging Christmas trees outside and I caught my hair in the branches more than once.'

He reached out and pulled another pine needle from her tumble of curls, almost hoping he'd see another and another. 'Here.' He handed her the iPad. 'Thanks for collecting it.' He was glad to see her. Any time.

'I needed the walk. I'm no longer a member of the gym on account of saving money so it's pounding the pavements for me from now on.' She registered him standing there, the way he'd gone out to the kitchen. 'You're walking without a stick.'

'Only short distances for now. My physio just left and I'm progressing well.' He gestured to the lounge. 'Can you stay a while? I can make us a coffee?'

'I can't today, got a few chores to do and then I'm on the late shift. And then tomorrow, it's the Christmas tree collection day so all hands on deck.'

Even from the confines of his hallway, they didn't miss the sound of a helicopter flying overhead. 'You're wondering who that is and where they're going?' he said.

'Don't you do the same when you see or hear a fire engine?'

'Guilty. I think it's in our nature, isn't it, to want to leap in and help? And on the hardest of jobs, when we achieve an unexpected positive outcome, that's the best feeling ever.' He was losing himself in his own thoughts, his own passions now.

'I'm sorry if you thought I was being nosy, by the way, when I mentioned Norm's comment about your doctor's visit.'

He wished they were having this conversation over coffee, that she could hang around. 'Please don't apologise. There's no need.' And it was nice that she cared.

'You seem positive today, though.'

'I am, mostly. I really want to get back to work but I'm in a good headspace. And if I'm not going to go back to climbing ladders, I'll have to think of something else.'

'Good for you.'

'What would you do? If you couldn't be a critical care paramedic?'

She thought about it. 'Bitch, moan, scream.'

That had him chuckling. 'Sounds like me.'

'I'd have to think of something else that involved helping people. I'd need the interaction, even if I couldn't quite do the same job. I'd miss it too much, I think. What about you? Is there anything else you'd think about doing?'

'I've no idea what else is out there. I'm going to have to consider my options in the next month or so, as I get more mobile. I can already see me going stir crazy without a focus.'

Although he could focus on her. That might make the time more bearable.

'Did you get any further sorting your finances out?' he asked, before grunting. 'Sorry, nosy bugger, tell me to mind my own business.'

'It's fine, I don't mind you asking; I did offload a lot on you. And actually, Mum's boyfriend has been a big help.'

'Really?'

'Really.'

She filled him in on how Malcolm had turned up out of the blue, lent her some money, how they'd sat down and hashed out a plan for her to get on top of things.

'He sounds like a decent bloke.'

'He is. He has a good heart and Mum seems really happy.'

He hadn't mistaken it, had he? The atmosphere between them… heated, with a pulse. It was difficult not to reach out and pull her towards him. Was she thinking that maybe they could find their own happy, with each other?

'Are you sure you can't stay?' he asked again.

She hesitated but only briefly. 'I have to go.' She held the iPad up. 'I'll give this to your mum.'

He leaned against the door jamb when she stepped outside but soon stood straight again, conscious of not assuming his knee was totally normal. He'd reached the stage where despite any discomfort, sometimes he could forget. It was as if the negativity at the doctor's office that day had made him let go of the ferocity with which he was pushing his recovery and as a result, he'd actually begun to move further.

'Can I help with the tree drive?' he asked quickly before she could leave him to it. He didn't want her to go. He enjoyed her company too much.

Her gaze fell to his knee but rather than an outright no, she said, 'You sure?'

'I can give it a go. Take me with you, we'll see how I am, I can always hobble off if it's too hard. Call it a different sort of physio session, if you like.'

'You're on.' She gave him a time to be at the airbase. 'But you tell me the minute your knee gives you trouble.' She held up a warning finger when his facial expression must have given away that he had absolutely no intention of doing that. 'I mean it, Gio.'

'On one condition. You finally agree to letting me take you to dinner.'

She looked surprised.

'Is that a yes?' he asked when she said nothing. 'Actually, don't answer me now, but promise me you'll think about it.'

She grinned, nodded and as she walked away, told him, 'I'll see you at 10 a.m. sharp.'

It wasn't a date, but it was a start. She'd admitted she'd worried about him, she cared, and now she was letting him in that little bit more. Plus, she hadn't turned him down flat at the suggestion of dinner either.

And it was the best feeling ever.

28

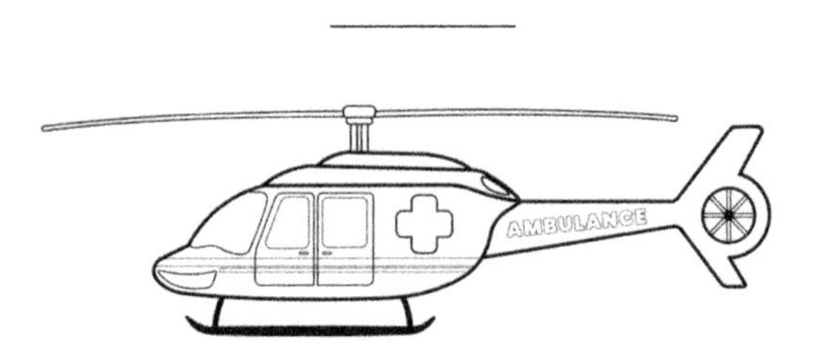

Bess walked to her mum's after delivering the iPad to Marianne. She was sure she was still smiling from Gio's company when she arrived for coffee and cake.

With Malcolm happily watching an overseas cricket match on the television in the lounge, Bess and her mum sat in the kitchen with their second slice of lemon drizzle each.

'You and Nadia could take on the world with your baking, you know,' Bess said.

'You need your sustenance for work later and the tree drive tomorrow. I can't believe how many people have their trees ready and waiting on the grass verge. I hope you've raised lots of money.'

'People have given very generously this year.'

'I am glad. I don't think a lot of people realise that the air ambulance isn't funded by the government – you need the generosity of the community.'

'We sure do and we've raised a few thousand pounds already.' Bess licked her fingers when she finished her piece of the soft, moist cake. 'Does Malcolm really not want a second slice? I'll take it to him if you like.'

'He's not got as sweet a tooth as me, love. He's all right with the cricket and the roaring fire.' They shared a giggle when they heard him cheer at the match from behind the closed door.

'The snow has almost melted.' Bess looked beyond the patio doors and into the garden.

'It'll be spring before we know it.'

Bess hooked her fingers into the handle of her mug of tea. 'Malcolm is nice, Mum. Really nice. I like him a lot.'

The brightness of her mum's smile said it all. She'd found a different and unexpected kind of happy and it meant a lot to have her daughter's endorsement. 'He likes you too, love. I'm glad you're giving him a chance.'

'I still can't believe he lent me money. I promise you, I won't let him or you down.'

'We both know that, love.'

Bess chose her words carefully. 'The way I was with Malcolm when we first met had less to do with him and everything to do with me.'

Fiona smiled kindly. 'I know. It's because of your dad; he's a tough act to follow.'

'He's a different act, Mum.'

'Yes, I suppose he is.'

'And he's similar in a few ways.'

'The financial expertise.'

'Not just that – the calm demeanour, his approach and the way he deals with the practical rather than flapping in a panic.'

'Like me,' said Fiona. 'You're like your dad, calm in a crisis, which is how you do your job.'

'I think I've got a bit of you in me too.' She'd certainly not handled her financial predicament so well. 'I'm glad you found Malcolm. I wanted you to know that.'

'I'm glad I found him too. I never thought I'd meet another man, let alone one who I wanted to spend so much time with.'

'Neither did I, and because I know you and Dad fell in love straight away, it was hard for me to see you with anyone else.'

Fiona's eyes twinkled. 'It was never that quick, your dad and me. I went out with him after a friend set us up. He ticked a lot of boxes – handsome, he made me laugh, but he was a bit too serious for my liking. I almost didn't go on a second date. But I did and after we'd been out four or five times, that was when I really began to fall for him.'

'So, it wasn't love at first sight?'

'Not at all. He took a while to grow on me and vice versa. I think that thunderbolt and lightning feeling happens sometimes but not always. It takes a while to get to know what a person is like beneath the surface. Those, Bess, are the most interesting layers of all.'

She thought about Gio, what her impressions of him had been only a few short months ago. They were vastly different to how she saw him now.

Fiona glanced over to the picture of the both of them. 'I think your dad and I were the yin to each other's yang or whatever the expression is. I was a throw-caution-to the-wind type of girl; he was one to keep his feet firmly on the ground. And somehow, it worked.'

She looked away from the picture and back to Bess. 'With Malcolm, it's different but it's a good different.'

Bess set her mug down after a warming mouthful of tea. 'I mean it when I say how happy I am for you, Mum. And he was so good to me the day he came over to my house and we sorted out my finances. Thanks to you and to him, I feel like I'm going to get on top of things once and for all. Overtime is my friend now; Marianne is staying a few extra months thanks to her job going so well and the fact we seem to get on living under the same roof.'

'It sounds as though everything is working out.' But she studied her daughter. 'What else is there, Bess?'

For the first time, Bess knew she was going to get all of this out in the open. 'When Dad died, I was really angry.' She hadn't wanted to share this part of her grief, she didn't want her mum to have to manage her feelings as well as her own, but she'd hidden it for too long. 'Angry for him because he was so careful financially but not just that, angry because I wasn't there. I couldn't save him. With all my training, my knowledge, I wasn't there.'

'Oh, love. No, you weren't. But you can't be angry about that.'

'I know, it seems irrational, but I am.'

'I suppose I can understand why but you need to let that go.'

'I know, it's just... well, I carry the frustration to this day if I let myself think about it. I sometimes dream about it, you know, that I'm saving him, that I resuscitate him and everything is okay. Then I wake up and realise it isn't.'

Her mum hugged her close. 'That must be incredibly hard. I have the dreams too, that he's around. It drains me when it happens.'

She wasn't sure whether that made her feel better or worse.

'Why didn't you ever tell me that this was how you were feeling, Bess?'

'I didn't want to make it harder for you in any way.'

'But it wouldn't have. I knew you had some sort of barrier up, that you weren't telling me everything. I wish you had. You don't always have to be the strong one.'

'I know that now. But I wanted to protect you from having to support me as well as yourself.'

'I'm your mum.'

And when Malcolm unleashed an even louder cheer from the lounge, they both began to laugh.

'I'm happy for you, Mum.' Bess nodded in the direction of the closed door behind which her mother's new boyfriend was sitting, part of their lives now.

'I'm happy for me too. And thank you, that means the world.' She held onto Bess a little longer. 'What about a happy ending for you, Bess?'

'For me?'

Fiona began to smile. 'I've heard you talk about your lodger, or more importantly about her son.'

'Gio? We're just friends.'

'You've been friends a long time.'

'I don't want anything to spoil that.'

'But you want more.'

'It's not that simple, Mum.'

Her mum squeezed her a little tighter, excitedly. 'Take a chance, Bess. That keyring you have, the one that says, *Live each day as if it's your last*? That doesn't only apply to holidays, spending, new things. It applies to love as well. And love is one thing that it's worth taking a risk for. Please believe me when I say that.'

'You make it sound easy.'

'It's never easy. Dating is hard at whatever age. You meet some people you wish you'd never taken a chance on. Oh, but when you meet someone who's worth it, as I suspect Gio is, or you wouldn't be tying yourself in knots over him, it's well and truly worth it.'

Bess cuddled her mum. So right about so many things.

Was there a chance she was right about this?

Was it time to take a chance on Gio?

29

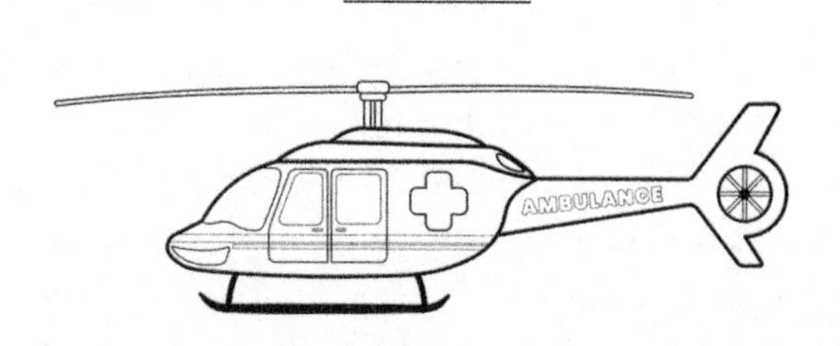

Gio got a taxi to the airbase for 10 a.m. sharp and found Bess in reception in her civvy clothes. He walked up behind her as she ran her eyes down a list attached to a clipboard.

'Reporting for duty,' he said.

She turned and met him with that beautiful smile. 'You came.'

'Of course.'

He liked the way she got a bit flustered; it reminded him of how things with Bess had evolved over recent months.

'Is that the list of collections?' he asked.

'Part of it.' She showed him the clipboard and the list with familiar street names around town.

'It's just the two of us?'

'For now.'

He wasn't at all sorry about that.

'We've got about a third of the addresses on this list. I'll drive the pick-up truck and we'll fit as many trees in as we can before we come back here and pass them on to be put through the shredder. The shredded trees will be taken to the garden centre and they'll repurpose in whatever way they see fit.' She handed him a pair of heavy-duty gloves. 'You'll need these.'

'I'm not a pansy. I can get my hands dirty.'

'We did this last year and believe me, you'll start off okay and then you'll wish you'd protected your skin.'

He relented, took the gloves. He hadn't brought his walking stick as he was starting to get used to moving around without it. It was an odd feeling after all this time.

She led the way outside and over to the pick-up truck and they left the airbase driving at the requisite 15 mph, making their way to the first address.

Gio looked up into the skies above, the weather still keeping them guessing from day to day as to what was coming next. 'Do you think it'll snow again?'

'Who knows? The snow we've had was quite the event.'

'School kids loved it.'

She pulled a face when she crunched the gears, unfamiliar with the truck.

'I wouldn't mind seeing some more,' he said. 'It always reminds me that seasons change, that we change, that nothing is static.'

'Since when did you think so deeply?'

'I think we all know the answer to that one.' The day of his accident changed things for Gio, at least in the short term and maybe even in the long term – perhaps physically and for sure mentally. Setbacks that stopped you doing the job you wanted to do would affect the toughest of people.

'So,' he said when she apologised for bunny hopping out of the junction. 'Rather than talk about how bad a driver you are with this—'

'Hey, new vehicle. Give me ten minutes and it'll be a smooth ride.'

'I've every faith it will be.'

'Appreciate the vote of confidence,' she said when she pulled out of the next junction without fault.

'So when should we go for this dinner?'

'You don't give up.' But if he wasn't mistaken, she didn't mind the question. It was progress.

'Nope. I'll keep asking.'

She jerked the truck out of the next T-junction. 'You've never been serious about anyone before; you're one of the lads. I'm not really up for just a bit of fun.'

'You want to marry me?'

She burst out laughing, the sound music to his ears. 'What on earth would you do if I said yes?'

'Probably run a mile. Or at least as far as I could run with a compromised knee.'

She pulled into their first street and parked up. 'It's complicated.'

'What's life without a little complication?' His eyes darted to her lips and then away when she clocked him staring. 'I get it. You're not interested in me because I'm an invalid.'

She got out of the truck. 'Gio Mayhan, you do talk some crap.'

Gio pulled on his gloves and took it easy dragging trees from their dumping ground back to the truck. Dragging wasn't so hard; a lot of the trees were under six foot and not particularly bushy. Between them, they lifted and loaded, but by the end of the next street, knowing they only had enough room to collect one more lot after this, he was relieved as he knew it would be the best thing for his knee if he soon gave it a rest.

'Okay, I know it's not that you think I'm an invalid,' he said when they both climbed back into the truck to head for the next street along. 'But you can't blame me for trying. And I think you think you know me but you don't really.'

She didn't say anything until she'd parked up again when she turned to face him. 'I've been dating longer than I care to admit even to myself, Gio. I'm not after a fling; I've had my time with those. I've been dating to try to find someone I connect with, but it hasn't happened, and I don't know whether it ever will.'

'You're dating the wrong guys.'

'Maybe.'

'We connect, don't we?'

Her silence told him she knew they did.

He wanted to keep her in the warmth of the vehicle a while longer. 'Why haven't things worked out with anyone you've dated, can you tell me that?'

'All I can tell you is that they weren't the *right* guys. I think I'd know when I met someone who was.'

'And I'm definitely not?' he ventured.

She hopped out of the truck and looked back once. 'You don't do serious, Gio.'

They collected the remaining trees and once the truck was loaded up and full, he stopped her from starting the engine just yet. If he didn't ask these questions now, he might not get the opportunity again.

'I haven't done serious,' he told her, 'but it doesn't mean I couldn't, if the right person came along.'

'I have this ideal,' she began hesitantly, 'and it's my own fault. I look at my parents' marriage and that's what I want, a soulmate, someone who will be there for me and whose side I will stand by no matter what.'

'You want the same instant fireworks they had?'

She wasn't watching him but he saw the glimmer of a smile. 'Actually, as it turns out, that wasn't exactly how it went for Mum and Dad. Their relationship was slow to develop; it took a while for them to get to know each other.'

'Has knowing that fact changed the way you think?' *Please say yes.*

'Maybe.'

As she switched on the engine and pulled away from the kerb, he knew that if he was ever going to get her to agree to go to dinner with him, he'd have to be honest about his own history. 'You're right, I've only ever had flings over the years. It's because I'm cautious about dating.' He quickly added, 'Don't laugh,' before she could do just that. 'I've always been one of the lads, loving life and my job, dating when I felt like it, not getting tied down, moving on when I needed to. But in the same way you think your parents' relationship is the ideal you're striving for, my parents' marriage is what I'm desperate to avoid. You know that my dad found someone else.'

'I do.' She risked a look at him before setting her focus back on the road.

'After that, my mum became a drunk, a bad parent. And I'm terrified that I could take after either one of them. That feeling has made me hold back over the years.'

'You're your own person, Gio.' She was concentrating too much to be able to look at him. 'You have control over who you are.'

'I do, but I've always wondered whether it will creep up on me, that I'll become one of them or a mixture of both. Don't get me wrong, Dad wasn't terrible when we were young but walking out on a family for someone else? That's unforgivable. And he broke Mum's heart. When he first left, she was overwhelmed, doing her best, but it wasn't long before she lost her part-time job because she'd taken so many sick days. The drinking happened slowly, I don't know for sure when it started to get out of hand, but the longer she went not able to get work, the more she drank and then she found herself in a place she couldn't claw her way out of.'

'For what it's worth, she's a pleasure to be around now, vehement about never drinking again. But at the same time, aware of temptation and risk.'

'She never was before. She wouldn't admit to her problem either; she went to AA a handful of times but it was never a part of her routine. I think she thought she'd go to a couple of sessions and she'd be done.'

'She always comes back from those sessions calm and happy.'

That pleased him. 'I forget you're getting to know her. I'm glad she isn't a terrible lodger; I'd have been mortified pushing her on you.'

'Well, no need to worry. It's all good. From both of our perspectives.'

'When Marco got married and had kids, I wavered. I thought maybe I could be happy too and not turn out like either of my parents. But I never met the right person.' He waited for her to take her eyes off the road for just a second and when she did, told her, 'Until now.'

And when she reached across to hold his hand as she drove, neither of them saying a word for the rest of the journey to the airbase, he got the feeling that she was beginning to understand how deep his feelings ran, how different he was to the man he'd been over the years. Was she finally beginning to understand that if commitment was what she was looking for then she might just find it with him?

30

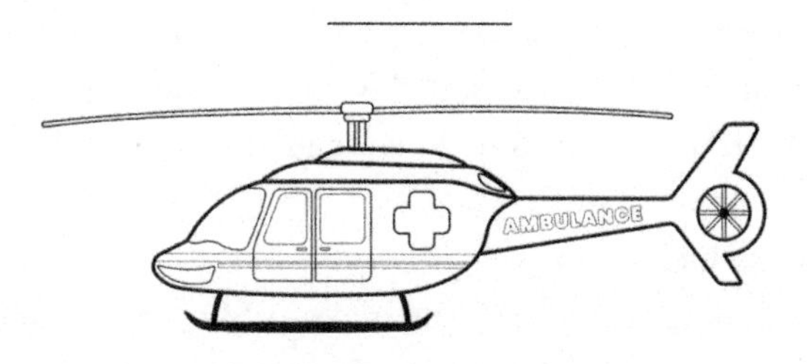

Bess parked around the back, adjacent to the helipad with the shredder set up on the other side for them, and climbed out.

She felt Gio come closer to her as she dropped the tailgate and they got ready to haul the trees across to meet their maker. She'd dropped his hand as she pulled into the airbase but she hadn't wanted to. She'd wanted to continue their conversation, to tell him that she believed him, to admit she wanted to give this a go as much as he did.

But right now, they had work to do.

The blue team were on duty today so the red team were free to do this part of the fundraising drive, but she couldn't help but be curious when she heard the phones ring – there was an outside ring to allow for calls to be heard wherever you were at the base – and Vik came out to start up the helicopter.

'You're itching to know what the job is.' Gio had got it in one. He'd probably seen her looking over at Hilda.

'Be quiet and take the other end of the tree when I drag it out.' She liked the way they could go from weighty conversation to inconsequential banter so smoothly.

'You get nervous that I know things about you.'

And now they were back to a more personal focus, but she let his teasing go. He was behind her as they walked the tree over to the guy in charge of the shredder and handed over the first tree before going back to get the next.

Once all the trees had been transferred, Bess picked up on Gio's discomfort – his pace had slowed and every now and then she noticed him wince. 'Your knee is giving you jip. Don't even think about denying it.'

'It's not so bad.'

She pulled out the keys to the pick-up. She wasn't going to let Gio try to prove himself because that's what she suspected he was about to do.

'What's going on?' Hudson was bringing out coffee for the guys at the shredding machine.

'Hero here is suffering,' she said, much to Gio's frustration.

Hudson didn't give Gio a chance to argue; he simply thrust the two cups of coffee forward and Gio took them on reflex. 'I'll help Bess. You take those to the workers, then get yourself inside. Sit down in there, take the weight off that leg of yours and eat something. Let's go, Bess.'

She grinned at Gio. 'Can't argue with that.'

'I suppose not.'

'Save me a scone?'

'After you dump me for another guy?' he called out after her.

Bess laughed and she and Hudson jumped back into the pick-up for Bess's final round before Noah and Maya would take over.

She wouldn't be telling Gio, but Hudson was twice as quick and they were back in no time, all the trees over at the chipper at record speed.

'Thanks, Hudson. Appreciate the help.'

'I appreciate the escape.'

'The kids hard work at the moment?' She'd heard murmurings of it between Hudson and Nadia. Nadia was the mother hen of the team and always ready to listen to problems, work-related or personal.

'Something like that.'

She looked for Gio in the hangar, expecting him to have waited for her, but there was no sign of him.

She went through the hangar and into the main building and spotted him beyond the doors of reception out front.

She went outside and walked up behind him. 'It's freezing; why are you standing out here?'

The snow had started to fall in earnest even in the short time it had taken her to come from the back of the building to the front and when she saw the look on his face, she knew this was why he was braving the cold.

Bess, still wearing her big jacket, was warm enough. 'Did you save me a scone?'

He laughed. 'Nadia made enough for the whole town; you don't need to worry.'

She was about to say she'd go and get one, a cup of tea too to warm herself up. But she didn't want to leave his side.

'I thought of something else I can do,' he said, facing her. 'In case I never get back to full duties.'

'Really?'

'I could study to become a fire investigator. I've looked into courses and I think it's something that wouldn't bore me to tears. A job like that would involve working out the origins of a fire – whether it was arson, how it could've been prevented perhaps. It would keep me closer to the action than anything else.'

'That sounds great.' And it was good to hear him so positive. She wanted to reach for his hand again but felt suddenly nervous. Their friendship had lasted for years, she valued it too much to risk it, but the things he'd told her on the tree drive that morning had her realise he was as worried about being able to make this work as she was.

He looked up into the skies as the snow fell over them, its white flakes scattered in his hair the same way they were likely in hers. 'I could stand out here forever in this.'

'I couldn't; it's way too cold.'

'What about if I refuse to come in until you say yes to going out with me for dinner?' It was a Gio-like remark full of intent but at the same time, she knew his feelings ran as deep as hers.

'Then I'd say that's very childish.' She grinned. 'Are you sure you want this? I meant it when I said I'm not looking for a fling. If things don't work then that's one thing, but I want to go into this with eyes open and I want you to as well. If you're not up for trying to make this work, if we'll go on a few dates and you'll get bored, then please tell me now.'

'Bess, I—'

'I mean it, Gio. Don't string me along.' She blinked away a snowflake that landed on her lashes. 'I'm not up for that. If I'm honest, I've liked you for a lot longer than I realised. In the shared house, I thought it was a crush, but when we danced at the wedding and I suggested you come here, it wasn't only because of our friendship.' She gulped. 'Did you feel anything for me when we danced together?'

'I—'

'Do you think you're capable of giving us a shot?'

She didn't get another word out because with his hands either side of her face, he didn't waste any time pressing his lips against hers, tentatively at first, and then giving it his all.

When he pulled back, her face still in his hands, he said, 'If you let me get a word in, I'd tell you that I'm all in with this; I don't want it to be a fling. I've wanted you since the day you moved into the shared house when I helped you pick up the contents of the cardboard box which gave way because you'd packed too much in it.'

'I'm not the best at packing.' She loved feeling his hands against her cheeks, the closeness of his face to hers, the feeling that this might just be the start of something wonderful.

'No, you're not. You're terrible.'

She laughed and then shivered despite her layers.

He opened up his jacket and pulled her against his body, wrapping it around her too.

'So, dinner,' he said, a statement this time, not a question. 'Tonight, somewhere with a view.'

'Okay.'

He hugged her tightly and whispered into her hair. 'I knew you'd see sense eventually.'

'Oh you did, did you?'

'We were predestined to happen. Friends first – good friends – but the universe always had something else in mind for us. I think you and I were written in the stars.'

She looked up at him. 'That sounds a bit deep for you. And a bit cheesy.'

He laughed softly. 'I told you before, not working has given me a lot of time to think.' His hands tangled in her hair and he looked into her eyes. 'I've wanted to ask you out for ages. Never mind everything else I've wanted to do.'

'I've wanted it for a long time too.'

He kissed her again and they only pulled apart when they heard the beep of the pick-up truck as it passed them with another load, this time Hudson leaning out of the window with a cheeky comment.

'About time!' Hudson called over with a wave.

'I'd say he's spot on,' said Gio.

Bess no longer felt the cold, only the moment and the magic as the snow continued to fall. She couldn't speak when he reached out and put a hand against her curls as if he was trying to tangle himself up in her.

'I'm a lot more together than I ever was, Bess. And so are you. I'm ready for this. For us.'

'I'm ready too.' She felt his hand in her hair before it edged down to the nape of her neck and made her shiver. The feeling was so powerful, she couldn't say anything else.

And she didn't need to because he was kissing her again and she knew now that she never wanted him to stop.

31

ONE MONTH LATER

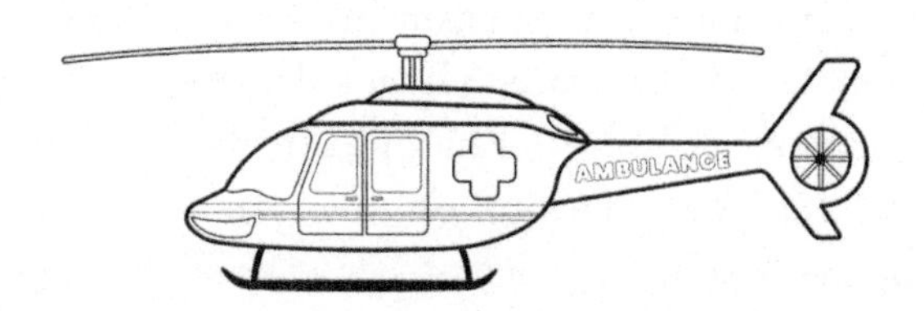

Winter was still putting in an appearance but today, it came with clear, blue skies and sunshine rather than the rain they'd had over the last few days, and the appearance of the first snowdrops in Wildacre Meadow. Bess had made good on her promise to pay regular instalments to her mum and to Malcolm and although she'd only just started, slowly but surely, she was seeing her debt decrease. And she wasn't adding to it, more to the point, which made her proud. She knew if her dad were here, he'd be feeling the same way. She missed him incredibly, she always would, but she was getting to know Malcolm more and more and it was hard to imagine not having him in their lives now. He made her mother so very happy.

A couple of weeks ago, Bess had gone for an appointment to have a routine breast screening. She always got nervous beforehand and this time, Gio had wanted to go with her.

'This is something I need to do on my own,' she'd told him. The checks had become less frequent as time went on and she hoped this one would come back as clear too but couldn't help being reminded of the day she'd found the lump, the days of worry that came after it and sent her world into a spin. And things with her and Gio were new; she didn't want this to be a part of the beginning of their relationship, not unless it needed to be.

The results had come back this morning and, apart from her mum, Gio had been the first person she'd wanted to tell. She'd come straight here to his place to let him know she'd been given the all-clear again. It hadn't taken long for them to tumble into bed and with a family meet-up on the cards in an hour, Bess finished up in the shower, pulled on her jeans and her pale-blue, roll-neck jumper.

Sitting on the bed, Gio reached out and tugged at the waistband of her jeans to draw her closer. 'I want to see my brother and his family but I'd rather stay here.' He lifted her jumper and planted a kiss near her belly button, right on the dolphin tattoo.

'Tempting, but we have to be there.'

He groaned.

'Your mum is nervous; I think it worked out well that I came over here, gave her a chance to get ready and get her head together.'

Gio pulled on his jeans and a charcoal jumper. Coffee and cake at a café meant he didn't need to dress up. It was a family-friendly, no-frills place, a venue where the kids could be kids and Marianne wouldn't feel too much pressure.

Gio was progressing every day. Now, it seemed that rather than suggesting that a return to the job he loved might not happen, even the doctors had begun to almost say – although they never categorically would – that he was likely to be able to return to full duties if he carried on this upward trajectory. He'd been determined throughout, pushed it when he needed to, taken it easy when that was required. He'd attributed a lot of it to Bess's bossiness and she didn't mind that at all.

When Gio and Bess picked her up, Marianne was no less nervous than she'd been when Bess left the house earlier. Her hands clutched her bag and she was quiet in the passenger seat as they made their way to the café. Gio and Bess tried to keep conversation going but they all did a deep intake of breath when they pulled up in the car park and saw Marco, Saffy and the kids climbing out of their vehicle.

'Do I look all right?' Marianne's voice shook. She didn't move from the passenger seat.

Gio waved to his brother and while he made his way over, Bess climbed out of the car and opened up Marianne's door. She held out her hand. 'You look wonderful. You can do this.'

Gio was already hugging his brother and then he moved on to Saffy before picking up Matilda. Bess could hear Billy asking for his turn as they walked over.

'Hello, Mum.' Marco's gaze had been fixed on Marianne ever since she got out of the car; Bess had been watching him.

Bess felt protective over her lodger, even though that wasn't her right. This meet-up had been a long time coming after Marco came down with a winter bug, as did the kids, and then Saffy had a family emergency with her parents. Marianne had seen for herself over FaceTime that things with Marco's family were tough during the rest of January, she hadn't assumed he was making excuses, and it had given them all a bit of extra time to work up to this day.

'Thank you for coming.' Marianne stopped a few steps in front of her eldest son.

And Marco opened his arms.

Marianne took a step closer, froze, but then closed the gap fully and fell against him.

Gio scooped Billy up now he'd set Matilda down and Bess introduced herself to Saffy and Matilda.

'Shall we get the kids settled inside out of the cold?' Saffy suggested. 'Maybe give them a moment,' she said just to Bess, nodding in the direction of Marianne and Marco.

Gio had already had the same idea and headed for the café and when they caught him and Billy up, he sneaked a look back at his mother and his brother, who were still hugging.

They settled the kids inside and they were given crayons and pads of paper straight away, which Saffy expressed her relief about. But when their grandma came inside, they immediately latched on to her, wanting her to help them draw. An argument nearly erupted as they fought about who got to have Marianne's attentions first so Bess stepped in with Matilda and it seemed to save the day. She felt Gio reach beneath the table to give her knee a squeeze.

After cake and two rounds of coffee for the adults, more paper for the kids to doodle on, Bess and Gio walked with Saffy and the kids to the local park so they could run off some energy. They didn't seem to care that it was freezing cold and it also gave Marco and Marianne a chance to have some time alone.

As the kids played and Saffy policed their time on the seesaw, Gio sat at the picnic bench next to Bess.

'Today has gone really well,' said Bess. To onlookers, they might have seemed like one big, happy family despite the trust that needed to be re-established. And Bess loved that she was a part of it all.

'It has. Starting with your good news.' He leaned across and placed a kiss on her temple, his lips warming her up. 'And the kids love Mum as much as they ever did; I don't think they're too scarred from her past behaviour.'

'I'm glad.'

Marco, Saffy and the kids were staying in a hotel for a couple of days but Marianne hadn't mentioned what she wanted to happen later. Perhaps she was waiting for the right moment.

Gio had his elbows resting on the tabletop behind them as they watched Billy and Matilda. Soon after he and Bess had got together, they'd talked about kids, whether either of them saw children in their future. Bess had admitted that when she was still in her thirties, she'd realised that every birthday, every time she turned another year older, the possibility was slipping further away. And she'd said that now she was in her forties, it was even more unlikely to happen.

'I love these two,' Gio admitted as they watched the kids play now.

'They're pretty amazing.'

He put an arm around her shoulders and pulled her in close. 'We could give it a try. If it happens, it happens. If it doesn't then it'll be just us two.'

She loved that he'd whispered those words in her ear. It showed her even more – not that he hadn't told her umpteen times how much he loved her and was glad they'd found their way to each other as more than friends – that he was all in when it came to their relationship.

'We might be too old, Gio.'

'Yeah, geriatrics, me and you.'

She grinned. 'It might be too soon. We only just started dating.'

'But we've known each other for years.'

'True.' She loved that she was discovering a new side to this man she'd always valued being in her life. 'How about we think about it?'

'I'm okay with that. And the practice we'll need to do, obviously.'

'Obviously.' She grinned.

'Uncle Gio, come on the roundabout!' Matilda called over.

'Auntie Bess, can you push me on the swings?' Billy shouted.

Gio and Bess looked at each other and as they went to their respective duties, Gio climbing on to the roundabout, Bess laughed, 'Maybe these two will be plenty.'

She went to the swings and Gio bellowed over to her in reply, 'I think you've got a point.' He looked like he was feeling a bit rough already, whatever he'd eaten and drunk likely churning around as his niece pushed the roundabout, her little legs going as fast as they could as she gave her uncle an experience he wasn't likely to forget in a hurry.

Marco, Saffy, Matilda and Billy came back to Bess's place. Marianne had made chocolate chip cookies for the kids and when she revealed that she wanted to cook a Christmas dinner for them all this evening despite it being well and truly past the festive season, the suggestion was met with a resounding yes. Billy and Matilda wanted to help with the preparations, Bess assured Marianne she was on hand if needed, Saffy said she'd do anything she could to help out too.

As Bess and Gio left the others in the kitchen, they overheard Marco invite Marianne down to their house in a couple of weeks.

Bess snuggled next to Gio on the sofa. 'This is nice, all of you together.'

'Yeah, it really is.' She heard a catch in his voice, the sign of emotion she wasn't going to push him to explain because she knew how big this moment had been for all of them.

The kitchen door opened, Marianne came through briefly, ran upstairs and returned with an inky-blue woollen dress.

'What's going on?' Gio asked.

'Never you mind, I want to show this to Saffy.' She disappeared with the dress and closed the door behind her.

'She's hiding something,' said Gio but for once, his voice didn't imply he was worried at all.

'She bought the dress for a special occasion,' said Bess.

'What sort of special occasion?'

Bess turned to him. 'Don't freak out... She has a date.'

'A date?'

'With Frank.' She hoped he wasn't going to find this difficult to handle. His mother needed his support and approval. Bess knew that if she didn't get it, Marianne would likely cancel and that would be a shame.

'Who's Frank?' Gio asked.

'Frank, who works with The Skylarks,' said Bess. 'He's a good man. You don't need to worry.'

'I'm not.'

'Liar.'

'You think it's a good idea?'

'I do.' Perhaps some background might help. 'They met one evening in town, after one of her meetings; they seemed to hit it off. They've been for coffee, chatted a lot, but this is their first official date. She's nervous, more about what you and Marco will think than anything else.'

He fixed his gaze on Bess. 'Should I be worried?'

'I don't think so. I can't guarantee it but my gut feeling is that this is a good thing. Frank is a lovely man, he's had his fair share of heartache, I've no doubt he'll do right by your mum.'

'I need to talk to her.'

But Bess leapt up when he did and pulled him back towards the sofa. 'Leave it for now; there's plenty of time to do that.'

When he sat down, Bess sat on his lap to stop him attempting to get up again.

'This is highly inappropriate with kids in the house, you know.' His hands settled on her hips.

Bess gasped. 'I didn't think.' But when she tried to move, he held her firm.

'Good tactic, though,' he praised. 'Don't mind you stopping me moving this way at all.'

Her lips grazed his, teased him. She couldn't help it. She wished right now that they were alone or that they could sneak off.

'You know how we could do this sort of thing permanently?' he asked after kissing her with the promise of more. 'Move in with me; think of the money we'll save.'

'I don't want to rush.'

'I think we've waited long enough.' He kissed down her neck. 'And you know it makes sense.'

'So you keep telling me.'

'I've found persistence pays off.' He kissed all the way up her throat and back to her mouth. 'Figured I should start dropping not-too-subtle hints; it took you long enough to say yes to a date. I need to start asking now if we're ever going to move forwards.'

'Hasn't anyone ever told you good things come to those who wait?'

He groaned with the frustration that they were alone in the room but likely to be interrupted at any given moment. 'We need to take this upstairs.'

'With your family here?' She laughed.

'We'll have a while. They're too busy eating cookies and talking about dresses and roast dinners to care.'

'You obviously have no idea how kids' minds work. They'll lose interest and seek you out.'

'How about we take the risk? Imagine this is our last day on earth; would you turn me down then?'

Bess giggled. 'Not a chance.'

He stood up, Bess still on his lap, her legs wrapped around

him. It was as if he was practising what it would be like to go back to work and take the stairs with the weight of a body in his arms.

And Bess didn't mind one little bit that he'd chosen her as his first rescue because she knew now that with Gio by her side, she really was living life to the full.

ACKNOWLEDGEMENTS

A big, big thank you again to Lauren Dyson, critical care paramedic with the Dorset and Somerset Air Ambulance, for answering all my questions. Lauren has been a godsend, giving me accurate information and little snippets here and there that really help me to create a realistic world for my very own air ambulance team right here in Whistlestop River.

Thank you to my readers who have chosen to embrace another new series from me – I'm so thrilled with all the positive reviews coming through for the first book, *Come Fly with Me*. It's always a nervous time introducing a new book and especially a new series which you put your heart and soul into. I hope you all enjoy this book just as much as the first and number three in the Skylarks series is already underway as this book hits the shelves!

As always, my thanks and gratitude to Rachel Faulkner-Willcocks for being such a fab editor, and to the entire team at Boldwood Books, who really are the best in the business. I look forward to putting more books out in the world with your unrivalled expertise and guidance.

And finally, thank you to my husband and my girls for supporting me every step of the way.

Much love,

Helen x

ABOUT THE AUTHOR

Helen Rolfe is the author of many bestselling contemporary women's fiction titles, set in different locations from the Cotswolds to New York. She lives in Hertfordshire with her husband and children.

Sign up to Helen Rolfe's mailing list for news, competitions and updates on future books.

Visit Helen's website: www.helenjrolfe.com

Follow Helen on social media here:

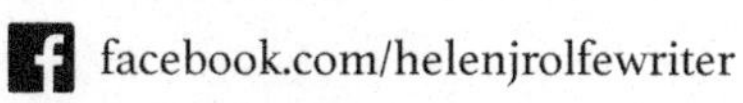
facebook.com/helenjrolfewriter

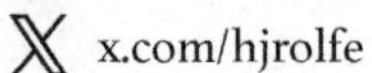
x.com/hjrolfe

instagram.com/helen_j_rolfe

ALSO BY HELEN ROLFE

Heritage Cove Series

Coming Home to Heritage Cove

Christmas at the Little Waffle Shack

Winter at Mistletoe Gate Farm

Summer at the Twist and Turn Bakery

Finding Happiness at Heritage View

Christmas Nights at the Star and Lantern

New York Ever After Series

Snowflakes and Mistletoe at the Inglenook Inn

Christmas at the Little Knitting Box

Wedding Bells on Madison Avenue

Christmas Miracles at the Little Log Cabin

Moonlight and Mistletoe at the Christmas Wedding

Christmas Promises at the Garland Street Markets

Family Secrets at the Inglenook Inn

Little Woodville Cottage Series

Christmas at Snowdrop Cottage

Summer at Forget-Me-Not Cottage

The Skylarks Series

Come Fly With Me

Written in the Stars

Standalones

The Year That Changed Us

Printed in Great Britain
by Amazon